MOTHERS AND DAUGHTERS

MOTHERS AND DAUGHTERS

Gwen Madoc

This first world edition published in Great Britain 2007 by
SEVERN HOUSE PUBLISHERS LTD of
9–15 High Street, Sutton, Surrey SM1 1DF.
This first world edition published in the USA 2007 by
SEVERN HOUSE PUBLISHERS INC of
595 Madison Avenue, New York, N.Y. 10022.

British Library Cataloguing in Publication Data

Madoc, Gwen
  Mothers and Daughters
  1. Poverty - Fiction 2. Wales - Social conditions - Fiction
  3. Domestic fiction
  I. Title
  823.9'2[F]

ISBN-13: 978-0-7278-6523-6   (cased)
ISBN-13: 978-1-84751-020-4   (trade paper)

All Severn House titles are printed on acid-free paper.

Typeset by Palimpsest Book Production Ltd.,
Grangemouth, Stirlingshire, Scotland.
Printed and bound in Great Britain by
MPG Books Ltd., Bodmin, Cornwall.

In memory of my wonderful parents,
William and Mabel Govier,
whose loving marriage was an inspiration.
True love never dies.

One

Swansea, June 1910

Lucy Chandler strolled down the slope towards Mumbles Pier with her younger sister, Eva, feeling self-conscious in her white-sprigged muslin blouse and cream linen hobble skirt. After dressing in mourning for only two months, she felt everyone was staring with disapproval.

'We shouldn't be doing this, Eva, so soon after Father's passing.' It did not seem right under the circumstances that they were intent on enjoying themselves on this sunny June day.

'Oh, don't be a spoilsport, Lucy,' Eva exclaimed impatiently. 'I'm fed up with wearing black and keeping a dour expression. After all, Father paid little attention to us when he was alive.'

That was very true. Joseph Chandler had been a well-respected businessman but to his daughters he had appeared cold and distant. Lucy always had the distinct impression whenever her father had bothered to look at her that he was secretly wishing she were a boy. Nevertheless, he had been their father.

'Just the same, Eva, we shouldn't act giddy,' Lucy cautioned. 'Lewis's mother was saying that she expected we'd be in mourning for at least six months.'

'Oh, bah! Lewis's mother should mind her own business,' Eva opined strongly. 'She's not your mother-in-law yet, Lucy.' She tossed her head. 'Besides, I don't see why I should waste the summer in mourning when I don't feel sad.'

'Eva!'

'Well, at least I'm not a hypocrite.'

'Neither am I!' Lucy retorted. 'But there're Mam's feelings to consider too, you know. She's worried enough about how long probate is taking.'

Lucy felt aggrieved that her deceased father had failed to leave a will, thereby causing her mother, Sylvia, so much anxiety over the settlement of his estate.

They reached the head of the pier, passed through the stile gate and on to the weathered boards. There were gaps between them where one could see the sea swirling beneath. It always made Lucy a little nervous.

'Look!' Eva said excitedly. 'There's a chap with a camera taking photographs.' She dashed forward. 'Come on, let's get ours taken.'

'Wait for me!' Lucy hurried after her, praying she would not catch the heel of her shoe between the boards and fall flying.

Eva ran helter-skelter along the pier. Sometimes she acted more like a seven-year-old instead of seventeen. Everyone in Oystermouth knew the Chandlers and the string of haberdashery shops the family owned in and around Swansea. Two years older than Eva, Lucy felt they should act with some decorum.

Hands holding on firmly to their wide-brimmed straw hats, they posed against the railings of the pier, the magnificent sweep of Swansea Bay behind them.

'You can pick up the prints from the shop in Oystermouth next week,' the young photographer told them as he handed them a ticket. 'That'll be sixpence each.'

'That's a bit steep,' Eva exclaimed, shading her eyes to look up at him.

The young man shrugged. 'You should've asked the cost before I took the picture,' he said smugly.

Having been paid, he walked off to find his next customer.

'Well! The cheek of it!' Eva said, staring after him.

'He's right, we should've asked. Our pocket money won't go far at this rate.'

There were lots of people on the pier today. Lucy and Eva strolled on towards the lifeboat house. All of a sudden Eva caught Lucy's arm.

'Look! A fortune-teller's booth. Oh! I want my fortune told. Come on!'

'Wait a minute!' Lucy said. 'Find out how much it costs first.'

The sign said sixpence for a brief consultation; one and six for a deeper analysis.

'I'm going to have a tanner's worth,' Eva said determinedly. 'It's all right for you, Lucy. You're already engaged to be married. I want to know when I'll meet the man of my dreams.'

Lucy had to smile. Eva was so pretty. There was always some boy trailing after her but she ignored them, saying they were too immature. Lucy blamed the silly romantic novels her sister read.

While Eva went in to the booth Lucy waited outside, staring out to sea at the faint smudges on the horizon: ships waiting to enter Swansea docks.

She had been engaged to Lewis Saunders for almost a year. Was he really the man of her dreams? She had never thought of him that way before. When Lewis had asked her to marry him she had been so surprised that she had said yes automatically. Every girl wanted to be married.

Eva came out of the booth, her eyes shining.

'Well, what did she tell you?' Lucy asked.

'I'm not going to say anything.' Eva grinned. 'Until you've been in and had your fortune told.'

'Oh, I don't think so.'

'I dare you!'

'Tsk! All right, then.'

Lucy went into the booth, sat down and crossed the woman's hand with a sixpenny piece. The woman, a red bandanna covering her hair, stared wordlessly into a much-fingered crystal ball.

'You'll meet a tall dark stranger very shortly,' the woman intoned at last in a bored voice. 'He will change your life completely.'

The woman covered the crystal with a dark cloth and sat silently.

Lucy stared at her. 'Is that all you have to tell me?' she asked. 'It's hardly worth sixpence.'

'You know more than you did before,' the woman said. 'It's money well spent.'

Lucy rose from the stool with a sigh. A fool and his money are soon parted, she reflected, and went outside to face an eager Eva.

'Well?'

Lucy repeated what she had been told and Eva's face fell.

'She told *me* the very same thing!' She put her fists on her hips. 'What a sell! I've a good mind to go back in and give her a piece of my mind.'

'Oh, come on!' Lucy urged pulling her sister away. 'It's time we got back home to Mam. I don't like leaving her alone in the house these days. She's so depressed. Haven't you noticed?'

Eva accompanied her back grudgingly. 'We've hardly had any fun.'

As they approached their home in Newton Road, a fine detached house in its own grounds, Lucy spotted a motor car in their driveway. Except for their father, hardly anyone they knew had a motor car. And then she recognized it as belonging to the family solicitor, Mr Jarrett. Eva spotted it too.

'Oh, look, there's old Jarrett's Humber,' she exclaimed pointing.

'Yes,' Lucy said, quickening her pace. 'Probate must be settled, and not before time too.'

Her mother had been having sleepless nights; although she had tried to hide it from them, Lucy had seen how nervous and distracted she had become.

The front door was ajar and Lucy pushed it open and went in, Eva close behind her. Voices could be heard from the sitting room: a man and a woman talking. The woman's voice was loud and belligerent in tone. It certainly wasn't her mother.

'Mam!' All at once concerned, Lucy called out, and walked swiftly into the room.

Mr Jarrett, short and rotund, stood before the fireplace. Beside him was a tall gaunt-looking woman probably few years older than Sylvia who Lucy had never seen before. She wore a shapeless hat and a poor quality knee-length herring-bone jacket over a long black skirt. It struck Lucy that everything about the woman looked second-hand.

Lucy glanced at her mother 'What's going on, Mam?'

She was dismayed to see her mother sitting in an armchair beside the fireplace, quietly sobbing into a handkerchief, her shoulders hunched.

'Mam, are you all right?' Lucy hurried to her side.

Sylvia Chandler looked up, her eyes and nose red with crying. 'Oh, Lucy, we're ruined. Your father has betrayed me, he's betrayed us all.'

There was an exclamation of anger from the woman. 'It's no more than you deserve,' she uttered waspishly. 'And a just punishment on you.'

'Don't you speak to my mother in that tone,' Lucy flared, straightening her spine and glaring at the older woman. 'What's the meaning of this, Mr Jarrett? Why have you allowed this person to reduce my mother to tears? Who is she, anyway?'

'It's not my doing, Lucy,' Mr Jarrett said hastily. 'Your mother has had a great shock.'

'She knew what she was doing,' the woman put in. 'She's only got herself to blame.'

'What's my father done?' Eva asked in a shrill voice. 'Left everything to charity, has he? Thoughtless of us as usual, that would be just like him.'

'No,' the tall woman said in a hard voice. 'He's left everything to me.'

'What?' Lucy was startled. 'Who *are* you?'

'I'm Mary Chambers, the legal wife of Joseph Chambers,' she said. 'And the sole beneficiary of his will.'

Lucy stared at Mr Jarrett, unable to make sense of what the woman was saying. 'What's she talking about, Mr Jarrett. Who is Joseph Chambers?'

Mr Jarrett fingered his collar as though it was too tight for him. 'Sit down, Lucy, and you too, Eva. I have something grave to reveal to you.'

'It's quite simple,' Mary Chambers cut in impatiently. 'Joseph Chambers married me twenty-five years ago and then when my daughter was three years old he upped and deserted us for her.' She threw up a gloved hand and pointed to Sylvia. 'That Jezebel!'

Sylvia gave a little anguished cry and buried her face in her handkerchief again.

'How dare you!' Lucy shouted at her. 'How dare you come into our home and insult my mother. Leave this house at once.'

Mary Chambers' lips tightened. 'This is now *my* house,' she said emphatically. 'Left to me in my husband's will. His entire estate is mine.'

'You keep mentioning a will,' Lucy replied angrily. 'But there is no will.'

'I'm afraid there is,' Mr Jarrett said apologetically. 'If Mrs Chambers here will allow me to explain.' He cleared his throat.

'Twenty-odd years ago Joseph Chambers, having deserted his wife Mary in Cardiff, changed his name to Chandler, removed himself to Swansea and entered into a bigamous marriage with your mother Sylvia.' He cleared his throat again. 'As you can see his first wife is still very much alive.'

Lucy stared at him speechlessly. She could not believe what she was hearing.

'Joseph Chambers made a will on his marriage to Mary,' Mr Jarrett continued. 'Leaving his entire estate, present and future, to her. That will has never been rescinded.' He lifted a hand as Lucy was about to protest. 'I've thoroughly checked the validity of the will, Lucy. It is legal and binding. There's no way of breaking it, I'm afraid.'

'But that's impossible!' Eva exclaimed. 'It's a trick, that's what it is! You're a dirty trickster,' she flared at the tall woman.

Mary Chambers sniffed disdainfully. 'I may have known the worst of poverty in my life since my husband left me but I've always kept myself respectable.' She glared at Eva and then at Lucy. 'I'll not be insulted by the likes of you,' she continued. 'Illegitimate offspring!'

'Oh my God!'

Eva fell back a step, and clutched at Lucy's hand, who felt a cold chill run up her spine at the shameful epithet.

Illegitimate? Her mother's marriage had been no marriage at all. She and Eva had been born out of wedlock. It was a terrible stigma that would ruin their lives.

'It's the end for us all!' Sylvia wailed, echoing her thoughts. 'We'll end up in the workhouse. Oh! How could Joseph do this to me?'

Lucy found her voice. 'If it's true that my father had committed bigamy, why didn't you come forward sooner and face him? Why wait until he was dead?' she asked angrily of Mary Chambers.

'I knew nothing of him for years,' she said. 'Not until a friend in Swansea sent me a cutting of an obituary and an article with a photograph from a local newspaper.' She nodded. 'I recognized my husband immediately even after twenty-odd years.'

Lucy was silent, remembering the article.

'If Joseph had died intestate, Lucy, you would be entitled to a one-third share each of the real property,' Mr Jarrett said.

'But as it stands Mrs Chambers will inherit. I'm afraid your mother has no claim whatsoever. Unless – unless Mrs Chambers will be generous and benevolent and make you an allowance.'

Sylvia rose hastily to her feet. 'Yes, surely, Mrs Chambers, think of my girls!' she began in an appealing tone. 'You'll not take *everything*. We'll be destitute. I have no money of my own. I relied on Joseph for every penny!'

Mary Chambers looked angry. 'You lured my husband away from me and our child,' she accused, her voice rising loud and relentless. 'You knew he was married. You're as guilty as he was.'

'I swear I didn't know about you,' Sylvia burst out. 'When I met Joseph he told me he was a bachelor. I had no reason to disbelieve him.'

'So you say!'

'Stop it!' Lucy shouted at the other woman. 'You've no right to accuse my mother. She's as much a victim as you are. If there's anyone to blame it's my father.'

Lucy felt her blood boil at the thought of it. All these years Joseph Chandler knew of the existence of the will he had made in Mary Chambers' favour. He had callously taken no action to provide for Sylvia, the woman he had wronged, and his daughters. Obviously, his daughters were less than nothing to him.

'Why did you show your face here today,' Lucy challenged Mary Chambers. 'Was it to gloat?'

'I'm the one who has the grievance. I came to face down the woman who stole my husband,' Mary Chambers said belligerently. 'When Joseph deserted me he took everything. I've had to scrub floors, even take in washing to keep me and my daughter from starving.'

'I'm sorry for that,' Lucy said. 'But it's not our fault.'

'Your mother—' she began in a shrill tone, but Lucy shouted her down.

'My mother is innocent! It was Joseph Chandler who lured her into a bigamous marriage; into shame, humiliation and poverty. Have you given a single thought as to how we will live from now on?'

'It's not my concern,' she said haughtily. 'I've known poverty because of Joseph all my life, so has my daughter. She's never had the advantages you've had.'

'Why did my father leave you?' Eva burst out furiously. 'You did something shameful, didn't you?'

'No, I did not!' Mary Chambers snapped. 'He deserted me because I couldn't give him the sons he yearned for,' she said. 'When my daughter was two years old I had a bad miscarriage. The doctors told me I would have no more children. Joseph blamed me. He was furious.'

'So you finally admit that my mother had nothing to do with his deserting you,' Lucy said triumphantly.

'I too failed to give him a son,' Sylvia exclaimed with a sob. 'I always knew he despised me for it.'

'Don't expect any sympathy,' Mary Chambers burst out furiously. She glanced around at the well-furnished room. 'You've lived in the lap of luxury all these years. I've had to work my fingers to the bone just to exist.'

Sylvia whimpered and burst into tears again.

'You should never have brought this woman here,' Lucy said to Mr Jarrett, concerned to see her mother so upset. She pointed a finger at the door. 'We want you out of our home now,' she told the other woman. 'You're not prepared to help us, so leave.'

Mary Chambers stood her ground stubbornly, her expression furious. 'This house is now my property,' she reminded them. 'My own solicitor is arranging to sell up everything, including the businesses. I'll have what should have been rightfully mine at last.'

'Sell up? Everything?'

'I'm determined my daughter will have all the advantages which have been denied her throughout her life,' Mary Chambers said vehemently. 'It's only right and just.' She lifted her chin aggressively. 'Consequently, I hereby give you all two weeks' notice to quit this house.'

'What?' Lucy glared at the solicitor.

'I say!' Mr Jarrett exclaimed. 'Turning them out is rather harsh, Mrs Chambers. Surely you can give a little leeway?'

'That's my last word,' she said emphatically. 'I've suffered enough already. Now it's your turn,' she said to Sylvia.

'Oh, my poor girls!' Sylvia cried out, and sank back into the armchair, her hands covering her face. 'What will become of us all?'

'I'll go now,' Mary Chambers said archly. 'But remember

this: the contents, fixtures and fittings of the house belong to me. You are to remove nothing but your personal possessions. Is that understood?'

'You can't do that,' screeched Eva. 'You can't turn us out on to the street with just the clothes on our backs.'

'I had little else when Joseph deserted me,' Mary Chambers snapped out the words. 'Work for your bread like I had to.' She glared around at them. 'You're trespassing, all of you. You've been duly warned.'

Two

S ylvia was sobbing pitiably. 'My life has been a complete lie all these years. Oh, Joseph, how could you do this?'

Lucy went to kneel at her mother's side and put an arm around her, comfortingly. 'Don't take on so, Mam,' she said gently. 'Things will work out, you'll see.'

She hoped she sounded convincing because she wasn't convinced herself. She realized now that they had led such sheltered lives. None of them really had any idea how they could earn a living or make their way in a workaday world.

'I don't think so, Lucy,' Mr Jarrett said solemnly echoing her doubt. 'I'm afraid your situation is very bad.'

Angry, Lucy glared up at him. 'You're our solicitor. Why can't you do something?' she said sharply. 'There must be a loophole somewhere.'

He shook his head. 'There's nothing more I can do for you.'

Lucy stood up, staring at him aghast. 'You're washing your hands of us,' she accused in a strained voice. 'How could you? You've been my father's solicitor for years.'

'Your father is dead,' he said flatly. 'His money has gone to his wife. My dear girl, you can't afford to engage my services any longer. And if you could, to what avail? Mrs Chambers' position is unassailable.'

Lucy felt floored.

Mr Jarrett walked towards the door. Lucy followed him into the hall, Eva hot on her heels.

'But what are we to do, Mr Jarrett?' asked Lucy, bewilderment numbing her mind. It was all very well to give her mother words of comfort but she had no idea how they would survive.

'Where will we go?' cried Eva, wringing her hands.

'Start looking for rooms to rent immediately,' he suggested as he took his bowler hat from the hallstand and put it on. 'The cheaper the better.'

'But we have little or no money. We owe shopkeepers in the village who gave us credit. We must settle those debts.'

Mr Jarrett sighed heavily, and reached into his inside breast pocket. He took out a wallet and extracted a ten-pound note.

'This will pay those bills,' he said. 'Use the rest for rent on cheap lodgings and to buy a little food until you can find employment.' He looked from one girl to another. 'You must both put pride aside,' he said. 'Take whatever work you can find, no matter how menial.' He paused. 'I'll write off what your mother already owes me, as I'm sorry for your predicament,' he said. He shook his head. 'But I can do no more.'

With that he turned to the front door and walked out, closing it behind him.

Lucy stood silently for a moment, not knowing what she ought to do next.

'Ten pounds will never last,' Eva said petulantly. 'Mam must've some money put away somewhere.'

'Father made her account for every penny of the house-keeping, as you well know,' Lucy said. 'There was never any left over. She had to ask for anything extra.'

'He never refused,' Eva said.

'No,' Lucy agreed. 'But he kept a tight hold on the purse strings.' And that meant he kept firm control of his family and kept them totally in the dark about their true situation.

Lucy returned to the sitting room where Sylvia was still sitting, crying again.

'It's my fault,' she wailed as the girls came in.

'Mam, don't say that,' Lucy said hurrying forward to her.

'I disappointed him,' Sylvia went on in a choking voice. 'He wanted a son to carry on his name and the business, and I failed in my duty.'

'His name! A false name,' Eva said scathingly. 'Everything about him was a sham.'

Sylvia wiped her nose on her handkerchief. 'He gave us a good life,' she said.

'Yes, it was good while it lasted,' Eva said petulantly. 'I'm only seventeen. Life should be opening out for me. Instead it's caving in. What have I got to look forward to now?'

'Oh, for goodness' sake, Eva,' Lucy snapped at her. 'Stop feeling sorry for yourself. We're all in this together.'

'It's all right for you. You've got Lewis. You'll marry him and he'll take care of you. But what about me?'

Lewis! In her anxiety at their situation Lucy had completely forgotten her fiancé's existence. What would he have to say about it? Or more to the point, what would his mother have to say?

If there was one trait in Lewis that made her uneasy it was that he was too much under his mother's influence. Lucy had wondered if that would change when they were married, but suspected it would not; it often made her doubt that she was doing the right thing.

'Oh, my poor girls!' Sylvia exclaimed, and sobbed, 'If I'd given Joseph a son he probably would have made a proper will, and we wouldn't be in this mess. I blame myself.'

'Nonsense,' Lucy exclaimed. 'Father has behaved abominably, criminally even. Eva and I are branded as illegitimate because of him, and he's left us all destitute. How could any caring father do that?'

'He never cared for us, that's why,' Eva put in bitterly. 'He was a bad father.'

Sylvia protested, 'He provided for us. We wanted for nothing.'

Lucy understood her mother's loyalty. After all, Joseph Chandler had provided a home, and perhaps Sylvia had loved him and perhaps still did. If so, Lucy thought sadly, his betrayal must be a bitter pill for her.

'He never gave his love,' Eva insisted. 'He ignored us, his daughters, as though we were a necessary nuisance.'

'Eva is right,' Lucy said, rallying. Despite Sylvia's love, her father had known all along that this would happen and had done nothing to prevent his wronged wife's humiliation. She could not forgive that. 'Father knew that everything would go to his legal wife . . .'

Sylvia gave a little cry, and Lucy tried to comfort her.

'I'm sorry, Mam, but we have to face facts no matter how hurtful. We're now on our own and must provide for ourselves as best we can.'

'How can we provide for ourselves?' Eva exclaimed. 'We're not trained for earning our living. That Mrs Chambers will want us out soon. We'll be on the streets!'

'We must start looking for lodgings first thing tomorrow

morning,' Lucy said. 'And then find work. All of us,' she warned.

'I'm too young to work,' Eva protested in a whining voice.

'You're seventeen and well old enough,' Lucy said firmly. 'We must all pull our weight.'

Eva always liked getting her own way and was lazy by nature. Previously that hadn't mattered, although Lucy was impatient with her attitude, but now they were on the edge of penury. She gave her sister a stern look.

'No work, no food,' she declared firmly.

'Who said *you* are in charge,' Eva challenged crossly.

Lucy glanced at her mother. Sylvia, sniffling into her handkerchief again, looked utterly defeated. Lucy realized she alone would have to manage their lives from now on.

'I say so,' Lucy told her sister sharply. 'Mam's too upset to take responsibility.' She spoke to Sylvia. 'Come along, Mam,' she urged strongly. 'We should start packing our things; decide what to take with us.'

'I intend to take my best tea set,' Sylvia said defiantly as she rose from the sofa. 'That was a wedding present from my mother.' She broke down again. 'Oh, what would she say if she could see the mess I'm in now?'

Lucy put an arm around her shoulders. 'I think you can take the tea set, Mam,' she said sorrowfully. 'After all that is your property not Father's. But the contents of the house have been left to Mrs Chambers so we might get into trouble if we remove anything that's not our personal property.' Lucy could feel her mother's shoulders shake with sobs. 'Take Mam upstairs, Eva,' Lucy said. 'Help her pack.'

Lucy rallied everyone the next morning, urging them to get ready as soon as breakfast was over, so that they could look for rooms. She wasn't sure how they should go about it, but decided that they must simply walk about, searching the streets of Mumbles village.

They were about to set out when a knock came at the front door. The sound made Lucy's heart jump, wondering what misfortune would land on them next. She was surprised when answering the door to see her fiancé standing outside.

'Lewis! I wasn't expecting you, and at this time too.'

'Good morning, Lucy,' he said. He did not look her in the

eye, but fidgeted with his tie as he spoke. 'Can I come in? I have to talk to you.'

Lucy was on guard immediately. His mother was behind this visit; she could sense it in his tone. 'Yes, come in, for a moment.'

He came into the hall and hesitated on seeing Eva and her mother with their hats and coats on.

'We're on the point of going out,' Lucy explained.

She walked into the sitting room and he followed.

'Going out?' He sounded surprised. 'I'd have thought, under the circumstances, you'd stay at home out of sight.'

Frowning, Lucy whirled to face him. 'What do you mean, Lewis?'

He shook his sandy-coloured head. 'It's all over the village,' he said a sour tone in his voice. 'Your parents were not really married.' He flicked a glance at her then. 'You realize what that means, don't you, Lucy? You're not legitimate. You can never hold your head up again, not in respectable circles.'

'Lewis!' She was shaken that he was being so frank, and stunned too that someone other than a member of her family had raised the subject of her illegitimacy.

'It's shocking – that's what Mother says,' he rushed on, his tone rising. 'Shocking and disgraceful.'

'Oh, does she?' Lucy bristled with anger. 'She's helping to spread the gossip, too, I expect.'

'Lucy, that's not fair,' Lewis said. He almost pouted. 'It's not Mother's fault that everyone's talking about your family's disgrace. You won't be able to face people around here after this, that's what Mother says.'

That gave Lucy pause for thought. With all this gossip and the bad feeling that went with it, they would be unlikely to find lodgings in the close community of the village. She realized they would have to look further afield; even Swansea itself.

'We've done nothing to be ashamed about,' Lucy said strongly. '*My* poor mother was betrayed. She's devastated. And people like your mother talking about her behind her back won't help.'

Lewis shuffled his feet. 'Mother says she can hardly believe your mother knew nothing of it, not after all the years she and your father were together. She must've . . .'

'How dare you, Lewis?' Lucy cried out.

It dawned on her that he was trying to start a quarrel. He wanted to break their engagement, or at least his mother did. Perhaps Mrs Saunders had never heard of breach of promise. Of course, if she ended it she would be in breach instead. But there would be no point in Lewis suing her. She hadn't a shilling piece to her name. She didn't even have a name, really. No, Mrs Saunders would not want an illegitimate pauper for a daughter-in-law.

Lucy felt her blood boil at the callous attitude of mother and son. She knew now that Lewis was the last man on earth she would marry, but she would not make the split easy for him.

'When we're married, Lewis, people will forget.'

He spluttered and his face went red.

'What's the matter, Lewis?'

'You can hardly expect a ch-chap to put himself in such a scandalous p-position,' he stuttered.

'I thought you loved me, Lewis?'

'I n-never made any such ad-admission!'

'No, you never did, did you?' Lucy said scathingly. 'It was more likely you, or rather your dear mother, were attracted to my father's money and position, especially as he had no male heir.'

'That's insulting . . .'

'It's meant to be!' Lucy shouted. 'Marry you, Lewis? Not if you begged me.' She lifted her chin proudly. 'You were never good enough for me, anyway,' she said pithily. 'I knew that in my heart.' She took in a gulp of air. 'My word, I've had a lucky escape.'

'You're being extremely offensive, Lucy,' he said. 'I'm not staying here another minute to be insulted by the likes of you.' He swallowed hard. 'I'll take my ring back, if you please!'

'By all means!' Lucy tore the engagement ring off her finger and held it out to him. 'Here!' she said mockingly. 'Save this for your next fiancée. I pity her.'

He grabbed the ring from her hand and turned towards the door, about to stride off, but turned at the last moment to face her. He opened his mouth to say something, but Lucy thwarted him.

'Get out, Lewis,' she shouted. 'We've nothing more to say to each other.'

His mouth snapped shut and he marched out. Lucy felt the tension leave her body and she sank exhausted on to a sofa. Strangely, she knew a sense of utter relief, recognizing for the first time that the prospect of marrying Lewis had weighed heavy. It had never seemed right.

Sylvia and Eva came rushing into the room.

'What was the shouting about?' Eva asked, her expression filled with curiosity.

'Lewis has jilted me,' Lucy said. 'Isn't it wonderful?'

'Oh my dear girl,' Sylvia said, coming to sit next to her, 'I'm so sorry.'

Lucy jumped up from her seat. 'I'm not. I've always had my doubts about Lewis,' she said triumphantly. 'He's not man enough for me.'

Eva laughed out loud gleefully but Sylvia looked shocked.

'Lucy! What an outrageous thing for an innocent young girl to say.'

Within the hour they set out on their search for lodgings.

'I think we'll start looking in Woodville Street,' Sylvia said. 'That's a respectable area.'

Lucy was cautious. 'Mam, we should go further afield. Let's catch the train for Swansea where no one knows us.'

'Nonsense!' Sylvia said. 'I was born and brought up in the Mumbles. I see no reason to move elsewhere.'

Lucy bit her lip. She could not bring herself to tell her mother of the awful things that Lewis had told her about the gossip in the village.

'And I don't want to be covered with sooty smuts from Puffing Billy, either,' Eva said petulantly. 'This is the only decent dress I've got left.'

'Everyone in the village must know what's happened,' insisted Lucy. 'I don't think we'll be welcome anywhere in the Mumbles.'

'Well,' Sylvia said, setting off at a brisk walk down Newton Road, 'we won't know until we ask.'

They turned off the main road and then on to Woodville Street, terraced houses with front doors that opened on to the pavement. The terrace climbed a gentle slope and halfway up Sylvia spotted a square of white cardboard propped in a window, announcing rooms to rent.

'What did I tell you,' she said to the girls. 'It looks quite clean, too.'

Before Lucy could say anything, Sylvia knocked at the door. The woman who answered looked them up and down. 'Yes?'

'My name is Mrs Chandler,' Sylvia said. 'I'm interested in your rooms to rent. Can I view them?'

The woman's eyes narrowed and she gave them another appraisal.

'I know you,' she said to Sylvia at last. 'You're that hussy from the top of Newton Road, the one with the two bastard daughters.' She began to close the door in their faces. 'This is a respectable house. There's no place for the likes of you here.'

With that the door was slammed shut. Sylvia fell back a step, her face turning pale. Lucy quickly put an arm around her shoulders, feeling her mother tremble.

'Are you all right, Mam?'

'Oh, Lucy!' There was shock and despair in Sylvia's voice. 'She called me a hussy. What's happening to us?'

'Well!' Eva cried out. 'What utter cheek! She can't talk to us like that. Who does she think she is?' She lifted a hand to knock again. 'I'm going to give her a piece of my mind.'

Lucy pulled her back. 'Things will be worse if you make a scene, Eva,' she warned quickly. There was nothing like a row in the street to bring people out on to their doorsteps. She would not be made a sideshow. 'It's no more than I expected.'

'What?' Eva frowned at her.

'Lewis warned me.' She glanced at her mother, unwilling to say more just then. 'I'll tell you later. Come on, Mam, let's go down to Oystermouth and get a cup of tea before catching Puffing Billy to Swansea.'

The tea helped. At least Lucy felt her frayed nerves ease a little. The sooner they moved away from the village the better.

They waited for the locomotive to make its return journey from the terminus at Mumbles Pier. Quite a few people were waiting also. The train was always packed. They were lucky to be boarding at Oystermouth, the first stop after the terminus.

'Have we enough money for seats?' Eva asked. 'I'm not riding on the railings or on the footplate. I'll fall off, I know I will.'

'We don't have enough money for seats on the lower deck,' Lucy said. 'We'll probably have to ride upstairs on the open deck.'

'Oh, bother!' Eva said crossly. 'We'll look like chimney sweeps by the time we get to town.'

Lucy was proved right. She had taken charge of the ten-pound note and had settled their outstanding bills. She was reluctant to break the five-pound note that was left. They used most of their change to raise the fare as far as the Slip, west of the town itself.

Lucy always enjoyed a ride on the Mumbles train as it hugged the sweep of Swansea Bay. In some places the rails ran so close to the lapping tide that she had the illusion of riding on the waves themselves. Today, there seemed little joy in the experience. Today she felt desperate.

They alighted at the Slip close to Brynmill, an area of mostly newer properties. It was unlikely they would find cheap lodging there.

'We'd better make for the Sandfields,' Lucy said in a practical tone.

Eva made a face. 'It's a very poor part of town; such mean little streets,' she said. 'Can't we do better than that?'

'We're poor ourselves, Eva,' Lucy said shortly. 'The sooner you accept that the better.'

Eva muttered under her breath, but trotted in their wake as Lucy and Sylvia made their way to the myriad narrow streets of terraced houses that were the Sandfields.

They traipsed up and down for a while, looking for a sign of vacancies. Halfway along King George Street they found one.

Sylvia was hesitant. 'What are the lace curtains like? Do they look clean?'

'According to Lucy we can't be fussy,' Eva exclaimed bitterly.

Without answering Lucy knocked at the door that was in need of a fresh coat of paint. After a few minutes it was answered by a buxom youngish woman in a grubby apron, holding a baby in her arms. The pleasant expression on her face was marred by an ugly bruise on her cheekbone.

'Yes?'

'You have rooms to rent?'

'Come in,' the young woman said eagerly.

They followed behind her as she walked down the passage. The house smelled of boiled cabbage and fried onions, and Lucy saw Eva wrinkle her nose in distaste.

They went into a cluttered back room with a small scullery adjoining. Even though it was summer the fire was blazing, making the room very hot. A galvanized bucket was perched precariously on the hob over the flames, the water bubbling furiously around what looked like nappies.

'Two furnished rooms upstairs,' the young woman said, jiggling the baby on her hip, 'and use of the scullery.'

'Where's the bathroom,' Eva asked haughtily.

The young woman looked blank for a moment. 'There's no bathroom, love,' she said at last. Her expression brightened. 'But there's a tin bath hanging on a nail in the yard. That's where the privy is.'

'Oh!' Eva looked crestfallen.

'How much is the rent?' Lucy asked.

The young woman wetted her lips. 'Seven shillings and six pence a week,' she said rather hopefully.

'We offer five and six,' Lucy said boldly. She felt uncomfortable bargaining, but their survival depended on how well she managed their money.

The young woman shook her head. 'Oh, no, my husband won't have that. He's laid down the law, he has. It's seven and six.' She tossed her head. 'Take it or leave it.'

'We'll leave it,' Lucy said firmly. 'Come along, Mam, Eva. We'll find something better.'

Lucy turned and strode down the passage to the front door, Eva and Sylvia following in her wake.

'Just a minute!' the young woman called behind them. 'Don't be hasty.'

Lucy turned to her. 'We can only manage five and six.'

'Tsk! Oh, all right!' The young woman shook her head. 'I don't know what Fred will say when he gets home from work.'

Lucy opened her handbag and took out the white five-pound note. The young woman's eyes opened wide at the sight.

'As soon as I change this note,' Lucy said. 'I'll give you two weeks' rent in advance. Will that help?'

'I should say so!' the young woman said. 'By the way, I'm

Doris, Doris Price. Fred, my husband, is a labourer at the gas works.'

'I'm Lucy Chandler,' Lucy said, watching carefully for recognition of their name, but there was none. 'This is my mother, Mrs Chandler and my sister, Eva.'

Doris Price smiled. 'Pleased to meet you, I'm sure.' She sounded eager again. 'When will you be moving in?'

'Tomorrow,' Lucy said quickly. There was no point in staying any longer in the Mumbles.

'Oh, good! Fred will get you a key and a rent book tomorrow,' Doris said.

'How many children do you have?' Eva asked with a sniff.

'Three,' Doris said proudly. 'Two boys and my little Alice here.' She hugged the baby and kissed her cheek. 'We're as quiet as mice, Mrs Chandler.'

Lucy was thoughtful. She had half a crown in her purse. Perhaps they should secure the rooms in case they were taken by someone else in their absence. She brought out the coin.

'Here's a down payment to secure the rooms,' she said to Doris. 'You'll get the rest tomorrow.'

'Oh, that's good of you.' Doris beamed at them. 'See you tomorrow, then. Oh, I am pleased that I've got such nice respectable-looking lodgers. There's a lot of riff-raff about these days.'

Their few bags, bundles and other possessions were stacked in the hall in readiness.

Sylvia sat on the sofa, wearing her hat and coat. She was crying again, and Lucy felt her heart break at her mother's distress.

'I can't believe it, Lucy,' Sylvia said, her voice breaking with emotion. 'I can't believe I'll never see the inside of this house again.' She looked up, her face streaked with tears. 'I've lived here since I was married . . . Oh! The shame of it all!'

Lucy sat beside her, taking her mother's hand and squeezing it. 'I know, Mam,' she said with difficulty, wanting to cry herself. 'I was born here, so was Eva. It's the only home we've ever known.'

'Oh, my poor girls!' Sylvia wailed loudly. 'What have I brought you to?'

'None of it is your fault, Mam,' Eva said. There was a touch of impatience in her voice. 'Besides, it's over and done with now. We have to move on.'

For once Eva made sense, Lucy thought. Her younger sister was often frivolous and thoughtless. This change in their lives might steady her; help her to grow up and be useful.

Lucy got to her feet. 'We must make a move,' she said gently. 'Hanging around here won't make us feel any better. As Eva said, we must move on. Everything will be all right, Mam. You'll see.'

She was trying to encourage herself as much as her mother, but in her heart she was afraid. None of them had any experience of earning their own living. The awful thought, no fear, was always at the back of her mind. It would be dreadful if they failed, and ended up in Mount Pleasant workhouse.

Lucy set her jaw. She would scrub floors and take in washing before she let that happen to her mother. For the first time she felt true hatred in her heart against her father. He had brought them to this penury. She wished she could face him one more time to curse him.

Three

When they arrived at King George Street later the next morning, their knock was answered by Doris Price, wrapped in a worn and grubby woollen dressing gown even though it was getting on for ten o'clock.

'Oh! You're early,' she said at the sight of them and their bags and bundles. 'The kids are just having their breakfast.'

They stepped inside and stood in the passage. The house seemed to be in uproar. From the living room came piping shouts of fury and scuffling. Doris's two young sons were obviously fighting while baby Alice was crying pitiably.

Lucy wondered if her mother and sister felt as uncomfortable as she did. Would they ever get used to living in someone else's home? This was a far cry from the life they had known in Joseph Chandler's fine house in Newton Road.

Lucy was impatient with herself for thinking of that again. That life was over and this was their reality now and the sooner she came to accept that the better.

'We'll go up to our rooms,' Lucy said. 'Out of your way, Mrs Price.'

'Call me Doris,' their landlady said cheerfully above the din coming from the other room. 'Let me know if there's anything you want and Fred will see to it.'

There was the sound of crockery smashing and a youthful scream.

'Kids!' Doris said mildly. 'Who'd have 'em?' She turned and scurried into the back room shouting at the top of her voice, 'Stop it, you little perishers!'

They stood at the bottom of the stairs. Sylvia's face was pale.

'I don't think I can stand living like this,' she said in a trembling voice. 'I'll go out of my mind.'

Full of sympathy, Lucy put an arm around her mother's

shoulders. 'It's hard for you, Mam, I know. You've always been used to better.'

'So have you!' Sylvia said sharply, lifting a small linen handkerchief to her nose. She sniffed. 'I can hardly believe we've come down to this.'

Lucy led the way upstairs, wondering in trepidation what they would find. The bedroom had a double bed, a knocked-about wardrobe and a chest of drawers on which stood a china bowl and water jug. There was hardly room to turn around.

In the other room Lucy viewed the horsehair couch with doubt. She would probably have to sleep there. It did not look very comfortable.

Sylvia opened a wooden cupboard in the corner. 'This must be the larder,' she said mournfully. It was empty except for some chipped cups, a few random saucers and some dusty plates.

Eva pulled out one of the chair and sat at a small round table. 'We ought to get more for our rent than this,' she said angrily. She looked up at Lucy accusingly. 'We shouldn't have taken the first thing that came along.'

Lucy put her carpet bag and a bundle of clothes on the couch. 'When we've earned enough money we can look for something better,' she said. 'Until then we'll have to make the best of it.'

'We'd better get some groceries in,' Sylvia said listlessly. Her voice sounded strained, but Lucy realized she was trying to come to terms with the situation.

'I noticed a grocers' on the corner,' Lucy said. 'We'll go there now. I'll break into the five-pound note.'

Sylvia straightened her spine. 'I'm still your mother, Lucy,' she said severely. She held out her hand. 'I'll take charge of our money and decide how it will be spent.'

'All right, Mam,' Lucy said meekly. She took the note out of her bag and handed it over. She thought that was a good sign. It would do her mother good to take over the reins again.

When they returned with a few essentials, Doris Price was waiting for them, baby in arms.

'Fred said I was to get the second week's rent from you straight away,' she said defensively. 'He was cross that I let you have the rooms for five and six.'

Sylvia handed over the money. 'When will it be convenient

to come through to the scullery to make a midday meal?' she asked.

'Any time you like,' Doris said, looking at the money in her palm, obviously checking it was the right amount. 'No need to knock. Just walk straight in.'

'What time does the milkman come around?'

'About eight o'clock in the morning.'

'Could we borrow a cup of milk from you?' Lucy asked awkwardly.

She knew her mother was longing for a cup of tea. Even the smallest everyday things now presented a problem, and she wondered how long it would be before they were used to living in someone else's pocket.

'There's a drop left from yesterday in the jug,' Doris said generously. 'You can have that.'

And so they drank their first cup of tea in their new home; tea made with milk that was already on the turn.

'It'll be all right, Mam,' Lucy assured Sylvia for the umpteenth time when she saw tears glisten in her mother's eyes. 'We'll survive somehow.'

Lucy had hoped that they might spend the rest of the afternoon searching for work, but Sylvia was looking exhausted.

'We'll start looking for something first thing tomorrow,' Lucy said. 'You take a rest, Mam, while Eva and I give this place a good clean.'

The next morning, her back still aching from sleeping on the couch, Lucy was up and, without bothering to wash, got dressed. She was on the doorstep exactly on eight to catch the milkman. Anxiously she waited as his cart was pulled along the length of the street by a tired-looking horse.

'Fill the jug, please,' she told him as he approached.

'That'll be eightpence, miss. Want any eggs? Fresh they are, straight from farms in Gower.'

Lucy bought three at tuppence each, putting them safely in the pocket of her apron, and felt lucky. At least they could have a decent breakfast.

As Lucy entered the passage she was startled when a man wearing a stained vest appeared suddenly from the Prices' living room. He was medium height and of stocky build, with a day's growth of beard on his chin.

He eyed the jug of milk narrowly.

'You owe my missus for the milk she let you have yesterday,' he said belligerently. 'That'll be fourpence.'

'It was sour,' Lucy said quickly.

'That's not my fault.' He frowned. 'You pay up,' he said harshly. 'I'm not having you sponge off me. You're getting the rooms for next to nothing as it is.'

Lucy hesitated and then decided it wasn't worth the argument. Like it or not Fred Price was their landlord. She handed over the four pennies.

'And another thing,' he said. 'You can't use our coal. I'm not running a charity by here, mind.'

'We don't want charity,' Lucy said angrily. 'We pay our way.'

'Well, see that you do,' he sneered. 'The coalman comes every Monday. Order your own.'

'Where can we store it?'

'In the coalhouse out the yard, along with ours,' Fred Price said.

'What?' Lucy stared at him haughtily. 'For you to help yourself to it,' she said sharply. 'Not likely!'

'Hey! You hoity-toity piece! Are you accusing me of stealing?'

'I'm not giving you a chance to,' Lucy said archly, pushing passed him and climbing the stairs. 'We don't need a fire.'

'Well, you've been warned,' he shouted up the stairs. 'Keep your bloody hands off my coal.'

Lucy waited until she heard Fred Price go off to work and then volunteered to go down to the scullery to make their breakfast of boiled eggs, tea and toast.

In the Prices' living room the two boys were causing uproar as usual, though Doris appeared unconcerned. She stood in the doorway, jiggling the baby in her arms and watching Lucy's preparations of boiling the eggs.

'The gas meter is a penny in the slot,' Doris told her. 'Or a sixpence,' she continued hopefully.

Lucy said nothing and got on with what she was doing. It took only pennies to boil eggs and the kettle, she judged. It would suit their landlords if she put in more. The Prices were a pair well-met, and would take advantage if they could.

It occurred to her that as soon as their backs were turned either Doris or Fred would be up in their rooms rummaging through their things. There were no locks on either door so there was not much they could do about it apart from making sure that they took what valuables they had with them.

Once breakfast was over and they had managed to have a wash each, they set off to search the town for work. Eva grumbled all the way into the town centre, and Lucy was angry with her.

'You'll pull your weight,' she told Eva sharply. 'If you want to eat.'

They decided it would be better if they split up and looked for work separately. They parted company outside Swansea market and arranged to meet up there again in two hours.

Lucy watched her mother walk away, shoulders bowed, while Eva skipped off eagerly, and she immediately had doubts about her intentions.

She turned in through the market gates and wandered around among the stalls. It was midmorning now and the stallholders were doing a roaring trade. She paused by an enclosed stall which sold curtain materials and smiled at the woman behind the counter.

'Is there work going in the market?' she asked.

The woman pursed her lips, looking Lucy up and down.

'You could try your luck lower down at the open vegetable stalls,' she said.

Lucy thanked her and strolled off to the lower level where open stalls crowded each other. There was a stall selling flowers and she paused. This would suit her down to the ground and she wondered if there was a chance.

'Is there a job going here?' she asked of a youth who seemed to be in charge.

'Boss isn't here,' he said gruffly. 'But I am, so push off!'

Lucy was angry but held her temper, and moved off feeling humiliated somehow as though she were begging.

A few yards on at a vegetable stall a stout woman was struggling with a sack of potatoes. Lucy quickly moved forward and helped her to lift it on to the boards of the stall.

'Thanks, love,' the stout woman panted, and Lucy saw that one of her hands was bandaged.

'I'm looking for work,' Lucy said quickly. 'I'm very strong.'

'Well, that's lucky,' the stout woman said. 'I've sprained my wrist so I'm hampered for the time being. I could use help for a week or two until this gets better.'

Lucy hesitated. 'I was hoping for something permanent.' The woman sniffed. 'A couple of weeks is all I can offer,' she said. 'Take it or leave it.' She turned away.

'I'll take it,' Lucy said quickly. 'I can start as soon as you like.'

The woman turned back to her, smiling. 'Start tomorrow morning,' she said. 'I can't pay much, mind; a bob a day. Business isn't all that good.'

Desperate as she and her family were for money Lucy knew she must seize the opportunity and nodded in agreement. A week's work here would at least pay the rent. 'That's fine with me,' she said. 'My name is Lucy.'

'And I'm Mrs Cooper. Eight o'clock tomorrow morning, Lucy,' Mrs Cooper said. 'The market closes at eight in the evening. You can finish sooner if the stock is sold up before that.'

Lucy said goodbye for the moment and walked off. Should she continue looking for work, she wondered. The place with Mrs Cooper was temporary. Could she really afford to be complacent?

She wandered aimlessly for a while and then it was time to meet Sylvia and Eva. Her mother was already waiting outside the market gate. Lucy could tell by her expression that she had news.

'Did you find anything, Mam?'

Sylvia hesitated. 'Yes. A cafe in Union Street – washing up.'

'That's wonderful!' Lucy said, but Sylvia did not look happy. 'Isn't it, Mam?'

'I suppose so,' Sylvia said listlessly. 'The pay is good; at least I think it is. Seven and six a week for the first month, rising to nine and six, if they keep me on.'

'Mam, you've done wonders!' Lucy exclaimed excitedly. 'I only managed to get a shilling a day, hauling sacks of potatoes.'

'Oh, Lucy!' Sylvia looked upset. 'Such menial work. It's not right.'

'It's honest work, Mam,' Lucy said staunchly. 'We needn't

be ashamed of it.' She looked around at the people surging
past. 'What's keeping Eva?'

Within a few minutes Eva was with them, her face glowing.
'I found a job,' she blurted out. 'Ten shillings a week. What
do you think of that?'

Lucy stared open-mouthed and she realized Sylvia was
stunned too. 'Where? What kind of a job?'

Eva lifted her chin proudly. 'I'm the new barmaid at the
Exeter Hotel on the corner of Oxford Street.' She turned and
pointed. 'You can see it from here. I can keep all the tips, the
landlord said.'

Sylvia gave a little scream and covered her mouth with one
hand. Lucy too was shocked.

'But you're only seventeen,' she said.

'I told the landlord I was nineteen,' said Eva with a laugh.
'He believed me and said I was pretty enough to draw in the
customers.'

'It's out of the question,' Sylvia said sharply. 'Apart from
you being underage, it isn't respectable. You'd be rubbing
shoulders with drunken men and loose women. I forbid it.'

'But ten shillings—'

'No, Eva! I won't have my daughter doing such unsavoury
work. It's bad enough that Lucy has to haul potatoes.'

Eva looked at Lucy with scorn. 'Is that the best you could
do?'

'It's better than going hungry,' Lucy said. 'Which is what
you'll be doing if you don't find sensible work.'

Eva pouted. 'I thought we were desperate.'

'We're not that desperate,' Sylvia said firmly. 'Let's find a
cafe. I need a cup of tea.'

It broke Lucy's heart to see her mother returning exhausted each
evening to their rooms in King George Street, so tired she could
hardly eat the scanty suppers that Lucy prepared. At thirty-eight
her mother wasn't old by any means, but she had never been
used to such taxing labour. And Lucy wondered in trepidation
how she would stand up to such a gruelling change of lifestyle.

Lucy was worn out herself. Mrs Cooper turned out to be a
slave-driver determined to get every ounce of Lucy's energy
for her shilling a day, but Lucy was determined to stick it out
to the bitter end.

Eva was the only one who was in a good mood in the evenings spent in their cramped quarters, and Lucy was angry that there was no sign of her sister finding work. On the Friday of their first week they quarrelled bitterly.

'You're a lazy little wretch!' Lucy stormed at her sister.

'Don't you talk to me like that,' Eva snapped back.

'I'll talk to you any way I like until you find work,' Lucy shouted. 'Mam is working her fingers to the bone while you waste your time window-shopping. Oh, don't deny it! I saw you lunch time today, gawping in the window of Miranda Fashions in Oxford Street.'

'I was looking for a job there,' Eva snapped.

'You little liar!' Lucy spluttered. 'You were just enjoying your-self as usual. I bet you didn't even try to get a position there.'

'They might've taken me on because I'm pretty and attrac-tive,' Eva said, raising her chin arrogantly.

'You'd better mend your ways, Eva,' Lucy said through gritted teeth. 'I won't let you ride on Mam's shoulders. You'd better find a job next week or you'll go hungry. I warn you!'

On Saturday morning early, Sylvia came upstairs from the back yard, crying and shaking all over.

'Mam! What is it?'

'It's that beast Fred Price,' Sylvia said, through sobs, sinking on the horsehair sofa. 'I was in the lavatory. He came bang-ing on the door, demanding that I hurry up.' Sylvia covered her face with her hands. 'Oh, I was so humiliated. And then, would you believe it, he waited right outside the door until I came out.'

'Mam, you mustn't take it to heart,' Eva said calmly. 'The man's an oaf. Ignore him.'

Sylvia stared at her. 'I can't ignore him. What do you think he said to me when I came out?' she swallowed. 'He said, get your own newspaper to wipe your . . . Oh, I can't repeat such vulgarity.'

'I'll have a word with him,' Lucy said. 'I'll get him to apologize.'

'Apologize!' Sylvia stood up abruptly. 'I never want to set eyes on the creature again.' She began to pace the small living room. 'We must leave. I can't stay here a day longer.'

'Mam, we paid two weeks' rent in advance,' Lucy reminded her. 'We can't afford to just leave.'

'We're leaving,' Sylvia said firmly. 'By hook or by crook, I'm going to find us another place with respectable people.'

After breakfast they went off to their various jobs, leaving Eva to her own resources.

'Don't forget the milkman,' Lucy told her sternly. 'He'll be here in half an hour, and get some eggs too.'

Together they caught the tramcar into town, and parted in Oxford Street.

'How do you feel now, Mam?' Lucy asked, searching her mother's face for distress.

Sylvia's expression was set; there was a resolute cast to her mouth. 'Determined, that's how I feel,' she said.

'It's twelve o'clock, Mrs Chandler. You can take your lunch break now.'

'Thank you, Mr Benucci.' Sylvia wiped her hands on a towel.

'What is it to be? Your usual hot pie?'

It was an added bonus of the job that Mr Benucci, a short well-rounded good-natured man, allowed her to have free food midday.

'I have to go out today, Mr Benucci, on business,' she said. 'I won't have time to eat.'

He shrugged. 'I'll put the pie in a paper bag. You can take it home with you.'

'You're very kind, Mr Benucci.'

'You're a good worker, Mrs Chandler.'

Sylvia put on her hat and jacket and hurried off to Mansel Street, where Mr Jarrett had his office. He had been Joseph's solicitor for years; he knew them well. Surely he would be willing to lend her some money?

Mr Jarrett's young clerk refused to let her see his employer.

'You have no appointment, madam,' he said officiously.

'But it's urgent,' Sylvia insisted. 'I've known Mr Jarrett for years.'

'I'm sorry,' he said and shook his head emphatically. 'Mr Jarrett is a very busy man, seen by appointment only.'

Sylvia was turning away in frustration when the office door opened and the solicitor appeared. She rushed towards him, despite the clerk's attempts to hold her back.

'Mr Jarrett! Mr Jarrett, I must speak with you.'

He looked startled. 'Mrs Chandler, I'm surprised to see you.'

'I'm desperate,' Sylvia exclaimed. 'I need your help.'

'I'm sorry, sir,' the clerk said, frowning furiously at Sylvia. 'I told her you were busy.'

'It's all right, Watkins,' Mr Jarrett said. 'Come this way, Mrs Chandler.' He ushered her into his office, and then sat down behind his desk. 'Do take a seat,' he said.

Sylvia sat down, clutching her purse. 'Mr Jarrett, you know that I am in straitened circumstances.'

He cleared his throat. 'I am well aware of it,' he said carefully.

'I've found work, and so has Lucy,' Sylvia rushed on. 'And we have found lodgings, of sorts. No, to be truthful, Mr Jarrett, our lodgings are atrocious; our landlord a bestial man. I can no longer tolerate it.'

'I fail to see what I can do about it,' Mr Jarrett said, sitting back and making a steeple of his fingers.

Sylvia lifted her chin proudly. 'We've known each other a long time, Mr Jarrett. You know I am respectable and trustworthy.'

He turned his head away a moment.

'The fault was with Joseph,' Sylvia exclaimed quickly, angered and even insulted by his gesture. 'The wrong that was done to my daughters and to me was none of my doing. Yet we are being hounded and punished for it.'

Mr Jarrett leaned forward, a shadow of a frown on his face. 'What is it you want of me, madam?'

Sylvia wetted her lips. It went against all her upbringing and her principles to beg like this but she must.

'I want you to lend me some money, Mr Jarrett,' she said frankly. 'I must find decent lodgings for my daughters and myself.'

'Lend you money?' He looked startled. 'But how would you pay me back?'

'I'm sure we could come to some suitable arrangement,' Sylvia said eagerly. 'I have a reasonable wage, and I believe my employer is pleased with my work. I will have an increase in pay shortly. Lucy, too, is gainfully employed. We live very simply. Over a period of, say, five years, we could pay you back with interest.'

Mr Jarrett rose from his chair and went to the window over-looking the street below.

'I'm afraid I can't oblige, Mrs Chandler,' he said carefully his back turned to her. 'To lend you money in your circumstances would be foolish in the extreme.'

'But, Mr Jarrett . . .'

'I'm sorry,' he said firmly. 'I'm not a moneylender. That is not the nature of my business. I am surprised you ask this.'

Sylvia felt her lips tremble and strove not to burst into tears. 'I'm at the end of my tether, sir,' she said. 'My daughters are in need.'

He turned then and Sylvia saw that his face was set against her, and her spirits dropped.

'I'm not your legal adviser and therefore no longer have responsibility to you or your family, Mrs Chandler,' he said coldly. 'I shall be pleased if you will leave my office now. You have already taken up a great deal of my time.'

Mr Jarrett took a seat at his desk once more, his head averted, ignoring her. Feeling cold and dismal, Sylvia rose to her feet and without a further word left the office.

As she walked from Mansel Street and into Craddock Street she had to keep a tight control of her emotions, unwilling to make a spectacle of herself by crying in the street. Her pride was the only thing she had left.

She lifted her gaze as she went, trying to pull herself together, and then she noticed a sign in a first-floor window of premises on the opposite side of the street. She stopped and stared at it.

Mr Jarrett had pointed out he was no moneylender, but the sign she spotted in the window above was that of a moneylender and it invited her to enquire within about a loan. Her spirits lifted immediately. Of course! This was the answer.

She hurried across the street and climbed a steep flight of dusty stairs. At the top was a small landing with two doors. One was marked private, but the other, a glass office door, bore a painted sign, Naylor Investments.

Hesitating only briefly, she knocked and walked in. The room, which overlooked the street below, was crowded with filing cabinets and shelves stacked with brown folders.

The man sitting at the desk, a cigarette dangling from his

lower lip, was probably in his early thirties, she judged; well-built with regular clean-shaven features. His dark hair was thick and wavy. He looked up as she came in but did not rise from his chair.

'Yes!' he said. His tone was clipped as though he was a man of little patience.

Sylvia wetted her lips. 'I've come about a loan,' she said tentatively.

'Have you now?' he exclaimed without bothering to remove the cigarette from his mouth.

His dark eyes took in her features, her figure and Sylvia wanted to squirm as his bold gaze ran over her.

'Well,' he continued. 'Let's see what we can do for you.' He indicated a wooden chair before the desk. 'Sit down. I'm Stan Naylor.'

'I'm Mrs Chandler,' Sylvia volunteered and sat, clutching her purse to her, watching him.

He was not ill-spoken, but there was an air of the working class about him; a man who had pulled himself up by his bootlaces, yet was still self-conscious of it.

He took the cigarette from his mouth, holding it between two fingers, and placed his elbow on the desk looking at her keenly.

'How much money are we talking about, Mrs Chandler?'

Sylvia wetted her lips. 'I haven't really thought of that.'

He raised his brows. 'Have you given it any thought? You understand what it means to borrow money?'

She shook her head. 'No, not really, but I must borrow. There's no alternative.'

Putting the cigarette back in his mouth, he leaned back in his chair, scrutinizing her through the drifting smoke, his eyes bright and knowing.

'Got yourself into a bit of trouble, have you, my dear?' he said smiling narrowly and then gave a soft laugh. 'Been a bit naughty, perhaps?'

Sylvia bridled at his implication and familiar tone. 'No, I have not!' she said sharply. 'The fact is my husband . . . I've been left a widow recently; poorly off, with two children.' Somehow she did not feel bad in lying to him.

'A widow, eh?' He inclined his head as he looked at her. 'You're a good-looking woman. The clothes you're wearing aren't new but they're of very good quality,' he observed shrewdly. 'You've been used to living well.'

'What has that to do with my borrowing money,' exclaimed Sylvia sharply. She was beginning to regret coming here.

'I'm trying to decide what kind of a risk you are.'

'Risk?'

'Whether you can pay me back.'

'I have a job,' Sylvia said quickly. 'And my daughters have found employment, too.' She hoped Eva would find something suitable soon.

'Daughters working?' He frowned. 'You gave me the impression you have small children.'

'Well, does it matter?' With all these questions and his forward attitude she was less and less sure she was doing the right thing.

He pursed his lips. 'No, I suppose not.' He paused. 'All right. How much?'

She had been thinking furiously as they had exchanged words and now knew what she wanted to borrow.

'Fifty pounds,' she said daringly.

He whistled. 'That is a lot of money, Mrs Chandler,' he said.

'I need to find good lodgings as soon as possible,' Sylvia said. 'Make a decent home for my daughters.'

'Your husband left you without a roof over your heads?' He sounded more curious than surprised.

Sylvia lifted her chin proudly. 'It's a matter I don't wish to discuss,' she said shortly.

His expression tightened at her curt reply. 'Are you being straight with me, Mrs Chandler?' he said. 'I could hand over the money and never see you again.'

Sylvia stood up abruptly. 'I didn't come here to be insulted, Mr Naylor. Do you treat all your clients in this way?'

He gave a soft chuckle, taking a puff from the cigarette. 'I can treat my clients any way I like,' he said. 'They put up with it because they've no choice. I have what they want and they're often pretty desperate, like you, Mrs Chandler.'

Sylvia gave him a hostile glance and got up to leave the office.

'Sit down, Mrs Chandler,' he said loudly. 'Don't be so touchy. In your situation you can't afford pride.'

Sylvia still hesitated.

'Don't be a fool, sit down,' he commanded. 'You're not going to leave your daughters in want just to save your dignity, are you?'

Reluctantly Sylvia resumed her seat while Stan Naylor opened the desk drawer and took out a thick bundle of banknotes secured in an elastic band. Sylvia could not stifle a gasp when she saw it. She had never seen so much money.

'Now, let's get down to brass tacks,' he said. 'You'll borrow fifty pounds. The interest is twenty-five per cent, payable monthly.'

'What?' Sylvia stared appalled. 'But that's usury!'

'That's business, Mrs Chandler,' Stan Naylor said in a hard tone. 'My business.' He waved the bundle of banknotes. 'Ready cash, Mrs Chandler. To spend any way you want.'

Sylvia hesitated for just a moment more, remembering the humiliating scene with Fred Price that morning. She could not suffer to live like that any longer.

She nodded. 'I accept your terms, Mr Naylor,' she said quietly.

'Good! Now give me your details, where you live.'

Sylvia told him. 'But I'll be moving soon,' she went on.

He paused. 'You must let me know any new address immediately, or you'll be in breach of my terms, and the entire amount of the loan will become payable plus interest,' he said harshly. 'Remember that. Now sign here.'

Sylvia signed the document he put before her, her hand shaking despite her determination to stay calm.

From the bundle he counted out fifty one-pound notes on to the desk and then pushed them across to her. Sylvia's hand closed over them eagerly and she put them carefully into her purse.

'Today is the twenty-first of June. Payment is due at this office the twenty-first of every month,' Stan Naylor reminded her. 'And remember this, Mrs Chandler, failure to pay or if you go into arrears means you automatically breach the contract. I've already outlined what to expect. The consequences can be very unpleasant.'

Sylvia swallowed. 'What if I fall ill and can't work?'

He shook his head, his expression darkening. 'Don't fall ill, Mrs Chandler,' he said; there was a harsh warning in his voice. 'It wouldn't be at all wise.'

All of a sudden she was frightened and put her hand protectively to her throat. Had she made a dreadful mistake?

'Get into arrears,' he continued in the same warning tone, 'and you and your daughters will be in a great deal of trouble.' He shook his head. 'Believe me, you don't want *that* kind of trouble.'

Four

Lucy was just finishing preparing their evening meal when her mother returned home from work. She was later than usual, and although she looked tired and strained there was some brightness in her eyes which Lucy had not seen for a long time.

Eva was setting the table. 'Come and sit here, Mam,' she said, indicating a place at the table. 'Lucy is just making a pot of tea. I expect you could do with one.'

Sylvia sat and kicked off her shoes. 'Yes, the cafe was really busy today. I thought I'd never finish the washing up.' She took a brown-paper bag out of her purse. 'Here's a pie Mr Benucci gave me.'

'That's kind of him.'

'He says I'm a good worker. I think he'll keep me on.'

Lucy put a cup of tea in front of her mother. 'It's not too much for you, is it, Mam?'

She had been thinking of taking her mother's place at the cafe while Sylvia found work less back-breaking than bending over a stone sink filled with hot water and soda crystals. It had been a week and already Sylvia's hands were red.

Sylvia smiled up at her. 'I'll be all right, Lucy dear. Mr Benucci has given me a stool to sit on at the sink. He's very considerate of his employees.'

'I don't suppose he needs a waitress?'

'He already has three girls, I don't suppose he'll take on another just now. And what have you been up to, Eva? I hope you're looking for work and not wasting time.'

'I look every day!' Eva said smartly, sitting down at the table. 'I haven't found anything to suit me.'

Lucy was impatient. 'We can't afford to be too finicky, Eva,' she said flatly as she sat down to eat. 'I expect the money is getting low. Isn't that right, Mam?'

Sylvia bit her lip and then put down her knife and fork.

'As a matter of fact,' she said, 'we've had a piece of good fortune.'

She picked up her purse from the floor at her feet and reaching inside brought out the bundle of banknotes. Lucy stared and so did Eva.

'Mam! Where on earth did you get that?'

'I went to see Mr Jarrett during my lunch break,' Sylvia said. 'I explained our predicament and he loaned me . . . er . . . thirty pounds.' She quickly put the money back in her purse out of sight.

'He did?' Lucy was astonished.

'Well, he's changed his tune,' Eva exclaimed. 'He was reluctant to give us even ten pounds a week ago. I wonder what's made him so generous all of a sudden.'

'Yes, but this is a loan,' Sylvia said quickly. 'It has to be paid back with interest. We can't expect him to do it for nothing.'

'Well,' Lucy said with wonder. 'I renew my opinion of Mr Jarrett.'

Sylvia's glance slid away from hers. 'This means we can look for better lodgings straight away,' she said. 'Perhaps we could go out after we've eaten.'

'Mam, it'll be near enough half-past nine before we clear up. That's rather late.'

Sylvia looked disappointed.

Lucy touched her arm. 'I'll stand guard outside the lavatory in the morning,' she said encouragingly. 'I won't let Fred Price come anywhere near.'

'I know I'm being silly . . .'

'No you're not,' Lucy said quickly. 'Your modesty is important to you and our landlord is an ignorant oaf.'

Sylvia smiled. 'He is, isn't he? And I'll tell him so to his face when we give notice. But how soon can we start our search for a new place?'

'We paid two weeks' rent in advance, Mam, remember. He's not getting away with that,' Lucy said firmly. 'Thursday is half-day in Swansea. We'll meet at the cafe and tuck into some of Mr Benucci's hot pies before we go looking. We'll have all the afternoon.'

'We must find something,' Sylvia said. 'I won't stay here in this awful place.'

'We should write to Mr Jarrett,' Lucy suggested thought-fully. 'To thank him for the loan.'

'Oh! No!' Sylvia said quickly. 'He asked me to keep it confidential. He doesn't want it generally known that he loaned me money in case others ask. It was a special favour, you see. Please leave it to me, Lucy dear.'

'Of course, Mam.' Lucy got to her feet and began to collect the crockery. 'I'm so proud of you, Mam, the way you're coping with everything. You're being so brave.'

Sylvia put her elbows on the table, a thoughtful expression on her face. 'I relied on your father all those years; he took care of everything. But now we're on our own and it's sink or swim, I do feel a sense of freedom.'

'Yes, it's going to be all right,' Lucy said.

She had said that so often lately, usually without meaning it, but suddenly she did feel that things would get better for them.

'Roll on Thursday,' Eva said.

Sylvia had insisted on looking for lodgings in the Brynmill area. The terrace houses were newer there and quite large. They had been walking the streets unsuccessfully for a while and Eva was beginning to complain.

'My feet are aching, Mam,' she said. 'And I need a cup of tea.'

'Don't we all,' said Lucy.

They were walking along Marlborough Road when Eva spotted the sign. 'Look! A flat to rent. A whole flat!'

The house was very well kept. A short paved path led to the front door. Beside it a flight of steps ran from the pavement down to the basement area. It looked out of their price range.

'We can't afford it,' Lucy said emphatically.

'I'll enquire,' Sylvia insisted, hurrying to the front door to knock.

The door was opened by a tall, well-corseted woman in a dark blue Jap-silk flowered blouse and black tailored skirt. She smiled at them pleasantly.

'Yes?'

'It's about the flat to rent,' Sylvia blurted out. 'Can we view it, please?'

'Yes, of course. This way.' She came out and descended the side steps, lifting the hem of her skirt as she went. 'It's a furnished basement flat, quite self-contained you know.'

They trooped down behind her, Lucy feeling doubtful. They could never afford this, so why torture themselves with what was unobtainable?

The woman had a key chain attached to her belt and opened the door. 'Your own entrance, you see,' she said leading the way forward into a rather dark passage. 'Two bedrooms, living room with a very good range. A scullery.' She waved them around. 'The lavatory is in the yard.'

'Is it shared with other tenants?' Sylvia asked quickly.

'Oh, no,' the woman said shaking her head. 'This flat is very private.'

And very expensive, Lucy thought gloomily. She was watching her mother's excited face and felt sorry that she would be disappointed.

'Is there a bathroom?' Eva asked airily.

To Lucy's surprise the woman nodded smugly. 'Oh yes, all modern conveniences. It's along the passage there and it's fitted with a hot-water geyser.' She appeared very proud of that. 'There's also an outhouse with a boiler for doing your laundry,' she went on. 'So you see there's plenty of hot water.'

'It's wonderful!' Sylvia said. 'And so clean.'

'Why, thank you.' The woman beamed at her and touched her coiffured hair self-consciously. 'I am rather particular.'

'So am I,' said Sylvia companionably. 'I can't abide mess or disorder.'

'My name is Mrs Grant,' the woman said eagerly. She looked around all three of them. 'Well, what do you think?'

'It's very nice, Mrs Grant,' Lucy said. 'But I doubt we can afford the rent.'

'That's not for you to say, Lucy,' Sylvia said severely, lifting her chin. 'I'm the head of our household.' She turned to Mrs Grant. 'How much is the rent?'

'Ten shillings a week.'

Lucy's shoulders drooped and she stepped closer to Sylvia to comfort her in her disappointment.

'We'll take it!' Sylvia exclaimed with alacrity, astonishing Lucy. 'It's just what I'm looking for.'

'Oh goody!' Eva chortled.

Lucy was floored. 'Mam! What are you thinking of? We can't afford it.'

'We're taking it, Lucy,' Sylvia said vigorously in a tone that brooked no argument. 'My mind is made up.'

She reached into her purse and took out two ten-shilling notes, holding them out to Mrs Grant.

'Here's two weeks' rent in advance, Mrs Grant. We'll move in at the weekend, if that's all right with you.'

Mrs Grant took the money. 'As soon as you like, Mrs . . . er . . .'

'Mrs Chandler,' Sylvia said. 'These are my daughters, Lucy and Eva.'

'Very nice to meet you, I'm sure,' Mrs Grant said amicably. 'I hope you'll all be very happy here.'

Sylvia was determined to give notice to the Prices as soon as they returned home.

'Why not wait until tomorrow,' Lucy advised. She suspected Fred Price would turn nasty and make their last few days in King George Street quite uncomfortable. He might even take it into his head to lock them out while they were at work and confiscate their belongings. She wouldn't put anything past him.

Sylvia was adamant. 'I'm going to do it straight away,' she said firmly. 'And Lucy, I want you to be with me.'

Fred Price was in his living room when they returned, sitting before the fire in his vest, his feet resting on the brass fender.

He ignored them as they came in, chewing on the stem of his pipe, although Lucy could see there was no tobacco in the bowl.

'Mr Price,' Sylvia began loudly, her voice shaking. 'I'm giving you notice. We're moving out tomorrow evening to other lodgings.'

'Hey! You can't do that!' He scrambled to his feet, his expression belligerent. 'I know my rights as a landlord,' he blustered. 'I need at least a week's notice to find a new tenant and a week's rent to cover my loss.'

'You can whistle for it!' Lucy blurted. 'You've had all the rent you're entitled to.'

'I'll have the law on you!' he shouted. 'You hoity-toity lot

are the worst kind; doing down an honest man of what's rightfully his.'

'And you're an oaf!' Sylvia exclaimed bravely, although
she clutched at Lucy's hand as she said it. 'An uncouth, vulgar
oaf. I wish I'd never set eyes on you.'

With that she turned and hurried out of the room, pulling
Lucy along with her. They climbed the stairs quickly, while
he stood at the bottom, shouting and cursing. Lucy was relieved
when they reached the comparative safety of their rooms.

'What's all the shouting?' Eva asked.

'I wish you hadn't insulted him, Mam,' Lucy said, feeling
quite out of breath. 'Fred Price is not a man to let it lie.'

'I couldn't help myself,' Sylvia said. She flopped on to the
sofa. 'I've suffered indignity at his hands. Now I feel better.'

Lucy was disturbed. 'We should've waited until after
supper,' she said. 'I think the scullery might be out of bounds
for us from now on.'

Anyway none of them would dare go down to the scullery
to even boil water after that altercation.

'I might have lost courage if I'd waited,' Sylvia said. 'I can
manage without, just knowing we have a wonderful flat to go
to tomorrow.'

'All the same,' Lucy said. 'Eva had better remain here all
day tomorrow until we come home from work.'

'What!' Eva exploded. 'I'm not sticking in here all day
alone.'

'Do you want what few clothes you have to be taken by
the Prices? Doris would be around the pawnbrokers as soon
as our backs were turned. We need you to occupy the rooms,
Eva; keep guard.'

'It's not fair!'

Lucy was angry. 'Father making us illegitimate wasn't fair,
but it's a truth we have to live with. You're the only one
without a job. It must be you.'

They went to bed hungry that night but it was not hunger
that kept Lucy awake until the early hours. Her mother
seemed to be acting in a very reckless way. The loan money
would not last very long with food and fuel as well as a
heavy rent to pay. Eva was still without work and it was her
last day with Mrs Cooper tomorrow. Once she had been paid
her daily shilling, she too would be out of work. Lucy could

not help feeling that the future looked dark. There was trouble ahead.

Eva was furious that she had to stay indoors the whole day. She did not feel guilty that she hadn't found work. Plenty of time for that. The town was bustling and exciting and her new found freedom was exhilarating and she intended to make the most of it.

From their window she watched her mother and sister hurry to catch the tram into town and then an idea came to her. They had planned to pack that evening, but there was no reason why they should not move straight away. Eva set about packing their few belongings with gusto until she had all their bags and bundles ready just inside the bedroom door.

Fred Price had left early as usual. Now, if only Doris would go out for a while she believed she could put her plan into action without a hitch.

She went downstairs and into the Prices' living room. Doris Price was there in the usual turmoil. She glared at Eva as she came in.

'What do you want?' Doris asked belligerently. 'Don't think you can use the gas without paying.'

'I don't want anything,' she said. 'The fact is I'm fed up. My mother says I have to stay in all day to watch you don't pinch our belongings while we're out.'

'What?' Doris looked furious but her cheeks turned pink. 'Of all the cheek! The thought never entered my mind.'

'That's what I told my mother,' Eva said innocently. 'And I particularly wanted to go down to town today. Peacocks are having a summer sale. Everything half-price. I'm missing so many bargains, it's not fair.'

'A sale?'

'There'll be crowds there, crowds,' Eva emphasized. She gave Doris a knowing look. 'It'll be so crowded the shop assistants can't watch everyone.' She winked at Doris. 'I could've got myself some real bargains free of charge.'

Doris half smiled and then straightened her face. 'The very idea!' she said.

'Tsk!' Eva bobbed her head. 'I won't get a chance like this for a long time.' She turned, her shoulders drooping. 'Oh well, I'd better get back upstairs I suppose.'

She went up to their rooms and stood at the window over-looking the street. Within three-quarters of an hour Doris stepped out of the front door, her children with her. She had on her best hat and coat, and was carrying a copious canvas bag.

Grinning to herself, Eva waited until she was sure Doris had left the area, and then donning a hat and coat left the house, making for the dairy on the corner of the next street.

She strolled into the yard at the back, which stank of spoiled milk. Her target was hauling a heavy milk churn and placing it with several others.

'Hello, Cecil,' she said.

The youth, tall, loose-limbed and gangly, spun around, his face reddening at the sight of her. 'Hello, Eva.'

She sidled up to him, smiling and fluttering her eyelashes. 'Do you have anything for me today, Cecil?'

He swallowed spasmodically, his gaze fixed on her face.

'There might be a drop of milk and an egg or two,' he breathed. He glanced back toward the door of the dairy. 'I don't want the gaffer to catch me, though.'

'It's all right. I don't want those today,' Eva said softly, moving closer to him knowing she could make him tongue-tied and trembling in a moment. 'I want to borrow a handcart.'

'What?'

'A handcart, Cecil, dear, just for a few hours.'

'I don't know . . .'

Eva moved even closer and put a hand on his chest, looking up into his face, seeing perspiration on his upper lip. 'Oh, Cecil, you told me the other day you'd do anything for me.' She pouted prettily. 'Were you teasing me?'

'No, I meant it, Eva,' he gasped.

'It's just an old handcart,' she said smiling. 'I'll bring it back, I promise.'

'Alright but promise to meet me on Sunday afternoon for a stroll on the prom,' Cecil said eagerly. 'You won't let me down, Eva, will you?'

'A promise is a promise,' Eva said lightly.

Eva trundled the handcart back along King George Street. It was not as easy as she had expected because it seemed to have a will of its own.

She was out of breath by the time she reached the Prices' house. She had been gone no more than half an hour and was certain Doris could not have returned in that time, but just the same she was cautious as she let herself in. To her relief blessed silence reigned inside.

Leaving the cart just outside the front door, Eva made short work of getting all the baggage downstairs and loaded. Without a backward glance, she set out for their new home. The cart was heavier now, and even less manoeuvrable, but she was determined to master it. It was a fair step to Marlborough Road, but she had plenty of time. There might be one or two Sir Galahads on the way who would give her a helping hand for a smile.

'This is the house, Bert,' Eva said to the stockily built youth who had pushed the cart from Rhyddings Park Road.

He stopped, puffing and leaning on the cart. 'I'll give you a hand unloading if you like, Eva,' he said generously.

'Oh, you're so kind, Bert.' She beamed at him. 'My knight in shining armour.'

He reddened. 'Oh, go on!'

Eva knocked on the door, which was answered by Mrs Grant.

'Mrs Chandler sent me,' Eva said. 'It's all right to move in now, is it?'

Mrs Grant eyed the loaded cart and the youth. 'Yes, of course. I didn't know you had a brother.'

'Bert is an acquaintance, in fact we've only just met,' Eva said casually. 'The cart was too much for me. He very kindly helped me.'

'I see.'

Mrs Grant went down to the basement door, opened it and waited while Bert unloaded the cart and took everything into the flat.

'I think I should lock up now and hand the key to your mother later,' Mrs Grant said, casting a glance at Bert.

'That's a good idea,' Eva said as she climbed the basement steps to the pavement. 'I'm going into town now to look for work.'

'What about this cart? You can't leave it here.'

Eva flashed a brilliant smile at the young man standing on

the pavement. 'Bert will take that back to Benson's Dairy in the Sandfields, won't you, Bert?'

He shuffled his feet, his face reddening. 'Anything for you, Eva.'

'You are a dear,' she said warmly.

'And I'll meet you next Sunday afternoon by the Slip, two o'clock sharp,' he said eagerly. 'We'll stroll on the prom.'

'I'll be there, Bert,' Eva said. 'I always keep my promises.'

Lucy did not finish her last day at Mrs Cooper's stall until half-past seven. She received her daily shilling without a word of thanks from her former employer, and was glad to get away.

She went straight to the cafe to meet her mother so that they could take the tram home together, but it was another half hour before the last of the customers left and Mr Benucci said Sylvia could leave.

He pushed a brown-paper bag into her hand. 'Here's something for your supper, Mrs Chandler.'

'Thank you, Mr Benucci,' Sylvia said gratefully.

Lucy thought her mother looked very tired and was sorry that they had to make an effort to move to Marlborough Road that evening, probably without eating first.

When they reached the Prices' in King George Street they found the door locked and bolted.

'Oh, no!' Lucy's worse fear was confirmed. Eva had gone out after all their warnings, leaving the rooms unattended. 'I knew this would happen.'

Sylvia was near to tears. 'All our things; our clothes gone. We're left with just what we stand up in. Oh, Lucy, what are we to do?'

Lucy was furious with her sister for allowing this to happen. It would take a big chunk out of Mr Jarrett's loan to fit themselves out with their most basic needs.

Lucy banged vigorously on the door and then shouted through the letterbox, 'Open up, Mr Price, or I'll call the constable.' It was an idle threat and Fred Price probably knew it.

'Where's Eva?' Sylvia said tearfully. 'She's such a wilful girl. How could she let us down like this?'

Lucy felt her shoulders sag with weariness and despair.

'There's nothing for it but to go to Marlborough Road,' she said. 'At least we'll have a roof over our heads.'

'I'm so tired, Lucy,' Sylvia said dismally. 'So tired of it all. I don't know if I can go on.'

Lucy put a comforting arm around her mother's shoulders. 'I know you're tired, Mam,' she said gently. 'You must rest. Stay in bed tomorrow. I'll go to the cafe instead of you. I'm sure Mr Benucci won't mind.'

'I can't ask you to do that,' Sylvia said. 'I must do my part, no matter what I feel. If only Eva would find work.'

With one final look at the Prices' house, Lucy took her mother's arm and led her away.

It seemed a long walk up to Marlborough Road in Brynmill and Sylvia was visibly trembling when they reached the house and their rented flat.

Sylvia waited at the top of the basement steps, leaning on the railings, while Lucy rang the bell.

Mrs Grant answered almost immediately. 'I saw you coming up the road,' she said. 'I was on the lookout for you.'

Lucy was confused. 'I know we said we would move in later this evening, Mrs Grant,' she began. 'But unfortunately circumstances have changed.'

'Yes, I know, your sister told me.'

'I don't understand, Mrs Grant.' She was totally confused. 'Was my sister here today?'

'Well, yes,' Mrs Grant said. 'She came this morning with a handcart loaded with bags and bundles.' Her expression showed disapproval for a moment. 'But I wouldn't give her the key,' she said pulling in her chin. 'Not while she had that young man with her.'

Lucy could only stare. Eva had come here and brought a man with her? What on earth was she up to?

Mrs Grant held out the key. 'I know she's young,' she said, 'and young girls are often giddy, but I expect my tenants to act respectable.'

'We are respectable,' Lucy said firmly. She took the key. 'I don't know what my sister has been up to, but I can assure you it won't happen again.'

Mrs Grant sniffed. 'Well, all right, then.'

Lucy nodded, feeling piqued that their landlady might be having second thoughts about them. Eva had a lot to answer for. She unlocked the door of the flat, walked into the dark passage and immediately tripped over something heavy lying on the floor.

'What on earth . . .?'

'Oh, Lucy, what is it?'

'Careful, Mam, you might fall,' Lucy said bending down to examine the object in the dimness. It was a carpet bag and she recognized it as her own. Her eyes growing used to the dimness, Lucy saw that other bags and bundles were strewn on the passage floor.

'Good gracious!' she exclaimed in astonishment. 'It's our things from King George Street. How on earth did Eva manage it?'

'Oh, thank heavens!' Sylvia exclaimed. 'Lucy, I can't believe it.'

Lucy could hardly believe it herself. Eva had managed an extraordinary feat in rescuing their belongings from Fred Price and she was astonished at her sister's ingenuity. But she was still angry with her for leaving them in the dark about the move.

'You go along to the kitchen, Mam, and put the kettle on,' said Lucy. It was lucky they were renting the flat fully furnished. 'I'll put these bags in the bedrooms.'

When she joined Sylvia her mother had a pot of tea ready.

'Mrs Grant left some milk for us,' Sylvia said indicating a small white jug on the table where an open packet of tea also stood. 'That was kind of her, wasn't it? I think we'll be happy here, Lucy. I'm sure of it.'

'We might if Eva behaves herself,' Lucy said and then told her mother of Mrs Grant's remarks about the young man Eva had brought to the flat with her.

'Oh dear. Where can she be?' Sylvia said in a worried tone. 'It's getting late.'

They had just finished the tea when the front door opened and Eva flounced into the kitchen.

'Oh, there you are,' Sylvia said. 'I was worried.'

'Eva, I've a bone to pick with you.' Lucy's pent-up anger burst out. 'Why didn't you let us know you managed to move our things?'

'What does it matter?' Eva shrugged. 'You found your way here anyway.'

'It matters because Mam was very upset when we found ourselves locked out of King George Street, and so was I,' Lucy flared. 'We thought we'd lost everything.'

'Well, we didn't, thanks to me,' Eva said petulantly.

'Don't go on at her,' Sylvia said. 'We're all safe now.'

'I'm not going to let her off that easily,' Lucy persisted. She remembered the despair she had felt and knew it had been so much more acute for her mother, but Eva seemed to be insensitive to Sylvia's suffering. 'Eva is far too selfish,' she declared. 'She never gives a thought to what you're going through, Mam.'

'You should be thanking me, not criticizing,' Eva said.

'It was thoughtless of you,' Lucy said. 'Mam has had so much to bear since Father died and the shameful truth came to light. Losing our things seemed like the last straw.'

Eva poured herself some of the tea. 'I think I was very clever outwitting the Prices,' she said archly. '*You* would never have been clever enough.'

That was probably true, Lucy thought. Eva was always so much cannier than she was. But anger with her younger sister still rankled.

'And what about this man you brought to the flat?' Lucy snapped. 'Mrs Grant was scandalized. Who was he?'

'Scandalized! What rubbish!' Eva flipped a hand in dismissive gesture. 'He was just some bloke I met on the way who gave me a hand with the cart. It was heavy, I can tell you,' she said. 'I needed someone with a bit of muscle and he volunteered . . .' She grinned. 'After I smiled at him.'

'Eva, you're turning into a hussy. We moved away from the Mumbles to get away from gossip. Your behaviour will cause talk.'

'Piffle!'

'You're not to bring your men friends around to the flat,' Lucy insisted heatedly. 'It looks bad.'

'He's not a friend. Huh! I wouldn't bother with a labouring lad like him,' Eva said disparagingly. 'I'm only interested in men with money, who'll take care of me and give me what I want.'

'Eva!' Sylvia was shocked to hear such talk.

'Well!' Eva tossed her head. 'I deserve it after what Father did to me.'

'What he did to us all,' Lucy reminded her. 'We all suffered, Eva, and Mam more than anyone. She was the one he betrayed most and left penniless.'

Eva paused and glanced at Sylvia. 'I'm sorry, Mam,' she said. 'But I'm going to make sure I don't end up like you.'

'Oh, Eva!' Sylvia's voice cracked as though she was going to burst into tears again.

'You little horror!' Lucy exclaimed. She felt like slapping her sister's face for those insensitive words. 'How could you?'

'You don't want to hear my good news, then,' Eva said unabashed. 'I've found a job. I start Monday.'

'Where?'

'Ernest Mason, the gents' outfitters in the Uplands.'

'What?'

'I saw an advert in the newspaper yesterday for a sales assistant.' Eva wrinkled her nose. 'They wanted a young man, but I persuaded them I was better. They've never had a female shop assistant before.'

Sylvia looked apprehensively at Eva. 'But you can't go into the fitting rooms and measure gentlemen's inside . . .' She stopped, flushing with embarrassment.

'No, of course not, Mam,' Eva said calmly. 'I'll sell them items over the counter – socks, handkerchiefs, shirts, things like that.' She preened. 'Men, especially older ones, like a pretty face to talk to.'

'What's the wage?' Lucy decided someone must be practical.

'Seven and six a week.' Eva looked proud of herself. 'I think that's very good indeed.'

Lucy had to admit that it was. With Eva's wage and her mother's at the cafe at least the rent would be covered. It was up to her now to find employment to pay for food. And in the long run Mr Jarrett's loan would have to be repaid.

Lucy sighed deeply at the thought. There was no doubt about it, though. They'd be living on the edge of penury for a long time to come.

Five

'I'll take your place in the cafe today, Mam. Mr Benucci will understand,' Lucy said to her mother the next morning. 'You must rest. I heard you tossing and turning all night.'

'I didn't get much sleep,' Sylvia admitted. 'But I don't want to lose that job.'

'I'll hold it down for you until you're better.' Lucy paused. 'Or you find something less exhausting.'

Sylvia shook her head. 'I'll manage it somehow.'

Lucy set off for the tram into town, confident that Mr Benucci would accept her as a substitute.

She thought there was a fleeting look of disappointment on his round face as she explained the situation.

'I'm so sorry Sylvia is ill,' he said quietly.

'I'll stand in for her, Mr Benucci,' Lucy said quickly. 'If that's all right with you?'

It was hot and steamy in the kitchen, the atmosphere growing even denser as the morning wore on. Lucy was perpetually on her feet, up to her elbows in hot water and soda crystals, and by midmorning her back ached through bending over the sink. She was reminded that Sylvia had to put up with this day in day out, and realized why her mother was so exhausted. She would have to do something about it.

Mr Benucci came into the kitchen about eleven o'clock.

'Take a ten-minute break, Lucy,' he said, kindly. 'Get yourself some tea.'

Lucy was thankful. She drank her tea leaning against the worktop in the kitchen while her employer inspected some of the food being prepared.

'Mr Benucci,' Lucy began hesitantly. 'I wonder if you'd consider letting me take my mother's place here permanently.'

He turned and stared at her and she thought she saw dismay in his expression. 'She has complained?'

'Oh, no!' Lucy hurriedly reassured him. 'My mother is very happy here, but I think it may be too much for her. You see, Mr Benucci, she's never been used to hard physical work. She's beginning to feel the strain.'

'I understand,' he said nodding. 'Sylvia is a lady. I saw that straight away and I was sorry she was down on her luck.'

'She was very grateful, too,' Lucy said then hesitated a moment. 'Then you're willing to take me on instead of her?'

He smiled, his bushy moustache stretching on his top lip in a curious way. 'Glad to, Lucy. You're a good worker like your mother.'

Lucy went back to washing dishes, relieved that she had taken the load from her mother's shoulders.

At one o'clock Mr Benucci told her to take her lunch, a hot meat pie and tea on the house. She sat at one of the tables in the cafe, glad to take the weight off her feet and ease her back for a while.

Having finished her meal she was just about to return to the kitchen when Mr Benucci came to her table and waved her to sit down again. He sat too, and looked at her earnestly.

'Is Sylvia too ill to do any kind of work?' he asked, his tone a little uncertain.

'No, Mr Benucci,' Lucy said. 'She'll find something else; something less strenuous.'

He shifted uneasily in his chair. 'Could she cope with a little light housework and simple cooking for a few hours each day?' he asked.

Lucy looked at him with interest. 'That would be ideal,' she said eagerly. 'Do you know of such a job going?'

'I need someone at my home in the Uplands,' he confided in a lowered voice. 'I have an invalid wife and an elderly mother. My older spinster sister looked after them until recently, but suddenly she ran away to be married! At fifty-five!' He looked both scandalized and astonished.

'I'm sure my mother would be willing to take that on,' Lucy said quickly. 'When would you like her to call and discuss details?'

'Next Thursday at early closing,' he suggested. 'If she could be here then, I could take you both up to my house to meet my wife and mother.'

Lucy smiled happily. 'She'll be here, Mr Benucci.'

He looked doubtful for a moment. 'Maybe Sylvia would rather not work for me at my house?'

'My mother likes you very much, Mr Benucci,' Lucy said. 'She thinks you're a kind and generous man.'

He beamed. 'Take some meat pies home for supper, Lucy,' he said rising from his seat. 'And some Eccles cakes.'

On Thursday, Sylvia came in just before the cafe closed its doors for the half day. Lucy was amused to see how solicitous Mr Benucci was with her mother, and how eager he was to please.

He had a motor car which he kept parked in the yard at the back of the Exeter Hotel opposite. As they drove up Walter Road he explained about his wife.

'Maria has been sickly for years, and my mother is getting on for eighty-two.' Sylvia was sitting next to him in front and he gave her a quick sideways glance. 'You mustn't mind Mama's sharp tongue,' he said. 'She's from the old country and has never learned the ways of her adopted country.'

'I'm sure we'll get on,' Sylvia said.

Lucy thought she was looking better after her short rest and was glad of it.

Mr Benucci's home, a tall gabled terraced house, was situated in a leafy street just off the Grove in the Uplands. He let them into a wide hallway with parquet flooring.

'The basement kitchen is along the passage and down the stairs,' Mr Benucci said, pointing. 'Mama sleeps in a room next to the dining room along here. She can't manage the stairs now.'

Lucy was dismayed to see that everything looked dusty and rather dingy. Mr Benucci's sister had obviously taken very little trouble with the housekeeping. There was a great deal of work in this house and Lucy was worried that her mother would be unable to cope.

'Mama is probably in the sitting room,' Mr Benucci said. 'But first I want you to meet my wife.'

He led the way up the staircase to a front bedroom on the first floor. The room was large and filled with heavy dark furniture and had the musky odour of illness. Although it was just past midday heavy curtains were half drawn across the tall windows.

Maria Benucci was a small figure in a vast bed. Lucy could hardly make her out in the dimness.

'Maria, my dear, here is Mrs Chandler,' Mr Benucci began. 'She is to keep house and see to your meals.'

'Please call me Sylvia,' she said to Maria.

'Open the curtains, Mario,' a small voice said from the bed. 'I want to see her.'

Her husband did as he was asked. In the bed Lucy saw a painfully thin woman with a mass of dark hair in need of combing. The front of her nightdress was stained with food. Maria Benucci cut a pathetic figure and Lucy's heart was touched with pity.

Dark eyes stared from the pale face at Sylvia. 'You're a handsome woman,' Maria said weakly. 'I was handsome once.'

'Have you an objection, Maria, my dear?' Mr Benucci asked quickly.

'None. I want only peace now, Mario.'

'Then it's settled,' he said. 'Sylvia will begin her duties as soon as possible.' He moved towards the door. 'We'll leave you to rest now, Maria.'

There was no answer and so they left the room.

As they went downstairs Lucy was worried. Perhaps they had been too hasty in accepting this work. Should she speak up and tell Mr Benucci?

'I want you to meet Mama now,' Mr Benucci said eagerly when they were standing in the hallway again.

'Before we do that, Mr Benucci, I must speak with you,' Lucy began quickly. She could not let Sylvia take on something that would be too much for her.

'Lucy, what's the matter?' her mother asked.

'This house is very large,' Lucy continued quickly, 'and frankly, Mr Benucci, it has been neglected to a bad degree.'

'Lucy!' Sylvia exclaimed. 'How could you be so rude?' She turned to Mr Benucci. 'I do apologize for my daughter, Mr Benucci. Young people are so outspoken these days.'

Mario Benucci shook his head. 'Lucy speaks only the truth, Sylvia, and I should apologize to you,' he said sadly. 'My sister was a bad housekeeper. She was resentful and lazy. I had no right to expect you to . . .'

'But I want the position,' Sylvia said. 'And I could begin immediately.'

His eyes brightened. 'Oh, can you? Well, that's wonderful.'

'Wait!' Lucy exclaimed. 'My mother can't manage it alone.' She swallowed hard, wondering if he would resent her interference. 'You'll need to take on extra help, Mr Benucci. A woman to do the rough work and a maid.' She realized he could well afford it.

His eyes opened wide as though surprised that he hadn't thought of it himself. 'If you really think it necessary, Lucy, then so be it. I'll see to it first thing tomorrow morning.'

Mama Benucci, a wizened little woman with wrinkled olive-coloured skin, was sitting in a deep armchair near the front bay window watching the world go by outside.

'Sylvia, this is my mother, Mrs Bianca Benucci,' Mr Benucci began as they entered the room.

Bianca Benucci turned to stare at them, defiance in her dark shrewd eyes. 'Mario,' she said sharply. 'Where is Sophia?'

'I told you, Mama, she has gone away.' Mario Benucci sounded exasperated for a brief moment but quickly checked himself. 'Mama, this is Sylvia, our new housekeeper. She will take care of you from now on.'

Mrs Benucci stared at Sylvia. 'We want no outsiders here, prying into our business,' she said in a tone that brooked no argument. 'Sophia must be fetched home immediately.'

Mario Benucci sighed deeply. 'She has married, Mama. I told you. I cannot interfere between husband and wife.'

'Bah!' She glowered at Sylvia. 'My son may be a trusting fool but I am not,' she said. 'Do not think to rob us. I shall be watching your every move.'

'Mama!' With a helpless shrug he turned to Sylvia. 'I apologize. She is old, you understand.'

'Do not apologize for me, Mario!' Bianca Benucci burst out in a surprisingly strong voice. 'I will not be belittled in front of strangers. Now leave me!'

Out in the hallway, Mario Benucci looked thoroughly embarrassed. 'I hope you're not offended? She means no real harm.'

'She'll get used to me,' Sylvia said. 'I can start tomorrow if you like.'

He let out a long sigh of relief. 'By all means, Sylvia. Now we must talk terms.'

Mr Benucci's terms were quite generous, Lucy had to admit,

but she still wondered if it would all be too much for her mother. However, for the moment she would say nothing more.

Mario Benucci was as good as his word and the next day engaged a maid, who would live in, and a day woman to see to the rough work, leaving Sylvia in charge. It seemed ideal. With Sylvia's wage of two guineas a week, Eva's, and her own from the cafe they might just manage to live decently. They had no debts except what was owed to Mr Jarrett, but she was sure he would not press them for repayment, at least not just yet.

Lucy had been working at the cafe for a month and was getting used to the hard work, made even harder by the hot July weather they were experiencing.

She felt she had a lot to be thankful for. According to her mother everything ran smoothly at Mr Benucci's house in the Uplands, and he praised Sylvia to the skies, telling Lucy that her mother was a miracle worker.

It was Eva who was causing problems. Knowing Sylvia had the loan money, she pestered her mother continually for new clothes. 'But, Mam, I look a fright in these rags,' she burst out petulantly on the second Sunday in July. 'How can I go to church looking like this?'

'You look clean and respectable,' Lucy told her severely. 'Mam's not made of money.'

'But she is! She's still got most of that money from Mr Jarrett,' Eva snapped. 'I'm earning. I deserve a new dress. And my summer jacket is a disgrace.'

'I need that money to keep a roof over our heads,' Sylvia said. She looked a little distressed at the mention of the loan, Lucy thought. 'New clothes will have to wait.'

'I don't see why I should suffer.' Eva tossed her head angrily. 'It wasn't me who displeased Father,' she said nastily. 'I blame you, Mam. You should've made sure we were taken care of properly.'

'Don't speak to Mam like that,' Lucy said, angry at her sister's cruel words and selfishness. 'She has suffered more than either of us.'

But the following Sunday morning Eva appeared ready for church resplendent in a new dress. Lucy was astonished and stared accusingly at her mother.

'Mam, you gave her money for clothes after all!'

'Eva was right,' Sylvia said, looking sheepish. 'It was because of me that your father treated us so poorly. I disappointed him.'

'You've no reason to feel guilty,' Lucy declared. 'Eva is playing on your sympathy. Oh! she makes my blood boil. She's so selfish.'

The start of August gave no let up in the heat and the cafe's kitchen felt like a cauldron. At midday, when Lucy felt herself wilting, Mr Benucci came in to speak to her.

'Lucy, take your lunch break now,' he said.

Thankfully she wiped her soda-reddened hands and followed him into the cafe itself, which was packed to capacity, and buzzing with chatter as it always was on Friday, market day.

As Lucy waited at the counter for her usual hot pie, a man with a half-smoked cigarette dangling from his lower lip came into the cafe from the street and stood next to her. He wore a fashionable and expensive-looking three-piece suit and a homburg hat, but he did not have the air of a gentleman.

'Hello, Mario,' he said without taking the cigarette from his mouth. 'How's business?'

Mario Benucci looked up at him, and Lucy saw a momentary flicker of dislike in his eyes which surprised her.

'Fine, Mr Naylor, just fine,' her employer answered stiffly.

Mr Benucci pushed Lucy's plate towards her across the counter. 'Here's your food, Lucy. You can eat it in the kitchen if you like.'

Lucy was nonplussed. Mr Benucci had a strict rule that employees should not consume food in the kitchen itself. Yet here he was suggesting it. It was very odd.

'That's all right, Mr Benucci,' she said. 'I'll take that corner seat over by there. I won't be long.'

She walked away and sat down on the one unoccupied seat at a crowded table where she had a clear view of the counter.

Mr Naylor was tall and well built, probably in his early thirties, and as she glanced up at him she was disconcerted to see that while he continued to speak with Mr Benucci, he was watching her closely.

He appeared to be asking her employer a question yet never took his eyes off her. Mr Benucci shook his head vigorously and scowled. She had never seen an angry expression on his face before.

Dismissing Mr Naylor as extremely rude, Lucy got on with eating her pie, ignoring him. One of the young waitresses brought her a cup of tea and then, as two people at her table got up to go, he came across and without asking sat down opposite her.

She glanced up at him and then looked away quickly on seeing the disturbing expression in his eyes.

'Hello, Lucy,' Mr Naylor said. 'What's a pretty girl like you doing in a place like this?'

Lucy kept her eyes lower to her plate and did not deem to answer. She would ignore him. He was a complete stranger and had no right to be so familiar as to use her first name.

'The shy type, eh?' he said. He took a draw on the cigarette and then exhaled, letting the smoke drift in her face.

Trying to ignore it, Lucy took a sip of her tea and looked at him over the rim of the cup. There was confidence and arrogance in his expression and she took a dislike to him instantly.

In silence she put the cup down in its saucer and cut into her pie again.

'Don't you know it's rude not to answer when spoken to?' he said. His tone had an edge to it now. 'Or did your mother tell you not to talk to strangers, little girl?'

This was too much for her. Lucy took his glance directly and then had a qualm at the boldness of his gaze. But he angered her so she screwed up her courage to answer.

'You're right,' she said sharply, looking at him haughtily. 'I don't talk to strangers, especially rude ones who blow cigarette smoke in one's face and push their attentions where they are not wanted.'

His eyes widened at her directness. He looked annoyed for a moment and then recovered. 'Ah! Spirit and pluck,' he said. 'I like that in my women.'

'Ooh!' Lucy tightened her lips disapprovingly. She was insulted that he was trying to strike up an acquaintance with her; treating her no better than he would a common street woman.

He gave a thin sardonic smile at her reaction and then turned towards the counter and lifted the hand that held the cigarette.

'Mario!' he called out loudly. 'A cup of tea over here.'

Out of the corner of her eye Lucy saw Mr Benucci hesitate before waving his hand to one of the waitresses. He was watching them closely and she saw he was worried.

'What's your name?' Stan Naylor asked Lucy.

'You already know it,' Lucy said quietly.

She wasn't used to men pressing their attentions on her and was unsure how she should react. She did not want to kick up a fuss and make a fool of herself before all the customers.

'I mean your last name,' he said. 'Where do you live?'

'It's none of your business,' she said smartly.

'I could make it my business,' he said provocatively.

Lucy had had enough of him. The remainder of her pie was uneaten but she had lost her appetite for it. She attempted to rise from the table.

'Excuse me,' she said quickly.

'Where are you going?'

'If you must know, back to my work in the kitchen,' she said pertly. 'I have to earn my bread.'

'There are better ways to earn a living for a good-looking girl like you,' he said slyly. 'You deserve more than this third-rate cafe.'

'This job suits me fine,' she answered shortly and turned away. To her astonishment he grasped hold of her arm tightly, preventing her from leaving.

'I haven't finished talking to you yet,' he said loudly. 'No one walks away from Stan Naylor.'

She realized that the continuous hum of conversation around her had quietened abruptly and almost all the customers in the cafe were watching them. She felt her face flush with embarrassment and dismay. 'Let me go! How dare you put a hand on me?'

'Oh, don't be so coy,' he smirked, pulling at her arm. 'A nice piece of fluff like you must have plenty of men chasing her.'

'Let me go!' Lucy struggled, feeling desperate, not knowing what she should do.

The next moment Mario Benucci was at her side.

'Take your hand off my employee, Mr Naylor,' he said, his face darkly flushed. 'I want no trouble here. Please leave my cafe now.'

Stan Naylor rose to his feet. 'You'll keep out of this, Mario, if you know what's good for you,' he snarled.

Mario Benucci straightened his shoulders in a challenging gesture.

'I'm not afraid of you, Mr Naylor,' he said hoarsely. 'You're on my property and I want you out. If you don't go, I'll call a constable.'

Stan Naylor was obviously incensed and looked dangerous, as though he might strike Mr Benucci. 'No greasy little Itie is going to tell me what to do,' he exploded.

There was complete silence in the room as all the customers seemed to hold their breaths. Lucy felt mortified and afraid for Mr Benucci. Stan Naylor was obviously a bully.

Sweat broke out on Mr Benucci's upper lip and he looked angered and defiant. 'I mean it, Mr Naylor,' he said. 'I'll call the law. You can't afford that.'

'Damn you!' Stan Naylor snarled. He turned to look at Lucy, his eyes flashing anger at her as though she was responsible for his public humiliation. 'I'll see you again, Lucy, don't worry.'

He glanced around at the people seated and then with an oath strode from the cafe. Immediately the customers resumed eating and chatting. The show was over.

Trembling all over, Lucy sank on to the seat she had just vacated. 'Thank you, Mr Benucci,' she said sincerely. 'I'm so sorry about that awful scene in front of the customers.'

'Go back to the kitchen,' Mr Benucci murmured. 'I want to talk to you.'

Lucy rose shakily and walked to the back of the cafe and into the kitchen, her employer following her. Did he blame her for the insults heaped on him by that awful man? Was she about to get the sack?

Nervously, Lucy turned to face him. 'It wasn't my fault, Mr Benucci,' she began quickly. 'I did nothing to encourage him.'

'I know. Stan Naylor is not a good man, Lucy. He has a bad reputation where . . . the ladies are concerned. Have nothing to do with him.'

'I don't intend to,' Lucy assured him earnestly. Her instincts had told her that Stan Naylor was a person to be avoided. She bristled. His behaviour was unforgivable.

'He's a moneylender, among other things, with an office at the top of Union Street,' Mario Benucci said. 'So be careful.'

That was too close for comfort, Lucy thought.

'He's dangerous and unscrupulous,' her employer continued in a warning tone. 'I've heard he has unpleasant ways of dealing with clients who fall into arrears. That's why my threat of the law sent him on his way.'

'He's a criminal?'

'Undoubtedly. He has very dubious acquaintances. I've heard talk that he may be a fence for stolen goods.'

A criminal. That frightened her. 'I hope he won't come back,' Lucy said apprehensively.

Mario shrugged his thick shoulders. 'Most likely he will,' he said seriously. 'Now he has a grudge against me.'

'Oh, Mr Benucci!' Lucy was dismayed that she had brought trouble on this gentle man. 'It's all my fault.'

'No, you're the last one to blame, Lucy. Stan Naylor has a eye for a pretty face and is unprincipled. As he told us, no one walks away from him if he doesn't want them to.'

Lucy lifted her chin. 'He'll get nowhere with me,' she said firmly. 'I despise men of his type.'

Lucy decided not to tell her mother, or even Eva, what had happened at the cafe. Things seemed to be going well at the moment. Her mother was obviously happier working at Mr Benucci's house and Eva also seemed settled in her job. There was no need to worry either of them with something that might never come to anything.

The next morning when Lucy turned up at the cafe she had a shock. Mario Benucci was standing on the pavement giving directions to a workman who was covering the window with hardboard.

Lucy rushed to her employer's side. 'What's happened, Mr Benucci?'

'A brick through the window in the night,' he said heavily. 'The till has been opened but luckily I took the takings home with me.'

'Who could've done this?'

Mario looked at her seriously. 'You can guess who I suspect, Lucy.

'Oh, no!'

He nodded. 'Naylor didn't do this himself, of course. He has some unsavoury friends who would do it for him.'

Lucy was filled with disquiet. 'This has happened because of me.' She could not let Mr Benucci take the brunt of Stan Naylor's malice any longer. 'Perhaps I should give up my job, Mr Benucci,' she said in a dispirited voice. 'When I'm gone he won't victimize you any more.'

'No, you stay,' Mario said in a strong voice. 'I won't let Naylor intimidate me. This is merely a nuisance. I am insured. My cafe has a good reputation. This won't keep customers away.'

'I hope not, Mr Benucci,' Lucy said earnestly. 'I wouldn't want to be responsible for damaging your business.'

Mario smiled. 'Come along,' he said, urging her inside. 'Business goes on as usual, you'll see. There'll soon be plenty of work to take your mind off Stan Naylor.'

Lucy smiled back weakly. She did not think so. Stan Naylor had become a worrying threat in her life, and she knew she was ill-prepared to deal with such a ruthless man.

Six

Mr Benucci was right about his customers. They were loyal and Lucy was certain the boarded window brought in many others who were curious. The dirty crockery seemed to come in an endless stream. What with an aching back and aching legs she had little time to think about her own problems.

At closing time Mario Benucci slipped a half-crown into her hand. 'You've worked well, Lucy. I told you my customers would come.'

Tired as she was after the long day, Lucy was grateful. With wages coming in from three jobs they were just about keeping their heads above water, but still, every shilling counted.

The waitresses had left. Lucy and Mr Benucci were the last to leave. She waited as he locked up the door, rummaging in her handbag for some coins ready for the tramcar.

'Goodnight, Mr Benucci,' she said. 'See you in the morning.'

'Goodnight, Lucy.'

With a smile he crossed the road to the yard at the back of the pub opposite where his motor car was parked. Lucy walked down Union Street, and turned the corner into Oxford Street to go to the tram stop outside the market gates.

As she passed the front of the Exeter Hotel on the corner, she saw a man lounging in the pub's doorway smoking a cigarette, and with a shock recognized Stan Naylor. It came into her mind that he was waiting for her, and turning her glance away quickly, hurried on past.

'Lucy!' he called out.

She did not stop but quickened her pace and then heard his footsteps behind her. The market and most of the shops were shut at this time of an evening and so there were few pedestrians about.

Frightened, Lucy broke into a run, desperate to get to the

tram stop further up the road where she could see a few men were waiting. He wouldn't dare accost her there.

Suddenly her arm was seized from behind and she was jerked to a standstill. He swung her around to face him.

'You're a stubborn little piece, aren't you,' he said harshly flicking away the half-smoked cigarette.

'Let me go!' Lucy blurted.

'Not likely!' He grinned. 'There's no one to interfere now.'

'How dare you accost me like this,' Lucy cried out, struggling to free her arm. 'I'll call a constable.'

'Don't be silly. I just want to talk – for now.'

'I've nothing to say to the likes of you,' Lucy panted. Her heart was racing like a steam engine, and she looked about her, frantic to find a way of escaping him.

'The likes of me? What does that mean?' His tone was harsh.

'You've a grudge against Mr Benucci because he stood up for me. I know you're responsible for smashing the cafe window,' she accused unwisely. 'You're no more than a criminal.'

'Benucci has been telling tales, has he?' he snarled. 'Listen, I'm a businessman, I am, nothing more, see?'

'You're no gentleman, that's for sure,' Lucy said brusquely. His fingers were digging into her arm. There were bound to be bruises. 'No decent man would waylay a woman in the street. Let me go!'

He glanced around and then abruptly pulled her roughly into the doorway of Fanbury's dress shop. The entrance formed a deep semicircular well, with a central display window. He pushed her behind this, effectively screening them from the street.

'Now listen,' he said, leaning close, crowding her. She could smell tobacco on his clothes. 'Why are you making things difficult, Lucy? I only want to get to know you better.'

Lucy pressed her back against the glass door, straining to avoid physical contact with him. 'I don't want to know you,' she said breathlessly and swallowed hard. She felt like a small trapped animal.

'Now that's no way to behave when a man is paying you the compliment of being interested.'

'Why *are* you interested in me? I'm nobody.'

'Have you looked in the mirror lately?' He grinned. 'You're the best-looking woman I've seen in a long time.' He lifted a hand and touched her cheek with the back of his forefinger and Lucy cringed, terrified. 'Apart from your looks, there's something about you that makes my mouth water,' he went on, an underlying huskiness in his voice. 'You've got mettle. You're like me.'

'I'm nothing like you,' Lucy declared strongly. 'I'm hard-working and law-abiding.'

She strained further to keep a space between them. She was really frightened now. What did he want? What did he mean to do?

'Forget what Benucci told you about me,' Stan Naylor said heavily. 'He's jealous. He probably fancies you himself.'

'You're disgusting!'

He caught hold of the tops of her arms in a hard grip and gave her a little shake. 'Listen, you wouldn't think that if you knew me better,' he said. 'I treat my women well.'

'That's not what I heard,' Lucy blurted. 'You're not a good man.'

'I'd be good to you if you'd let me,' he said throatily, pulling her against his chest. Lucy felt sick with fear. 'Nothing would be too good or too much for you, Lucy, nothing.'

'Let me go!' Lucy sobbed in her fear. 'I want nothing from you.'

He shook her again. 'Give me a chance, for God's sake!' There was a hard edge to his voice now as though he was losing patience. 'I could give you anything you want – the best clothes, I'd buy you a flat or even a house. Just say the word.'

'No! I'm a respectable girl,' Lucy cried out, offended. 'I want nothing to do with you, Mr Naylor.'

'You stubborn little slut!' He released her and took a step back, his face darkening with anger. 'You think you're too good for me, is that it?'

'Yes! That's it!' Lucy shouted.

He scowled in rage and she thought he was about to strike her. But all at once she saw through the glass of the shop window a familiar outline: dark blue uniform and a spiked helmet.

'Help!' Lucy shouted. 'Help!'

Instantly the constable dashed into the doorway, confronting them.

'What's going on here?' he said sternly glancing from one to the other. 'You've no business in here when the shop's shut.'

'This man has accosted me,' Lucy cried out. 'He won't let me go. Help me.'

'Now then, sir?'

Stan Naylor laughed softly. 'Lovers' tiff, officer,' he said jovially. 'She dragged me in here to see that fur coat there.' He pointed at the article displayed in the window. 'Now she's cross because I won't promise to buy it for her.' He winked. 'You're a man of the world, officer. You know what women are like.'

The constable smirked, and sent Lucy an amused glance.

'He's lying!' Lucy cried out.

'Lucy!' Stan Naylor sounded hurt. 'Now you're taking things too far. This officer has more important matters to deal with than one of your tantrums.'

The constable stopped smirking and looked more closely at her. 'Is your name Lucy?'

'Yes, but . . .'

'I understand, sir,' the constable said, smiling again. 'But just the same, you must move on. You can't stay here.'

'We were just leaving, officer,' Stan Naylor said pleasantly.

He took Lucy's arm forcefully and led her out of the doorway, the constable following.

On the pavement, out of earshot of the police officer who continued to watch them, Stan Naylor whispered close to her ear. 'Make more trouble and you *will* be sorry.'

He propelled her quickly along the pavement, Lucy staggering forward on legs made stiff with fright. She must get away from him somehow.

They turned the corner into Park Street. Here he stopped. The planes of his face were hard with suppressed anger as he looked at her.

'You're playing a dangerous game, Lucy,' he said gutturally. 'And you're making me angry. If you knew me better you'd know that is unwise. Be sensible, and listen to what I have to offer.'

'You're wasting your time,' she answered breathlessly.

She glanced towards the corner. The constable was probably still in Oxford Street checking the shop entrances. If she made a dash for the tram stop now, Stan Naylor wouldn't dare chase after her.

'I never waste my time,' he said. 'I always get what I want, and I want you, Lucy, badly. Now listen, will you . . .'

At that moment Lucy decided to act. She put a hand against his chest and pushed. He momentarily lost his balance and staggered back. Lucy took flight. She sprinted to the corner and dashed across the road.

'I know where you work, Lucy,' Stan Naylor yelled after her.

She did not pause in her run and was thankful to see a tram just then stopping to pick up passengers outside the market gates. Leaping forward like a gazelle, she was on board in a moment, and panting, tottered along the aisle to find a seat. As she collapsed on to it she glanced out of the window. Stan Naylor was standing on the corner, his expression livid.

The tram moved off and Lucy sighed with relief. But his last words echoed in her mind. He could always find her again at the cafe.

That gave her pause for thought. There was no help for it. She would have to give up that job straight away. It would be a blow losing that good money but it had to be done.

While she would never contemplate for one second giving in to Stan Naylor, he was dangerous and he could make her life a misery from now on.

Although she was not in the least hungry after her upset, Lucy made an attempt to eat supper. Later she knew she had to be frank about what happened. She was sure Sylvia would understand that she had to give up the well-paid job at the cafe. All the same, it was a lot of money to lose from their income.

'Mam, I'll be coming with you to Mr Benucci's house tomorrow. I'd like to get there a bit earlier than usual before he leaves for business.'

Sylvia looked puzzled. 'What on earth for?'

Eva looked at Lucy with a smirk on her face. 'Has old Benucci tried to make up to you, or what?'

'Be quiet, Eva,' Sylvia said. 'Now, what's this all about, Lucy?'

Biting her lip for a brief moment, Lucy related what had happened.

'So a man with a bit of go in him tried to pick you up,' Eva said scornfully. 'That's nothing. It happens to me all the time. You should be flattered.'

Lucy ignored her. 'Mam, this man is dangerous,' she said earnestly, looking appealingly at her mother. 'He has a bad reputation. Mr Benucci knows him; says he has his finger in all kinds of pies, moneylending and so on. He's on the edge of being a criminal. His name is Stan Naylor.'

'What?' Sylvia started. Her face drained of colour and she clutched at the arm of her chair. 'Oh, no!'

Lucy was alarmed. 'Mam! Do you know him?'

Sylvia put her hand to her throat and shook her head vehemently. 'No, of course I don't!' she said quickly. 'It's just that I've heard talk too.'

'Is he good-looking?' Eva asked. 'He sounds as though he might have a bob or two.'

'You're doing the right thing in leaving the cafe,' Sylvia agreed. 'A respectable young woman like you can't be too careful.'

'I'll find something else, I'm sure I will,' Lucy said lightly, although she did not feel at all hopeful. 'I'll ask Mrs Grant if she knows of a job going around Brynmill.' It would not be wise to look for work in town, she decided. Stan Naylor might find her again. She shuddered at the idea.

'Did . . . did you tell him your last name?' Sylvia asked. Lucy thought her voice trembled. 'Does he know where you live?'

'No,' Lucy said firmly. 'Stan Naylor knows nothing about me, and I'm going to stay out of his way.'

Eva sniffed. 'Well, I think you're throwing away a good chance of making something of yourself,' she said. 'You're so stand-offish. I mean, it's no wonder to me that you lost Lewis Saunders. You don't know how to handle men, that's your trouble. Now, I—'

'Eva, be quiet, do!' Sylvia shouted. She looked distressed. 'That's a disgraceful way for a young girl to talk.'

Eva tossed her head. 'This is the beginning of the twentieth century, you know, Mam,' she said scornfully. 'We've left Victorian ideas behind.'

'I'll hear no more of it!' Sylvia exclaimed with energy. 'I'm going to bed. I've a bad headache.'

'Lucy, I'm so sorry to lose you,' Mario Benucci said when she told him her decision the next morning. He shrugged his heavy shoulders. 'But I do understand. You're wise. Stan Naylor is not the sort of man to associate with in any way.'

He gave her the money that was due to her for the days she had worked that week, and then she left and went back to their flat.

At the first opportunity she went up to see Mrs Grant. When she knocked at the front door, the landlady answered the door. She raised her eyebrows. 'Lucy! I'd have thought you would be at work at this hour.'

'I've left the cafe,' Lucy said shortly. 'I'm looking for another job. Do you know of anything around here?'

Mrs Grant drew in a deep breath, contemplating. 'Well,' she said, 'the only position I know of is with my friend Mrs Pettigrew. She has that big house on the corner of Rhyddings Park Road; keeps a boarding house for commercial travellers.'

'Oh, that sounds ideal,' Lucy said eagerly.

Mrs Grant looked her up and down. 'Yes, well . . . I don't know whether the work is beneath you, you being so refined, like.'

Lucy shook her head. 'I'll take anything,' she said.

'Mrs Pettigrew needs a woman for heavy work. Lugging coal scuttles up the stairs to the rooms, lighting fires and cleaning grates, and so on.'

'I'm stronger than I look,' Lucy said in a positive tone.

'Well, I hope you're more nimble on your feet than the last woman. Fell down the back stairs and broke her leg. So inconvenient to everyone! My friend was quite put out.'

'I'll go and see her right away,' Lucy said, backing away from the door. 'Before she takes on someone else.'

Mrs Pettigrew was a small, thin, sharp-nosed woman with a permanently worried expression.

'I take only gentlemen – commercial travellers,' she announced loudly on seeing Lucy standing on her doorstep. 'No ladies at all.'

'I'm here about a job,' Lucy said quickly. 'Mrs Grant, Marlborough Road sent me.'

'Oh, Elsie? Well, that's different.' She paused, inspecting Lucy carefully. 'I want a woman for heavy work.' She sniffed. 'Not much substance to you, is there?' She shook her head. 'It's hard work, you know.'

'I'm used to that,' Lucy said quickly. 'I'm very sturdy really.'

'Better come inside then and we'll talk about it.'

Lucy followed her would-be employer along a wide very clean passage and down some steps to a basement kitchen which gave exit to a small back garden.

'I do the cooking around here and the cleaning,' Mrs Pettigrew said. 'I want someone to carry coal scuttles up to the rooms, see that there's always plenty of coal too. My gentlemen expect comfort.'

'I can do that,' Lucy said.

'There's a great deal of laundry in a boarding house. That would be your job too, boiling, mangling and scrubbing the kitchen floor.' She looked at Lucy dubiously. 'Do you think you're up to it?'

'I'm a hard worker, Mrs Pettigrew.' Lucy paused. 'What's the wage?'

'Five shillings and sixpence a week,' Mrs Pettigrew said.

Lucy smiled weakly, trying not to show her disappointment. She would have to take it. She could not afford to be out of work for long.

'That suits me, Mrs Pettigrew,' Lucy said. 'I could start as soon as you like.'

Mrs Pettigrew studied her. 'You're a tenant of Elsie Grant's, are you?'

'My mother is the tenant,' Lucy said, and then hesitated to mention her mother's name. Had the gossip they had left behind in the Mumbles caught up with them? 'My mother is Mrs Sylvia Chandler. She's a widow,' she ventured at last.

'Oh, well,' Mrs Pettigrew said. 'If you're good enough for Elsie you'll suit me. When can you start?'

Lucy was relieved. 'I can start now, if you like,' she said eagerly, glancing around the kitchen.

'Right you are!' Mrs Pettigrew pointed to a cupboard. 'You'll find a sacking apron in there. Coal house is out back.'

Lucy quickly took off her hat and coat.

'Collect the coal scuttles from the rooms – six bedrooms on three floors,' Mrs Pettigrew instructed. 'Oh, and by the way, always knock first in case the gentleman is in.' She gave Lucy a warning look. 'And never loiter in the bedrooms.'

'I understand, Mrs Pettigrew.'

'When you've done that let me know. There's plenty more work. I want the laundry done every day, for example. You'll find the boiler and the mangle in the outhouse.'

'Yes, Mrs Pettigrew.'

Her employer sniffed. 'Right! Well, I'll leave you to it.'

It was gone nine o'clock that evening before Lucy got back to the flat, tired out. Sylvia ran anxiously into the passage when she opened the front door.

'Oh, thank goodness!' her mother said. 'I thought something had happened . . . that awful man . . .'

Lucy smiled wearily as she sat down at the table. 'I found myself another job, Mam,' she said. 'In a boarding house nearby. Not so well paid as the cafe, but it's something to keep the wolf away.'

'Come on, have your supper,' Sylvia urged. 'And then get off to bed. You look worn out.' She gave a little sob of misery. 'Oh, Lucy, what have I brought you to?'

Lucy gratefully ate what was put before her as she was ravenously hungry despite being weary. 'Mam, you mustn't blame yourself,' she said between mouthfuls. 'Father betrayed us all. We have to make a life for ourselves as best we can.'

Seven

Mrs Pettigrew did not seem to know the meaning of the phrase 'pause for breath', keeping Lucy on the go continually. At last it was Thursday and Lucy was glad it was her half day off.

As she approached the flat she saw Mrs Grant standing at her front door, and had the feeling the landlady was waiting for one of them to come home.

'Hello, Mrs Grant,' Lucy said as she reached the top of the area steps. 'Did you want to speak to my mother?'

The landlady's lips were a thin line as she looked at Lucy. 'I should say I do,' she said harshly. 'And you know why.'

Lucy was nonplussed at the animosity in her tone. 'Sorry, I don't,' she said shaking her head. 'Do you have a complaint?'

Mrs Grant drew in her chin. 'Arrears!' she said flatly.

'Arrears?' Lucy frowned at her, bewildered.

Mrs Grant's glance was frosty. 'I thought you were a respectable family when I let you have the flat. I never thought you were dishonest. I'm disappointed.'

Lucy blinked. 'What are you saying?'

'Three weeks' rent, that's what's owed to me,' Mrs Grant said loudly. 'And I want my money now or out you go on to the street, the lot of you. Tell your mother that!'

On those words she turned and stepped quickly into the house, slamming the door in Lucy's face.

Lucy was stunned and stood where she was for a moment more trying to understand what had just been said. How could they possibly be in arrears?

She let herself into the flat and put the kettle on. As she waited anxiously for Sylvia to come home, she mulled over Mrs Grant's accusation. Although their combined income was not so much it covered the rent with a little over for food, and surely there must be some of Mr Jarrett's money left.

Sylvia and Eva arrived at the same time. Her sister was talking non-stop about the day she had had at the shop and the distinguished gentlemen clients she had attended to.

Sylvia looked weary, but as Lucy looked more closely she could see tiredness was not the only thing weighing heavy on her mother. She put cups of tea before the two of them and then sitting herself, burst out with what was uppermost in her mind.

'Mam, how did we get into arrears with the rent?'

'What?' Sylvia's hand jerked and she spilled her tea. 'What did you say?'

Lucy reached across the table and took her mother's free hand.

'Mrs Grant says she'll turf us out on the street if the three weeks' arrears aren't paid straight away. Mam, what's going on?'

'Out on the street?' Eva exclaimed. 'What blooming cheek!'

Sylvia's face was white. 'It's a mistake. I'll talk to her,' she said in a voice that quivered. 'I'll straighten it all out.'

'We're not children to be protected, Mam,' Lucy said seriously. 'If we're in trouble you must tell us. Eva and I have a right to know.'

Sylvia covered her mouth with her hand and her head dipped for a moment. Lucy could see she was really upset.

'I'm a little short at present,' she said at last, her voice a mere murmur. 'It's only temporary, I'm sure.'

'But Mr Jarrett's loan?' Lucy said. 'Surely that's not all gone?'

Sylvia nodded, gazing at Lucy with tears in her eyes. 'It's almost gone; just a few pounds left.' She touched a handkerchief to her eyes. 'It seemed to melt away, Lucy, just melt away. Rent, food, clothes for Eva . . .'

'Don't you blame me, Mam!' Eva exploded. 'We should never have left you in charge of the money. Father always said you were scatterbrained.'

'Eva!' Lucy was furious with her sister. 'Mam needs our support, not criticism. And Father was hardly a paragon of virtue himself, was he?'

Eva pouted and folded her arms across her chest, looking

petulant. Lucy ignored her. She had to sort this out. Without a roof over their heads they were done for.

'How much do we owe Mrs Grant?'

Sylvia swallowed. 'Forty shillings with this week's rent.'

'How much is left of the loan?'

Sylvia sniffed in misery. 'A couple of pounds, that's all.'

'But enough to settle with Mrs Grant?'

Sylvia looked up, alarm in her eyes. 'No, Lucy! I need that money for . . .'

Lucy stared at her waiting for an explanation. 'For what, Mam? Nothing is more important than keeping a roof over our heads. We've nowhere else to go.'

'Well, I'm not leaving,' Eva said, lifting her chin aggressively. 'I'll barricade myself in before I do.'

'Mam, are you in some kind of trouble?' Lucy asked gently.

Sylvia burst into tears and refused to speak again. She left the room and Lucy heard her running along the passage to her bedroom. After a moment Lucy followed. She knocked on Sylvia's door and went in.

'Mam, I must have that money for Mrs Grant,' she said quietly. 'Please give it to me now.'

Without a word, Sylvia indicated the top drawer of the chest. Inside Lucy found a brown-paper bag with just three pound notes inside. Astonished and concerned she glanced across at her mother. 'This is all that's left of the thirty pounds Mr Jarrett loaned you?'

Sylvia nodded, sobbing, and seemed not to be able to speak.

'Mam, how could we possibly have spent so much?'

'I'm not used to handling large sums of money,' Sylvia mumbled miserably. 'Your father always gave me just enough to pay for our household needs. The loan ran between my fingers like water.'

Lucy sighed heavily. She could not blame her mother. Joseph Chandler might have been a deceitful husband but he had always shielded his family from the harsher realities of life.

'I'll give this to Mrs Grant right away,' she said quietly. 'The extra pound will pay the rent for the next two weeks in advance, just to show good faith.'

Sylvia turned away and buried her face in her pillow, weeping. Lucy gazed at her trembling form. She realized there was a lot Sylvia was not telling them and began to feel frightened herself.

Mrs Grant received the back rent huffily. 'How do I know this won't happen again? I can let that flat over and over, you know.'

Lucy offered the extra pound. 'I promise we won't fall behind in future,' she said. 'And here's two weeks' rent in advance.'

With a toss of her head Mrs Grant took the note from her fingers.

'Well, I hope I shan't have more of this unpleasantness, for your sakes.' She lifted her chin and gave Lucy an arch look. 'Many families have ended up in the workhouse for owing less. Bear that in mind.'

Lucy took charge of their income from that time on, putting aside the rent every week and doling out to her mother just enough money for necessities such as food.

Eva complained bitterly that her purse was always empty, and Lucy guessed that her sister had done her share in squandering the loan money.

Although they were out of debt with Mrs Grant, Sylvia seemed a bag of nerves always. Lucy discovered her crying quietly several times and she jumped out of her skin every time someone knocked at the door. Lucy was very worried for her.

It was the last Thursday in September, half day in Swansea. Eva wanted them all to take the train to Neath market, but Lucy was adamant that they would not spend one penny over their budget. They were arguing bitterly about it when someone knocked at their door.

Sylvia immediately sprang to her feet, her face turning pale, her eyes frightened. 'Who's that?'

'Probably Mrs Grant or a hawker selling something,' Lucy said, watching her mother's agitated expression. 'Go and see, Eva.'

'Tsk!' Eva tossed her head. 'It's always me. I'm a proper skivvy in this house, I am.' But she went to answer the door. 'Yes?'

Lucy could hear a man's voice.

'Is this the home of Mrs Sylvia Chandler?'

'Yes. What do you want?'

Sylvia heard the words too and clutched a hand to her throat. 'Oh, my God!'

'Hey!' Eva's voice suddenly rose angrily. 'Wait a minute! You can't barge in here uninvited.'

Sylvia gave another distressed cry, her expression terrified as heavy footsteps came down the passage.

Lucy leaped to her feet. 'Mam, what is it? What's the matter?'

Before her mother could answer, a tall man strode swiftly into the room and confronted them.

'Mrs Chandler,' he said loudly. 'You know why I'm here. Where's my money?'

Lucy stared at him, her mouth agape. Stan Naylor, as large as life. She was rooted to the spot. Despite all her precautions he had found her again.

Eva had followed him in. 'Get out,' she yelled. 'Get out whoever you are, before we call a constable.'

Stan Naylor ignored her. 'Well, Mrs Chandler,' he said heavily, 'I told you what would happen if you got into arrears. The whole debt becomes payable; the loan plus interest.' He held out his hand. 'I want my money; near enough a hundred pounds.'

Lucy drew in a loud gasp. 'A hundred pounds! That's absurd! What do *you* want with us?'

'Mrs Chandler knows why,' he said keeping his gaze on Sylvia. 'I warned you that if you reneged on the terms of your loan you'd face severe consequences.'

Lucy stepped towards him. 'What loan, Mr Naylor?' she demanded angrily.

For the first time he looked briefly in her direction, and then his glance snapped back to her, his eyes widening.

'Lucy!' He sounded as astounded as she was and he stared at her in disbelief.

Lucy was petrified for a moment but then Sylvia's frightened whimpering spurred her into action. She went to her mother and put an arm around her protectively.

'Don't you browbeat my mother,' she exclaimed hotly, trying to sound in control although she was trembling from head to foot. 'You've no right marching in here demanding money. Get out!'

'I've every right,' he said grimly. His gaze was fixed on her face, his expression calculating. 'Your mother borrowed money from me, fifty pounds, and now she has reneged. I've every right to demand what's due to me.'

Fifty pounds! Lucy was stunned. Her mother had lied about Mr Jarrett lending her money. Sylvia's worried behaviour was now explained. They were in worse trouble than ever. She decided to try and bluff their way out.

'We can't pay you,' Lucy said boldly. 'So you'll have to whistle for it.'

'The law is on my side,' he warned. He glanced around. 'I can seize your goods and chattels in lieu.'

'This flat is let to us fully furnished,' Lucy said. 'We own nothing here. You're wasting your time.'

He looked at her keenly for a moment. There was a cunning gleam in his eyes.

'I told you before, Lucy, I never waste my time,' he said evenly. 'Your mother owes me almost a hundred pounds to date. That's quite a sum. A labourer doesn't earn that in a year.' He smiled then, a smile of triumph. 'If your mother can't repay then I'll take it in kind.'

Lucy started. 'What do you mean?'

A smile still played on his lips. 'You know what I want, Lucy,' he said. 'I'll write off the debt if you'll agree to my terms.'

Lucy swallowed, suddenly afraid. 'Terms? What are you suggesting?'

'Lucy, what does he mean?' Sylvia asked, her voice quivering.

Eva gave a hooting laugh. 'I know what he means. He wants Lucy for his mistress.' She giggled. 'Isn't that just ripe!'

'His mistress! Oh my God!' Sylvia collapsed on to a chair. 'What I have brought my children to?'

'I guarantee to write off the debt, Mrs Chandler,' Stan Naylor said. 'If Lucy will be accommodating.'

Sylvia covered her face with her hands and sobbed. 'Oh, the shame of it. What have I done?'

'This is outrageous,' Lucy burst out, totally affronted. 'I utterly refuse. The proposition is insulting and degrading. How dare you suggest such a thing?' She felt her fury rise. 'Get out!' she stormed at him. 'Get out of my sight!'

'I wouldn't be too hasty, Lucy,' Stan Naylor warned. 'You haven't heard me through. I'll take care of all of you; provide a house, pay your expenses. You'd all live well.'

'Get out!' Lucy screeched. Her hands itched to strike him with something. She had never felt such humiliation, not even when she had learned she was illegitimate. 'Leave, before I do something I'll regret.'

His expression became grim again. 'The alternative is the workhouse, Lucy,' he warned. 'Your mother would never survive it. You think you're shamed now. You don't know the half.'

'I'd rather die than let my daughter live in such degradation,' Sylvia cried out. 'I'll . . . I'll kill myself if she agrees.'

'I've no intention of agreeing, Mam,' Lucy assured her. 'You've had my answer, Mr Naylor,' she said. 'You can do your worst to us, but I'll never agree to submit to you.'

His jaw worked furiously. 'You'll regret this, Lucy, I promise you.'

'Get out!' she yelled. 'You turn my stomach!'

There was cold rage in his eyes as he looked at her for a moment more and then he turned and strode out, slamming the front door behind him.

Lucy collapsed on to the nearest chair, her legs too weak to support her. That had been the worse moment of her life. To think that that evil man had propositioned her in front of her family as though she were nothing more than a common streetwalker. She felt besmirched to the very core of her being.

'You're a fool, Lucy,' Eva said scathingly. 'You've missed a great chance. You could've twisted him around your little finger in no time.'

'Be quiet, Eva,' Lucy cried out in anguish, hurt and astonished that she did not seem to appreciate the base insult Stan Naylor had heaped on her. Their world was tumbling down around their ears, but now she realized her sister was too shallow and self-centred to understand the tragedy of it.

Eva's lips twisted. 'I wish it was me he fancied. I'd be off like a shot.'

'Eva!' Sylvia was scandalized. 'Don't say such things, not even as a joke.'

'I'm not joking, Mam,' Eva said pertly. 'If Lucy wasn't so goody-goody, we'd be living in the lap of luxury. Did you see his suit? Cost thirty guineas, at least. He's got plenty of money, I'll bet.'

'Oh, Eva, how could you be so callow?' Sylvia whimpered. 'I've failed you both. I deserve to be punished.'

In trepidation, Lucy looked at her mother. Sylvia had her arms on the table, her head on top of them and she was sobbing as though her heart would break.

'Mam,' Lucy said, reaching out to her. 'Don't take on so. Eva's just a silly thoughtless girl who doesn't know what she's talking about.'

'Yes I do!' Eva exploded. 'I've got more gumption than either of you. I know how to get on, how to get what I want out of men.'

'Oh, my God! I've ruined us,' Sylvia cried. 'I've brought my daughters so low. Oh, I wish I were dead.'

'Don't say that!' Lucy cried, getting to her feet to comfort her. 'I'll never give in to Stan Naylor, and he can do what he will about it.'

Sylvia lifted her tear-stained face. She looked older and haggard with worry and strain. 'It's the workhouse for both my poor girls,' she said miserably. 'And perhaps prison for me.'

'Well, I'm not going to the workhouse,' Eva said loudly. 'I'm going to fight.'

'We've nothing to fight with,' Lucy said despondently.

'No, you haven't,' Eva said disparagingly. 'But I have a weapon, and I'm not afraid to use it either.'

Lucy shook her head. 'Eva, be quiet. You're upsetting Mam more,' she murmured tiredly. 'You don't know what you're talking about, anyway.'

Her sister's inane chatter wearied her. Since Stan Naylor's departure the knowledge of what was in their future had sunk in. Her mind had become numb with misery and worry.

'We'll see,' Eva exclaimed haughtily. 'I've got more guts than you have, Lucy, and more ambition. I know what I want, and I'm going after it.'

Lucy ignored her. 'Come on, Mam,' she said gently. 'Let's get you to bed. You're exhausted.'

She felt that way herself and longed to be in bed, but was doubtful that she would get any sleep. The future was now so bleak and uncertain. What little hope she had struggled to keep alive in her heart was now gone.

Eight

S tan looked up as the office door opened and a tall fashionably dressed woman in her mid-thirties walked in.

'What do *you* want, Maisie?' Stan asked testily, stubbing out a cigarette in the ashtray.

'Well, that's a nice way to speak to your wife, I must say.'

With a rustle of skirts Maisie sat down in the clients' chair opposite him. Stan sat back in his seat, scowling at her.

'You never come here,' he said irritably. 'You're spying on me, is that it?'

Nonchalantly she lifted one elegant shoulder. 'As it happens, no,' she said. 'I want some money.'

'What, again?'

'My word, you are irritable,' Maisie said mockingly. 'One of your floozies has given you the elbow, has she?'

Stan's jaw tightened. That was closer to the truth than he liked. He was still fuming at Lucy Chandler's rejection and the stark look of hatred she had given him. But it made no difference to the way he felt. He could not stop thinking about her. The more she appeared to despise him the hungrier for her he became. Lucy was a challenge and he was determined to possess her. She *would* be his.

To conceal his unrest he reached into the desk drawer, took out a packet of cigarettes and lit up.

'Why didn't you ask me for money this morning?' he asked, drawing deeply on the cigarette. 'Why come here?'

'You'd left before I got up,' she said. 'I was in town anyway. Why shouldn't I come here? Have you got something to hide, Stan?'

'Why don't you use your own money?' he asked, trying to change the subject. 'You've got plenty of it.'

'Now you know mine is all tied up in investments,' she said

with a smile. 'Anyway, it's a husband's place to provide for his wife.'

Stan stared at her. A few years older than he was, Maisie was still a looker. She had been stunning ten years ago when he had married her, a young widow, with money to burn. She had helped him get started in his various businesses, but she had proved too canny to allow him to take over her finances completely. She still had control of the bulk of her money. He knew her well enough now to realize she would never trust him with it.

Her wealth was substantial and maybe he would outlive her. It was for this reason that, although he had grown tired of her, he would never leave her. It would mean leaving all her money too. He wouldn't be such a fool.

'How much do you want?'

She told him.

His lips tightened as he flicked the ash from his cigarette. 'Are you thinking of buying up the town or what?' he asked sarcastically.

'It's no more than you spend on your loose women,' she said waspishly. 'Give me the money and I'll be gone.' She glanced at a small fob watch pinned to the bodice of her jacket. 'I've an appointment with the hairdresser in ten minutes.'

With a heavy sigh Stan rose from his seat and turned towards the safe behind his chair. He glanced at her. 'Before I open the safe, turn your back, Maisie.'

She gave a mocking laugh. 'You don't even trust your own wife?'

'Especially not my wife,' he said testily. 'Now, do you want the money or not.'

She turned in her chair and he watched as she took out a powder compact and pressed the powder puff gently to her nose.

'I look a fright,' she said archly peering at her reflection.

Satisfied, Stan turned the knob of the safe's lock to his secret combination and opened the door. Taking a bundle of notes out of the safe, he counted the amount she had asked for. He could well afford it, but it galled him to give her money when she was so well off.

He handed the money to her. She snapped her powder compact shut and rose from her seat, smiling at him as she accepted it. It was a fixed smile, he noted, cold and without any humour or feeling. But then he had no feelings for her.

'Good,' she said. 'I'll be off now.' With that she turned and walked swiftly from the room.

Stan closed the safe and spun the lock. Then he sat down again, sighing heavily. Lucy Chandler. She was so fresh and innocent, not hardened like Maisie. He had to find a way to tighten his hold on her mother; force Lucy to give way to him.

His jaw tightened. He would have her body and soul, and it would be one day soon.

Maisie Naylor walked to the corner higher up the street where a small carriage and horse were waiting. As she drew level the carriage door opened. Maisie glanced around to see if she was being observed and then quickly climbed in.

'Did you get it?' asked the man seated inside.

She fumbled in her purse. 'Quick, give me a pencil.'

He passed her the stub of a pencil and she wrote something on a piece of paper before handing it to him. He looked at it keenly.

'You're sure this is the combination?' he asked. 'I don't want to take any risks and come away empty-handed.'

'I'm not a fool, Ben Hopkins,' she snapped at him. 'So don't take me for one.'

'All right! Don't get shirty with me.' He paused. 'Did he notice you watching?'

'I watched him in the mirror of my powder compact.' She smiled. 'Stan is not as clever as he thinks he is.'

'Are you sure you want to do this?'

She lifted her chin. 'He has cheated on me for years. I know he thinks nothing of me, never did. It's my money he wants.'

'Why the hell did you marry him in the first place?'

Maisie had often asked herself the same question. Loneliness in being a young widow, she suspected.

'It's too late to think about that,' she said. 'All I want now is to hit him where it hurts most – his pocket. I'll teach him to neglect me for cheap whores!'

But neglect was not her only grievance. Since early in their marriage she had longed for a child, but Stan resolutely denied her. His excuse was he did not want that kind of responsibility. She had grown to hate him for it. Now Ben Hopkins had come into her life. He was nobody, a petty criminal, but he wanted her, and there was still time for children.

'I don't know why you've stayed with him,' Ben said.

That was a question she could not answer herself. 'Neither do I. I've put up with humiliation and disregard long enough. Now I'm going to ruin him if I can.'

'You could divorce him,' Ben said. 'You've got plenty of evidence.'

'It's not easy for a woman to obtain a divorce,' Maisie said bitterly. 'Besides, I could not bear the scandal that comes with it.' She nodded. 'No, I want to ruin him,' she said in a hard voice. 'I want to see him squirm.'

Ben gave the reins a flip to get the horse started when Maisie put her hand on his arm. 'Wait a minute,' she said. 'Look at that.'

A girl was walking slowly along the pavement looking up enquiringly at the signs attached to the buildings. She had a pretty pert face and a good figure. She walked with the confidence of youth, her hips swinging insolently and Maisie felt her hackles rise.

'A pound to a penny she'll go into Stan's office,' she said harshly.

As they watched, the girl turned into the moneylender's doorway.

'So that's his latest bit of stuff,' Maisie continued bitterly. 'She must be really new. He hasn't had time to buy her a flashy new wardrobe.'

'I thought you didn't care what he did any more,' Ben said moodily. 'You said you were my woman now.'

'I don't care,' Maisie exclaimed sharply. 'But it makes my blood boil that he thinks I'm too stupid to know what's going on.'

'He . . . he doesn't know about me, does he?'

Maisie laughed. 'You'd soon know about it if he did. Stan associates with some nasty people, believe me, and he'd have sent them around to rough you up.'

'That's comforting to know,' Ben said sarcastically as he flipped the reins again and they moved off.

Stan was sitting at his desk still brooding when a knock sounded at the office door. He straightened his shoulders and assumed a businesslike expression. 'Come in!' he called out.

The door opened and a girl strode confidently in. Stan caught his breath for a brief moment thinking it was Lucy Chandler but then he recognized her younger sister.

'Don't tell me you've come to pay off your mother's debt,' he said sarcastically.

She looked at him under her eyelashes. 'Well, I might have, in a way,' she said pertly.

'It's no use asking for more time,' Stan said harshly. 'Your mother had her chance and she was warned. I'm a businessman, not a charity.'

Eva Chandler sashayed further into the room and took the seat that Maisie had recently vacated.

'I'm not here about the loan,' she said. 'It's about what you suggested to Lucy.'

He leaned forward eagerly. 'Has Lucy changed her mind about my offer?'

'No, the stupid girl,' Eva said deprecatingly. 'But I'm open to offers.'

Stan was taken aback. He stared at her; her bold gaze and provocative smile. 'What?'

'I'm prettier and I'm younger. You'd find me a lot more fun than my goody-goody sister.'

He was amused. 'You're not old enough.'

'I'm seventeen!' she exclaimed hotly. 'I'm a woman. More woman than Lucy is.'

He stared for a moment more. 'You're serious, aren't you?' He could not believe her nerve.

'Of course I'm serious.'

She was pretty and eager but he was suspicious. 'Did your mother send you here?'

'Good heavens, no.' Eva laughed. 'She'd have a fit if she knew what I was doing.'

Stan rubbed his thumb against his jaw, thinking. No woman had ever propositioned him before and he was not sure he liked it.

'I'm not used to women taking the initiative,' he said sharply. 'Is this some kind of a trick to wriggle out of paying back the loan?'

'No.' She smiled. 'I told Lucy she was a fool to turn you down. You've got passable looks.'

And money, he thought cynically, and smiled. 'Flattery will get you nowhere.'

Eva inclined her head, looking at him under her eyelashes again. He suspected she thought the gesture irresistible and provocative, and he was reminded of her youthfulness.

'I don't beat about the bush where men are concerned,' she said with such obvious impudence that he laughed out loud. Her candour was refreshing.

'And of course at your age you've had great experience of men,' he mocked.

'I know how to twist them around my little finger,' Eva said with a lift of her slim shoulders. 'I know I'm attractive, and I know men's weaknesses.'

Stan looked at her. 'I believe you do,' he said thoughtfully.

She was attractive and apart from her auburn hair looked so much like Lucy. It was an offer handed to him on a plate. He'd be a fool to turn her away. And it struck him then that taking Eva up on her offer might force Lucy into taking her place. He could have his fun either way, and there was nothing to lose, everything to gain.

'All right, then, Eva,' he said slowly. 'I'll make you the same offer as I made Lucy, with one exception. I won't write off the loan. That stays.'

'I don't care about the loan,' Eva said with a dismissive shrug. 'That's my mother's headache. It was her fault we're in this mess in the first place. No man is ever going to do the dirty on me.'

There was a fleeting hardness in her face which reminded him of Maisie. Any qualms he might have had about her youthfulness dispersed.

He leaned back in his chair, smiling. 'So, what do you want, Eva.'

She sat forward eagerly, her expression alight with excitement. 'You promised Lucy a house, and clothes, didn't you. Well, I want all that.'

Her avariciousness grated on him and yet at the same time he was aware of an affinity. He had no illusions about himself or her. Maybe they were two of a kind after all.

'All right, but remember this, Eva,' he said warningly, 'I don't share my women with any other man. I'll set you up in your own place, but you're exclusively mine.'

She smiled at him. 'Of course, Stan. I'm young but I'm not a fool.' She gave him a pouting glance. 'And you stay away from Lucy,' she said. 'A deal is a deal.'

He nodded agreement but his thoughts were already racing ahead. He would be shot of this scheming little madam in a flash if he could have her sister.

'What happens next,' Eva said, interrupting his contemplation.

'Do you want to go home and collect your clothes and things?'

She shook her head. 'No fear.' She gave him a brazen glance. 'You'll provide all the clothes I want, won't you, Stan. And I'll want the best.'

'All right,' he said, rising from his chair. 'I own a house in Ffynonne. I'll take you there now.'

'Goody!'

'Eva, this isn't a game,' he said seriously. 'I'm taking you as my mistress. You do understand what that means?'

Eva looked impatient. 'Of course I do.'

'You've had experience, then, have you?'

Eva tossed her head. 'Of course!' she answered glibly.

He knew she was lying. He would be the first man in her life. He liked the idea.

'Well, you can settle in the house for the rest of the day,' he said. 'I'll see you tonight. Do you understand what I mean?'

She flushed then. 'Yes,' she said breathlessly. 'And I'm ready.'

'Where can she be, Lucy?'

Twisting her hands together fretfully, Sylvia stood at the window which overlooked the area steps and gave a limited view of the feet of passers-by on the pavement above.

'She's dawdling somewhere,' Lucy said, trying to sound comforting, although she was beginning to worry herself.

'But it's gone ten o'clock!' Sylvia turned from her vigil at the window to send Lucy a distraught glance. 'She's never been out this late before. I'm so worried.'

'Don't distress yourself, Mam,' Lucy begged, feeling angry at her sister's inconsiderate behaviour. How could she upset Mam this way? She would certainly get a piece of her mind when she did get home. 'I'm sure she's all right.'

'I pray that she is,' Sylvia murmured. 'If anything has happened to her it'll be all my fault.'

'That's nonsense,' Lucy said quickly. 'Eva's old enough to know right from wrong.'

Lucy wondered if that was still true. Eva had changed since going out into the world to work. There was a flightiness about her and she was becoming more and more unpredictable. She was certainly more thoughtless and selfish.

'Why don't you go to bed, Mam. I'll wait up for her.'

'I could never sleep not knowing where she is,' Sylvia said with a quiver in her voice. 'Oh, Eva, where are you?'

'But your body would be resting,' Lucy urged. 'Mam, we can't afford for you to be ill. Eva and I depend on you so much. Come on now, go and lie down.'

Sylvia eventually agreed and went to her bedroom. Lucy waited and waited. About one o'clock she peered in. Her mother seemed sound asleep, and Lucy was thankful, but she dreaded the morning.

'What time did Eva come in?' It was the first thing Sylvia said next morning as she sat up in bed and Lucy handed her a cup of tea.

Lucy hesitated, afraid to answer, and instead opened the bedroom curtains. In the early light Sylvia's features looked strained and Lucy realized her mother had had little sleep.

'Now don't get upset, Mam,' she said as calmly as she could. 'Eva didn't come home.'

'What?'

Sylvia dumped the cup and saucer on the bedside table and tried to struggle out of bed. 'She's missing. Oh, my God, Lucy, we must call a constable. They have to find her. Oh, Eva, my baby, where are you? What's happened to you?'

Lucy gently pushed her back on to the bed. She was very worried herself, but getting hysterical would not help.

'There's no reason to think anything has happened to her. Perhaps she's staying with a friend she met at the shop.'

'She's the only girl working at the shop,' Sylvia reminded her. 'As far as I know she has no friends; she's never mentioned any.'

That was true. Lucy had had many friends when they had lived in the Mumbles, but Eva had always kept herself apart, apparently despising the friendship of girls of her own age.

'We must call the law,' Sylvia said tearfully. 'She could be lying in a ditch somewhere.'

'Oh, Mam, that's going too far. I'll go to Eva's work first,' Lucy said. 'Perhaps I can find out something.'

Sylvia began to weep.

'You can't go to Mr Benucci's today, you're too upset,' Lucy said. 'I'll pop into the cafe to explain the situation to him.'

'I hate letting him down.'

'I know, but this is different, Mam. He'll understand.'

Lucy had a wash, but did not bother with breakfast; she was too worried herself.

She hurried around to Mrs Pettigrew's first to explain that she would not be able to work that morning. Her employer looked annoyed, her lips thinned.

'Very well, Lucy,' she said stiffly. 'But I hope you won't make a habit of this kind of behaviour.'

Lucy caught the tram to the Uplands and called into the gentlemen's outfitters where Eva worked. A tall thin man in a frock coat came forward as she entered. He looked down his nose at her.

'If you've come for a position, my girl, we have no work for you here.'

'I'm enquiring about my sister, Eva Chandler,' Lucy said quickly.

His expression turned even stonier. 'I said it was a mistake to hire a mere girl like her. Mr Benson thought otherwise, but I was right. Miss Chandler did not put in an appearance yesterday or today. Why, may I ask?'

'She's ill,' Lucy said on the spur of the moment.

'Well, you might have let us know before this.' He sniffed disdainfully. 'All right. I'll inform Mr Benson. When can we expect her to return?'

'When she's recovered,' Lucy said firmly and then turned and left the premises.

She was trembling as she stood on the pavement. From what she had just learned Eva had been missing for the best part of two days. Where could she be? Perhaps her mother was right. They should inform the law. But she hesitated, not quite believing there was anything sinister in her absence.

She would speak to Mr Benucci and ask his advice. Another tram took her into the heart of the busy town.

The cafe was already doing a good trade with customers taking a late breakfast, and Mr Benucci seemed pleased to see her. 'Lucy! How good to see you.'

'My mother is not able to get up to the Uplands to see to Mrs Benucci today,' Lucy said apologetically. 'She's upset. Something has happened.'

Mario Benucci's face fell. 'Has Naylor been badgering her again over the debt?'

'Not so far,' Lucy admitted.

'He will.' Mario nodded. 'I know that one. He's bad. He's planning something.'

Lucy felt her heart jump in dread. Was Eva's disappearance connected to Stan Naylor? Had he abducted her? The sooner she told the law the better.

'Eva has disappeared,' she burst out. 'That's why Mam is upset. Do you think Naylor could have something to do with it?'

Mario rubbed his knuckle over his moustache thoughtfully, giving Lucy an unsure glance. 'I saw Eva yesterday morning,' he admitted. 'She was walking up Union Street and stopped outside Naylor's office. I wondered why she wasn't at work.'

Lucy's mouth felt dry. Stan Naylor *was* behind this. She felt anger surge in her breast. 'He's taken her!' she exclaimed. 'I'm going to call the police.'

'Wait, Lucy,' Mario said. 'You have no proof.' He hesitated and then began to take off his white apron. 'I'll go and speak to him,' he said. 'Ask him what he knows about it.'

'No, Mr Benucci,' Lucy said, holding up a hand. 'You'd better not get involved. He has already damaged your window for speaking up for me. I'll go and see him myself, right now.'

'Lucy, are you sure? He's a devious man, and a dangerous one too I suspect.'

Lucy swallowed hard. 'I'll be all right.'

She walked slowly up Union Street looking for a sign indicating the moneylending business. She saw it then protruding from a window on the first floor, and with her heart in her mouth she climbed the stairs. There were two doors at the top, one bearing Stan Naylor's name. Knocking, she marched into a small smoky office.

'Yes?' Stan Naylor, a cigarette dangling from his lip, looked up as she entered and then jumped to his feet. 'Lucy!'

He came around the desk quickly, taking a step in her direction; an imposing figure in the small office. Lucy flinched but she wasn't ready to run yet.

'Miss Chandler to you,' she said distantly. 'I want to know what you've done with Eva.'

He took the cigarette from his mouth and smiled thinly. 'And I thought you were here to see me. I thought you'd come to your senses.'

Remembering all Mr Benucci had told her, she felt very vulnerable alone with him in the room. She was ready to believe he was capable of anything.

'I won't bandy words with you, Mr Naylor,' Lucy said defiantly, yet trying to keep her voice from trembling. 'Eva hasn't been seen since yesterday morning when she was loitering near this office. She didn't come home last night.'

'I know,' he said. 'She spent the night at a house I own.'

'What?' Lucy took a step back, horrified at his admission. 'You abducted her? I'll have the police on you, you devil!'

The planes of his face hardened. 'I didn't abduct her,' he said harshly. 'The fact is Eva came here of her own free will. She threw herself at me; brazenly offered herself in your place.'

'I don't believe you! You're lying. Eva wouldn't do a shameful thing like that.'

'You don't know your own sister very well,' he said disparagingly. 'That little hussy has got her eye on the main chance.'

'How dare you say that of her,' Lucy cried out. 'She's only seventeen, still a child.'

He laughed. 'She's no child,' he said. 'I'm telling you, Eva begged me to take her instead of you,' he said. 'Audacious isn't the word for the way she behaved.'

'If she did that, it was because she was trying to save our mother,' Lucy said uncertainly. 'She made the supreme sacrifice and you took advantage of her. You're despicable.'

'Sacrifice, my arse!' he said coarsely, tossing the cigarette on the bare boards of the floor and stamping it out with the toe of his shoe. 'Eva doesn't give two pennies for the mess your mother has got herself into.'

'That's a lie!'

'Listen!' Stan Naylor said. 'I warned Eva I wouldn't write

off the debt for her. I'll do that only for you and I still mean that, Lucy.'

Lucy turned her face away, unwilling to look at him. She could not believe what he said was true. Surely Eva would not bring shame and humiliation on them after all they had suffered after their father's betrayal.

'Eva said she didn't care about the debt or what happened to her mother,' Stan Naylor continued in a harsh tone. 'She's only interested in what I can give her – money, clothes, good living.'

'Liar!' Lucy shrilled at him. 'Liar!'

'All right, then,' he said angrily. 'Call the police. Accuse me of abducting her, and you can hear it from her own lips.'

'You took advantage,' Lucy said despairingly. 'You persuaded her. What have you turned her into? You've ruined her.'

'Huh! I've not laid a finger on her. Not yet, anyway.' He smiled. 'I knew you'd finally work out she was with me. You can take her place any time you like, Lucy. Any time.'

'How dare you speak to me like this?' Lucy spoke as haughtily as she could but she began to shake. There was a gleam in his eyes that disturbed her. She edged towards the door. She should have called the police from the start, but it wasn't too late. 'You won't get away with taking my sister,' she warned timorously.

'It's you I want, Lucy,' he said fiercely. 'Damn it! I can't get you out of my head. I see your face everywhere I look.'

He took a quick movement towards her and Lucy jumped back.

'Keep away from me!'

'You don't really mean that,' he said hoarsely. 'Women always say no when they really mean yes.'

'I mean what I say,' Lucy declared. 'I wouldn't give in to you if my life depended on it.'

His mouth tightened. 'You don't know what you're missing with me,' he said. 'I can teach you things you've never dreamed of.'

Lucy's legs were trembling so much she thought she might collapse. Could she reach the door in time?

His eyes were glowing now and she felt fear race up her spine like an electric charge. He was big and strong and could overpower her in a moment. Yet in her fear she was still defiant.

'I despise you,' she gasped. 'I told you before, I want nothing to do with you.'

He snarled and leapt forward. Before she knew what was happening, she was in his grasp. With one strong arm around her he held her fast against him. His other hand knocked her hat off, and he clutched at a handful of her hair, forcing her head back.

Helpless in his hold, Lucy squealed with terror, staring up into his face.

'This is just a taste,' he said throatily.

His mouth clamped down on hers savagely. In horror Lucy felt his tongue try to force itself between her lips. She struggled in revulsion not only at his physical touch but also at the vile taste of tobacco on his lips.

And then one of her hands was free. Lifting it up towards his face she raked her nails down his cheek.

With a yell of pain he let her go immediately. Lucy did not wait to see what damage she had done. She turned, stumbled through the door and almost fell down the stairs in panic. Out on to the street, hatless, she ran and kept on running until she reached the tram stop outside the market.

Shaking in shock and horror, she leaned against the red-bricked wall of the market trying to catch her breath, hardly able to believe what had just happened.

Mr Benucci had warned her that Stan Naylor was dangerous, and perhaps now she had made things worse for her mother. Undoubtedly he was a man who would take his revenge and she dreaded what he might do next.

In the meantime, her mother had to be told about Eva. She would be heart-broken. Lucy sensed she had been teetering on the edge of a breakdown for weeks. Eva's disgrace might be the final blow that pushed her over the edge.

Nine

Lucy was still shaken when she got home, and she was glad to see that her mother was resting. She made a cup of tea before going in to her. She had no doubt her mother would take the news very badly and for once she wished they had something stronger than tea in the house.

As she entered the room Sylvia struggled up into a sitting position. She still looked drawn and tired and Lucy hated the fact that she would have to make her feel even more miserable.

Sylvia looked at her eagerly. 'Where's Eva? Any news?'

Lucy wetted her lips. 'Yes, I know where she is and she's safe . . .' But she could not finish. Eva was far from safe in the clutches of that monster Stan Naylor.

'What is it, Lucy?'

Lucy hesitated, trying to find the right words to explain. 'Mam, Eva has done a foolish thing.'

'What are you talking about? Tell me!'

'Drink this tea first. I'll explain.'

Sylvia ignored the proffered tea. 'Why didn't Eva come home with you? Where is she? What's happened?'

'Eva went to see Stan Naylor yesterday morning.'

Sylvia's face turned even paler. 'Oh, no!'

'She offered herself in my place . . . to clear the debt,' she said simply.

She could never tell Sylvia that according to Stan Naylor, Eva didn't give a fig about the debt but wanted only to feather her own nest. It might not be true anyway. She would give Eva the benefit of the doubt.

Sylvia fell back on the pillows. 'Oh, my God!'

'I'm sorry to tell you, Mam, he took her up on her offer and she's now living in a house he owns, but I don't know where.'

Sylvia gave a cry of anguish.

'He hasn't laid a hand on her,' Lucy burst out. 'At least that's what he told me . . .'

'You went to see him?' Aghast, Sylvia peered up from the pillows; her eyes had a haunted look. 'How did you know he had anything to do with her disappearance?'

'Mr Benucci saw her near Naylor's office yesterday. I thought he might be involved.'

Sylvia covered her face with both hands, sobbing. 'My baby, in the hands of that unscrupulous man. She's ruined, Lucy, ruined! How can we ever hold our heads up again?'

'We must try and get her back,' Lucy said desperately.

She had no idea how they could achieve that. She dreaded the thought of facing Stan Naylor again. As fond as she was of Eva, she could never do it. If only they had someone they could trust; someone to face Stan Naylor unafraid.

'Your tea is getting cold, Mam,' she said gloomily. 'Drink it. It'll make you feel better.'

'I'll never feel better, Lucy. With all that has happened since your father died, I wish I was dead.'

Lucy's eyes filled with tears. 'Don't say that, Mam, please. What would Eva and I do without you? We'll get her back. We'll ask Mr Jarrett to intervene.'

'Oh, him!' Even in her misery, Sylvia's tone was scathing. 'He'll do nothing. He wouldn't even lend me some money. That's why I turned to the moneylender. Oh, Lucy, I've been so foolish.'

'Mam, it's no good going over and over that now,' Lucy said. 'What's done is done. We'll go on somehow.'

Sylvia turned over in bed, her back to Lucy, and she knew her mother was weeping. No words could ease her wretchedness now.

Feeling helpless and hopeless, Lucy left the room. She ought to go back to Mrs Pettigrew's or she would lose her job. But she could not leave her mother alone at a time like this. There would be other jobs.

No coaxing would make Sylvia eat the simple midday meal Lucy had prepared, and she had to admit that, too upset to enjoy anything, the food tasted like sawdust in her mouth.

She was washing up when someone knocked at the front door. Opening it, she was surprised to see Mario Benucci.

'Come in, Mr Benucci,' she said quickly, wondering why

he had come. He followed her into the living room. 'Sit down, please,' she invited him.

He took off his hat and sat down. There was a grave look on his face and it occurred to her that he was here because of Sylvia's inability to care for his wife and mother. Perhaps she had forfeited the position. Lucy decided she would have to take the job herself, if he was in agreement.

'Mam is sorry she has let you down, Mr Benucci,' she said quickly. 'I'm afraid she's still very upset. We've just had some news about my sister.' She swallowed deeply, feeling ashamed to admit Eva's dishonour. 'You were right. Eva has placed herself in the hands of Stan Naylor. My mother is distraught.'

Mario Benucci shook his head sorrowfully. 'I'm so sorry to hear it, but I feared as much,' he said in a low voice. 'The man has a bad reputation where women are concerned.'

Lucy squirmed, not wanting to be reminded of it. 'We're going to try to get her back.'

'The police . . .'

'No!' Lucy exclaimed. 'The fact is, Mr Benucci, and I'm ashamed to tell you this, but my sister initiated the connection.'

'I see,' he said simply and looked down at the floor.

'If you're here about Mam's work at your house,' Lucy said eagerly, 'I'll take that over for her until she's more herself.'

Mario Benucci looked up and smiled. 'You're a good girl, Lucy, and I'd be grateful for your help. Start tomorrow morning, perhaps?'

Lucy nodded.

Mario hesitated and Lucy saw he had more to say.

'I'm pleased that you can step in for your mother, Lucy, but that's not why I called today.'

She looked at him waiting for him to continue but still he hesitated, and she could see that what he had to say was disturbing him greatly.

'I called to see Stan Naylor earlier today,' he said. He straightened his shoulders. 'I offered to pay off your mother's debt.'

Lucy was astonished. 'Mr Benucci!'

He held up a hand. 'I couldn't pay the whole amount at once, but offered it in two equal parts.' He gazed at her solemnly. 'Naylor refused.'

'What?'

'He told me that the debt had risen, and would continue to grow monthly until . . .' Mario paused, turning his glance away from her, and Lucy held her breath. She could guess Stan Naylor's terms.

'Until I capitulate,' she said quietly. 'Until I agree to his disgusting terms – take my sister's place.'

'I'm so sorry, Lucy. The man is an out-and-out swine.'

'I'll never give in to him, Mr Benucci. I won't prostitute myself. I'll go to prison first.'

'The police should be told about him,' Mario said. 'This is usury of the worse kind and he's blackmailing you for your favours . . .' His face turned red at his own words.

'Involving the police will bring scandal. My mother couldn't bear it.' She swallowed. 'She's already wishing she was dead. She's a young woman still, Mr Benucci.'

'I know.' He rose to leave.

Lucy rose to her feet too. 'Thank you so much for your help, Mr Benucci. My mother will be deeply touched that you tried to help her. No one else cares.'

'I wish I could have done more,' Mario said gravely. 'I'll see you tomorrow morning at the Uplands.'

'I'll be there early,' Lucy assured him. 'Thank you, Mr Benucci. You're a real friend.'

Sylvia got out of bed reluctantly, thankful that Lucy had taken over from her the week before in caring for the Benucci family.

It was midmorning and she should be up and about. But she wanted to stay asleep. Sleep was the only relief she had from her misery.

She blamed herself for everything. Joseph's betrayal must have been her fault. She had disappointed him; she suspected he had despised her too for her submissiveness.

She had exposed her daughters to the humiliation of illegitimacy, poverty and worse, the lust of an unscrupulous man.

The thought of Eva turning bad, offering herself to that man in a scandalous way, burned in her brain day and night. And it was all her fault. She had brought them to this degradation.

With a deep sob of wretchedness she turned back to the bed, desperate to find relief from her burden in sleep. As she was about to climb in, someone knocked at the front door.

Listlessly she pulled on her dressing gown and shuffled along the passage.

Their landlady stood outside. Her glance took in Sylvia's dishevelled appearance and she clicked her tongue disapprovingly.

'Still not bathed and dressed at this hour.' She lifted her chin haughtily. 'Well, it doesn't surprise me after what I've just learned.'

Feeling vulnerable, Sylvia clutched her dressing gown closer to her chest. 'What do you want, Mrs Grant?'

'Huh! I want all of you out of this flat by the end of the week,' said Mrs Grant loudly. 'That's what I want.'

Sylvia put her hand to her head in confusion. 'What?'

'Oh, I was taken in by you, all right,' said Mrs Grant gratingly, 'with your posh way of talking and your airs and graces. And all the time you were in debt up to your eyeballs and your daughters are no better than they should be.'

'That's not true!'

Sylvia took a step back in shock and Mrs Grant took the opportunity to push her way in. She hustled Sylvia along the passage to the living room.

'I saw that man who came along here last week,' Mrs Grant continued in a heavy tone. 'Today a neighbour told me who he is. He's a moneylender, and a really bad hat, so I understand. You owe him a lot of money.'

Sylvia tried to rally. 'It's no business of yours,' she said, her voice quivering weakly.

'Oh, it's my business all right while you're staying under my roof. I don't want his kind on my premises,' Mrs Grant said nastily. 'And if that isn't bad enough I'm told your youngest is living over the brush with him. Disgraceful!' She sniffed. 'But then, I suspected from the start that she was loose.'

'Please go away!' Sylvia cried out. 'I'm not well.'

'I'm not falling for that,' Mrs Grant said in a hard tone. 'You've got behind with the rent once. I'm not giving you a chance to do it again. I know your sort. You build up arrears and then you do a moonlight flit. I've been had before.'

'We're paying the rent regularly now,' Sylvia said tearfully. 'We won't go into arrears again, Mrs Grant, I promise.'

'How can you promise that with the debts you've got

hanging over your head,' scoffed Mrs Grant. 'No, I'm not chancing it. I want you out by Saturday, and that's final.'

'But you can't do that!' Sylvia exclaimed. 'We've nowhere to go.'

'Then you'd better start looking for a place, hadn't you?' said Mrs Grant loudly. She paused. 'But not around Brynmill. I've already spread the word that you're trouble. No one will take you in around here.'

Sylvia could not bear it any longer and began to sob. Their world was tumbling down around their ears. Where would it all end? She could not bear it any longer.

'Where's your other daughter?' Mrs Grant asked.

'Working,' Sylvia managed to mumble.

'Yes, but at what, I ask myself,' Mrs Grant said scornfully. 'I dread to think!'

'Get out!' Sylvia cried.

Mrs Grant tossed her head, her glance at Sylvia disparaging.

'There's nothing worse than a woman gone bad,' she said with a sniff and then turned and marched out.

Sylvia burst into gales of tears and collapsed on to a nearby chair. She could not go on. She'd rather be dead; dead and out of it.

Lucy came home that evening to find her mother very near to collapse, weeping uncontrollably. When she was told of Mrs Grant's demand that they vacate the flat at the end of the week, Lucy was furious and was all for going upstairs and telling Mrs Grant off good and proper.

Sylvia begged her not to. 'She knows about Eva's disgrace,' she sobbed. 'And about the terrible debt I'm in. Quarrelling with her won't make anything better only worse.'

'Oh, I could kill Eva for what she's done,' Lucy declared angrily. 'Debt is one thing, immorality is another. Eva has added insult to injury in throwing herself at that man.'

'Is it my fault she's turned out this way?' Sylvia asked in a voice trembling with wretchedness.

'No, Mam!' Lucy exclaimed. 'Don't ever think that. Eva has always been strong-headed and wilful.'

And self-centred too, she thought, but she would not voice the words in front of Sylvia. Her mother was already taking too much of the blame on herself for what had befallen them.

Eva was going her own way, and there was nothing anyone could have done to prevent it.

Lucy was dismayed and Sylvia brought to tears again early that evening when Eva called on them unexpectedly. She flounced into the living room, parading her new finery as though nothing of consequence had happened.

Lucy thought she looked vulgar in the latest fashion, a style far too old for her, and even though the evening was still warm for September, she wore an expensive-looking fur stole around her shoulders.

'Well, what do you think?' Eva asked, twirling around, her face wreathed in complacent smiles. 'It's the best that Ben Evans' department store can offer.'

'Oh, Eva!' Sylvia burst into tears and collapsed into a chair. 'What have you done to yourself and us?'

Eva stopped preening, and looked impatiently at her mother. 'I'll tell you what I've done, Mam,' she said sharply. 'I'm making a better life for myself. I was never meant to be a skivvy.'

'You were never meant to be a loose woman, either,' Lucy said severely. 'You should be ashamed to show your face after what you've done. You look like a streetwalker.'

'I guessed you'd say that.' Eva made a moue and looked sourly at Lucy. 'You're jealous,' she said tetchily. 'I knew you would be.'

'Jealous! Of you and that beastly man?' Lucy said sarcastically. 'I'd rather be dead than be with him.'

'He gives me anything I want,' Eva exclaimed smugly. 'You should see the house in Ffynonne where I live. Furniture, fitting, everything first-class stuff. Stan's got pots of money and he spends it all on me because I'm his woman now.'

'Oh! Dear heaven!' Sylvia clapped a hand to her mouth and looked appalled. 'Eva, you realize no decent man will have you for a wife now. You're soiled goods.'

'I've got the man I want,' Eva said defiantly, tossing her head. 'I'm leading the life I deserve.'

'You disgust me!' Lucy exploded. 'You've sold yourself to him. That's what it amounts to.'

'How could you bring this disgrace on us, Eva?' Sylvia wailed. 'Lucy and I are humiliated and embarrassed at your behaviour.'

'Disgrace?' Eva looked angry. 'You're a one to talk, Mam. You lived in sin with a man for over twenty years!'

'Oh!' Sylvia covered her face with her hands.

'Don't accuse Mam of that,' Lucy said angrily. 'She had no idea Father had betrayed her.'

'So she says,' Eva flared. 'How do we know she's telling the truth? And what about the debts she's run up? Don't talk to me about disgrace.'

'Oh, to think my child has turned against me.' Sylvia jumped to her feet, her expression stricken. 'I can't bear this a minute longer!'

She hurriedly left the room and Lucy heard her mother running along the passage to her bedroom.

'Now look what you've done!' Lucy shouted. 'Mam is distraught. Because of you we're being evicted from this flat.'

'Stuff and nonsense,' Eva parried. 'It's the debt that's got people talking. No one will trust Mam now, and I don't blame them.'

'How could you say that?' Lucy asked. Looking at her sister's hard face she felt she was talking to a complete stranger.

'It's true,' Eva insisted belligerently.

'You'd better go,' Lucy said angrily. 'We don't want you here now. And don't come running back when Naylor slings you out, and he will when he's tired of you. He's just the type.'

Eva looked furious. 'Stan wouldn't dump me,' she said with certainty. 'He's going to leave his wife and marry me.'

'He promised you that?'

'He doesn't have to. He's madly in love with me, I can tell.'

'You poor little fool! He thinks nothing of you. The other day when I was at his office—'

'You went to his office?' Eva cried out. 'How dare you! He's mine. You had your chance—'

'Be quiet and listen,' Lucy stormed. 'I went there to ask him to leave you alone and to talk to him about Mam's debt.'

'You had no right . . .'

'He propositioned me. And then when I refused to have anything to do with him he forced himself on me. He grabbed me and kissed me. It was vile!'

Lucy paused as that awful moment was relived and instinctively she wiped the back of her hand across her mouth.

'You're lying!' Eva gasped.

'It happened just as I described,' Lucy persisted strongly. 'I was disgusted. I could have vomited. And you let that man touch you. Oh, Eva, how could you?'

'Liar! Liar!' screamed Eva.

With a sudden movement she flew at Lucy, hand extended, fingers flexed like a claw. Lucy knocked her sister's arm aside and quick as a flash she smacked her face. Eva recoiled, shocked.

'Stop it!' Lucy cried out. 'See what this evil man has done to us? He has set us at each other's throats. For Heaven's sake, give him up. Get back your self-respect before it is too late.'

'You jealous bitch!' Eva said in smouldering rage. 'I could kill you for this. You stay away from Stan. He's mine.'

'Get out!' Lucy shouted. 'And stay away. You're no longer my sister. I disown you.'

Eva's lips curled disdainfully. 'You and Mam will be in the gutter before long, or else the workhouse. I shan't want to know you then.' She turned on her heel and stalked out.

Lucy heard the front door slam. Trembling at what had just happened, she collapsed on to the nearest chair. Her family was disintegrating before her eyes. They were on the edge of penury and she could see nothing but misery in the future.

Sylvia's nerves were now so bad Lucy doubted her mother would be able to work for some time, or indeed ever again. They were to be evicted, and with only one wage coming in, how would they ever climb out of the shambles of debt and dishonour?

Rising wearily to her feet, Lucy made her way to her mother's bedroom. No matter how miserable she was herself, Sylvia was suffering even more. She must find a way to ease her mother's pain before she was tipped over the edge into insanity.

Ten

Sylvia rose from her bed, the silence of the flat unbearable. Silence let her thoughts torment her. She had blighted her children's futures; brought them to poverty and illegitimacy. She ought to be punished for what she had done. They would be better off without her and she could not live with what Eva had become.

But was she any better herself? Eva was right. She had lived in sin for years. She could not bear to think about it now; to remember. Thoughts were so painful, so agonizing.

Sylvia shuffled into the passage. Her coat was hanging on the rack. She had to get away from this place, from this intolerable life.

She shrugged into the coat over her nightdress and opened the front door, hardly noticing or caring that she was wearing only bedroom slippers. Up on the pavement she began to walk. She did not know where she would go but she had to get away from everything; block out everything. She wanted to get away from people; find an open space. She walked and walked . . .

On the seafront Sylvia crossed the railway track at the pedestrian crossing by the Slip and then felt the soft sand under the soles of her slippers. She shuffled forward, the sand enveloping her feet. It was surprisingly cool on her skin.

The wide sweep of Swansea Bay was before her, the beach almost deserted; other walkers were just dots in the distance. She looked out at the sea. The tide was coming in; it was coming to meet her; coming to help her escape the nightmare that was now her life. She was ready to let it embrace her.

Soon she was on solid wet sand, her slippers making strange rings in the moisture. She walked more surely now, almost eagerly. It would be over soon.

She gave a little sob but did not hesitate in her stride. She felt sorry for Lucy, left all alone. But she was doing the right thing, she knew she was. Lucy was young and strong, and she was good. She would never be tempted like Eva.

Wavelets were lapping around her slippers now. She gave a gasp as a small cold wave splashed around her shins.

Soon the hems of her coat and nightdress were sodden, the water weighing heavy. As the tide reached as high as her stomach Sylvia gave another gasp. It was so cold; as cold as death.

The water was at her shoulders; now covering her mouth. Just as she went under she thought she heard a man's voice, shouting. Was it Joseph come to meet her? She opened her mouth to call his name. Her mouth filled with the briny sea and suddenly she could not breathe. The water surged and she let herself go, giving herself to the sea. Darkness suddenly engulfed her and she knew nothing more.

Her mind stirred; pain was goading her into wakefulness. Someone was pummelling her mercilessly. She opened her mouth to protest and water gushed out, bitter salty water.

'That's it! That's it!' a man's voice cried urgently. 'Come on! Don't give up!'

She realized then that she was face down on wet sand. And then she vomited.

'Good! Good!' He sounded excited and breathless as though he had been running for a long time.

What was good about it, Sylvia thought sluggishly. She felt dreadful. Her ribs were aching and she had never felt so nauseated in her life.

Strong hard hands were pummelling her again. 'Come on! Let's get rid of it all.'

Sylvia moved her arms and hands and tried to push herself up. 'Don't!' she croaked. 'Leave me alone!'

He stopped his work immediately. 'Thank God!' he said hoarsely. 'I thought you were a goner.'

He helped her into a sitting position. She was wet and cold.

'What's happening?' she managed to mutter huskily, her mouth dry with salt water and sand.

'You tell me, missus,' he said.

She peered up at a well-built young man with pleasant features. He was soaking wet himself and red in the face from exertion. He grabbed a coat on the sand nearby.

'Wrap this around you,' he said, 'or you'll catch your death.'
He put it around her shoulders. 'Or was that exactly what you
were trying to do?'

In silence Sylvia huddled into the coat, shivering and feeling
sick again. She had failed to end it. Nothing had changed.
The nightmare was still with her.

'Are you a patient from the hospital?'

Sylvia shook her head, swallowing painfully. Her throat felt
raw, grazed.

'No, I came from home,' she managed to say.

Home? She had no home. Not any more. By the end of the
week she and Lucy would be homeless, in deep debt, cast out
on the street. There was nothing to live for.

'Your family must be worried out of their heads,' he
said.

'I have only one daughter now.' She could not forgive Eva
for what she had done and the things she had said. 'Lucy
doesn't know I'm missing.'

'I ought to take you up to the hospital, get you checked
over,' he said speculatively. 'The only thing is, missus, you've
committed an offence, you know that, don't you?'

Her insides were slowly easing in their churning and she
was taking more interest in what was happening around her.
She squinted up at him.

'What?'

'Suicide. Against the law, that is,' he said flatly. 'They could
have you up for it; send you to prison.'

'Oh!'

'What made you do it?'

Although frightened at his words, Sylvia was feeling a little
resentful that he had thwarted her purpose in walking into the
sea.

'It's none of your business,' she said quietly.

'Fair enough!' He flopped on to the sand beside her. 'I'd
better take you home. You need to get out of those wet things.
Where do you live?'

'You needn't bother any more,' Sylvia said. 'Leave me.'

'Oh, no!' He ran his fingers through his dark wet hair. 'I
don't feel like taking another dip, thanks.'

Sylvia looked over her shoulder at the oncoming tide. 'I
won't do that again, I promise.'

'Maybe not,' he said. 'But that railway line is too handy for comfort.'

Sylvia shuddered – either with horror or cold, she didn't really know.

He rose to his feet and held out a hand. 'Come on,' he said. 'We can't hang around by here much longer. Both of us need to get dry.'

He pulled her to her feet and Sylvia went quietly with him as he led her from the beach, her head bowed. She was a failure at everything; marriage, her children's welfare. She couldn't even end her own life successfully.

As they made their way to Marlborough Road, Sylvia was conscious of the curious stares of passers-by and sometimes their disapproving frowns. She realized they looked a strange couple; a man in his shirtsleeves, wringing wet, and a dishevelled woman in sopping bedroom slippers, huddled in a man's coat.

As they reached the top of the area steps Sylvia wondered if Mrs Grant was spying on her and what she would make of her bizarre appearance in the company of a strange young man. She would think the worst, that was for sure.

The flat door was standing open. She had not thought to close it behind her when she went out intent on ending everything.

She felt awkward now as she stood with him in the living room.

'You'd better have a bath,' he suggested. 'Get out of those wet things.' He paused. 'Have you a dressing gown I could change into? I'm beginning to shiver.'

She was concerned. Although she rather resented his interference, he had saved her life and she did not even know who he was.

Joseph's old woollen dressing gown was hanging in the back of the wardrobe. She was glad she had saved it now. She had brought some of his clothing with her from their old home, for what reason she wasn't sure. Sentiment, she supposed, because despite what he had done to them all she still had feelings for him.

She fetched it. 'You'd better have a bath, too,' she said. 'I'll call out when I'm finished.' She paused. 'I don't even know your name.'

'I'm Rob,' he said.

'I'm Sylvia Chandler.' She paused. 'Thank you for saving me.'

He smiled, his teeth visibly chattering. 'I was beginning to think you wished I hadn't.'

'I had my reasons,' she said and went along to the bathroom.

While Rob was having his bath, Sylvia made some tea. It was strange, she thought, being back here in the kitchen. She had never thought to see it again.

Rob's wet things were hanging before the range fire on a wooden clothes horse. Drying them would take ages, and although she was grateful she wanted him gone. A suit of Joseph's was also at the back of the wardrobe, and a shirt. Rob might as well have them – then he could leave.

As she passed the bathroom door she heard him singing to himself and could not prevent a smile.

'I've got a man's suit and shirt you can wear until your things are dry,' she called out. 'There's a pot of tea made in the kitchen. Help yourself.'

It was strange having a man in the house again, she reflected as she went along to her bedroom to fetch the clothes.

Lucy let herself into the flat feeling very anxious. Her mother had seemed so down after Eva's visit. When she had left for work earlier she was disturbed to see how depressed Sylvia really was and she had not stopped thinking about her all morning. At last she had left Mr Benucci's house to come home to make sure she was all right.

'Mam! Mam! Where are you?'

There was no reply, but she heard sounds from the kitchen and rushed in. 'Mam, are you all right?'

She pulled up short to see a tall dark-haired man with bare feet and wearing a woollen dressing gown standing there calmly pouring out a cup of tea. Her mouth dropped open in astonishment.

He had the grace to look embarrassed. 'Hello,' he said.

Lucy found her voice. 'Where's my mother. What have you done with her?'

'You must be Lucy,' he said.

Lucy began to tremble. 'Where's my mother,' she repeated. 'If you've harmed her . . .'

'Mrs Chandler is quite safe, now,' he said. 'She just went to get me some clothes.'

'Who are you?'

'I'm Rob,' he said, taking a long pull at the tea. He lifted the cup as though making a toast. 'I needed that,' he said with satisfaction.

'Rob?' Lucy felt confused. Was he a friend of her mother? 'Rob who?'

'Robert Naylor,' he said. 'I . . . er . . . met your mother on the beach this morning.'

'Naylor!' Lucy exclaimed angrily. 'Did you say Naylor?'

'Yes.'

Lucy ground her teeth. 'Any relation to Stan Naylor, money-lender?'

Rob paused. 'Stan is my half-brother, and step-brother too,' he said.

Lucy's blood began to boil. 'Get out!' she yelled at him. 'Get out before I call a constable.'

'What?'

She stepped further into the room and pointed at the wet clothes before the range fire, not understanding or caring why they were there. 'Get your things and go.'

'Don't be silly, Lucy,' he said in a reasoning voice. 'You don't understand. I haven't harmed your mother. Quite the reverse, I—'

'Get out!' Lucy was screeching now. 'We want nothing to do with the Naylors,' she continued. 'That family are nothing but a bunch of criminals.'

'What?'

'Stan Naylor has gone too far this time!'

Sylvia suddenly appeared in the kitchen doorway, men's clothes draped over her arm. 'Lucy, what in the world is happening? Why are you shouting?'

Lucy whirled to face her. 'Mam, why did you let this man into the house?' she asked. 'And why is he wearing nothing but a dressing gown?'

'He had to take a bath, of course,' Sylvia said as though it was obvious. 'He was wet through. I loaned him your father's gown.'

'Did you know he's a Naylor?' Lucy burst out accusingly. 'What were you thinking of?'

'Naylor?'

'He's Stan Naylor's brother.'

'His half-brother,' Rob corrected her.

'I don't care if you're his second cousin twice removed,' Lucy said through clenched teeth. 'That family is pure poison. I hate the lot of you and what you've done to my family.'

'Lucy, I don't know what you're talking about.'

Lucy lifted a hand and pointed to the passage. 'I want you gone from here, now.'

Sylvia hurriedly stepped forward. 'Lucy, you don't understand,' she said hurriedly. 'We . . . I owe Rob a debt of—'

'What!' Lucy stared at her mother in dismay. 'Oh, Mam! Not again?'

'No, no! Not that kind of a debt,' Sylvia said. 'Rob saved my life . . .'

Astounded and confused, Lucy took a step back. 'He did what? What are you talking about?' She intercepted a wary glance between Sylvia and Rob. 'Something is going on,' she accused in a heavy voice. 'I demand to know what it is.'

Rob reached for the clothing over Sylvia's arm. 'I'll just go to the bathroom,' he said quietly, 'and slip into these clothes while you explain.'

'Don't you loiter anywhere,' Lucy warned him.

He gave her a puzzled frown and looked somewhat offended, but Lucy didn't care. He was Stan Naylor's brother and that was enough for her. She glanced at her mother.

'He's here to spy, Mam, I know he is.'

'No,' Sylvia said. 'Please listen, Lucy.'

'I've no intention of spying,' Rob said stiffly and left the room carrying the clothes over his arm. When he had gone Lucy looked at her mother.

'Well, Mam?'

Sylvia looked embarrassed and nervous, her gaze was anywhere but at Lucy.

'Mam, I'm waiting to hear why you invited a Naylor into this house,' Lucy said. 'I deserve an explanation.'

Sylvia sat on a kitchen chair. 'Lucy, I've been a selfish and foolish woman and this morning I did, or tried to do, a terrible thing.'

'Go on.'

Sylvia bit her lip. 'I tried to end my life, Lucy, by walking into the sea, but Rob dragged me out. He saved my life.'

Appalled and stunned, Lucy could only stare at her mother, her mouth open.

'I was so terribly wretched,' Sylvia continued pleadingly. 'What with the debt and then Eva's shameless behaviour. It's all my fault, all of it, and I was so ashamed. I couldn't go on any longer.'

'What about me?' Lucy asked in a small voice. 'You were prepared to desert me? Leave me to face everything?'

'Oh, Lucy, I'm so sorry,' Sylvia cried out. 'I was selfish, I realize that now. And you would be alone if it wasn't for Rob.'

Lucy stood up and went to stand by the stone wash-up, resting her hands on the rim, her head bowed. She had nearly lost her mother. What would she have done if she had? She dared not contemplate it.

She turned. 'Are you really all right, Mam?'

Sylvia smiled quietly. 'Yes, thanks to Rob. He brought me home. I owe him my life.'

That might be so, but she could not bring herself to trust him. He was a Naylor. She had nothing but contempt for that family.

'It seems very strange to me, Mam,' Lucy said guardedly, 'that Rob Naylor just happened to be on hand when you . . . took that drastic step.'

'It was coincidence,' Sylvia said. 'How could Rob have known where I was or what I was doing?'

'Stan Naylor could've put him up to watching the house,' Lucy insisted. 'Rob might've been spying on us. I wouldn't put anything past his brother. He could have followed you to the seafront.'

'Lucy, I think you are being prejudiced.'

'Prejudiced? After what Stan Naylor has done to us? He's threatened us and he's seduced Eva . . .'

'I think it may be the other way about,' Sylvia said sorrowfully. 'That girl is a bitter disappointment to me.'

'Don't make excuses for *him*!' Lucy exclaimed. 'And don't try to justify encouraging Rob either.'

'But, Lucy . . .'

'Just think, Mam. Of all the people who could've been

passing at that moment it turned out to be Stan Naylor's brother.' She shook her head. 'No, it was no coincidence.'

'Well, you're wrong, Lucy,' Rob said emphatically.

He had quietly returned and was standing in the doorway fully dressed in her father's old tweed three-piece suit. It gave Lucy a confused sensation to see a strange man wearing her father's suit, but she shook off the feeling.

'Am I?' she asked aggressively. 'You may have taken in my mother,' she continued, 'but I'm no fool.'

'I can see that,' he said in a reasoning tone. 'And I can understand your enmity towards Stan. Sylvia has told me everything, even about Stan's attempts to . . . corrupt you, and I'm sorry for it.'

Lucy threw a glance of irritation at Sylvia. 'Mam, I thought you had more sense than to discuss our business with a stranger.'

'I know about the eviction, too,' Rob said. 'And I think I can help there. We could help each other.'

'Huh!' Lucy was sceptical. 'You're just like your brother,' she said. 'Quick to spot a chance to exploit someone in trouble.'

'That's not true,' Rob exclaimed. 'As a matter of fact Stan and I have been estranged for years, ever since our father died.'

'So you say!'

Rob pulled up a chair to sit at the table, resting his elbows on the top.

'Look,' he said earnestly. 'I have no love for Stan, nor he for me, especially not after the threats he's made to my mother to get her to leave her home.'

'He threatened his stepmother!' Lucy was incredulous.

Rob nodded. 'He has always resented her, hated her even.'

'But why threaten her?' Lucy said sceptically. She wasn't sure if she believed a word he was saying.

'In his will my father left the family home in Fleet Street to Stan,' Rob explained, 'but made provision that Nora would have the right to live in the house for as long as she wanted. This doesn't suit Stan.' Rob clenched his teeth, obviously angry. 'He wants to sell up or find a paying tenant, but can't while she's living there. He'd put her out on the street if he could.'

'He's a beastly man,' Sylvia opined. 'He has no conscience.'

'Nora's health is poor; she's bedridden,' Rob said. 'Stan can't evict Nora because of the terms of the will and because I make sure rent is paid even though no rent is required.'

'Who takes care of her?' Sylvia asked.

'I try the best I can,' Rob said. 'But it's difficult. Stan won't let me live with her to look after her properly and I do have a living to earn.'

'What do you do for a living, Rob?' Sylvia asked in a sociable tone and Lucy glared at her with impatience. Why was she encouraging him still?

His eyes lit up. 'I own a smallholding in Tycoch with greenhouses to grow all kinds of flowers,' he said eagerly taking a pipe out of his pocket and a packet of tobacco. 'I've a stall in Swansea market to sell them.'

Lucy thought back to that first day when she had looked for work in the market and had enquired at a flower stall. She wondered if it was the same one.

Rob was about to fill his pipe when he caught Lucy's disapproving glance. 'Do you mind?' he asked.

'Normally I don't mind a man smoking,' she said severely, 'but I resent you making yourself at home when you are obviously not wanted here.'

He put the pipe and tobacco away.

'As I was about to say,' he went on in an even tone, 'I've recently bought a piece of land adjoining mine at auction and I'm building a new greenhouse, bigger than any I've had before—'

'Why are you telling us this?' Lucy interrupted sharply.

She had a feeling he was merely talking to gain their sympathy for his own purpose.

He glanced at her. 'Sylvia did ask,' he said reasonably.

Lucy sniffed and turned away.

'What are you going to do about your mother?' Sylvia said.

Rob pulled his chair nearer the table. 'I'm looking for someone I can trust to look after her,' he said earnestly. 'I thought you would take on the job, Sylvia.'

'Me?' Sylvia looked astonished. 'After what I did today?'

'You were desperate, I know that,' Rob said. 'But now I've got a solution, for one problem anyway. In exchange for looking after Nora you could both live rent-free.'

'Oh, Lucy!' Sylvia exclaimed looking hopefully at her. 'This could be the best thing to happen.'

'Hold on, Mam,' Lucy said cautiously. 'It could be a trick, too.'

'I swear it isn't,' Rob said. 'Don't you see you'd be helping me?'

Lucy looked disdainfully at him. 'It doesn't make sense,' she said. 'If Stan Naylor won't let you live there he would certainly object to my mother and me occupying the house.'

'He won't know.'

'What?'

'He very rarely calls to see Nora,' Rob said. 'Her neighbours are sympathetic. None of them would tell him anything.'

Lucy shook her head. 'No, it's not possible,' she said emphatically. 'Besides, I wouldn't dream of living in a house owned by that vile man.'

She sent a suspicious glance at Rob. 'He's put you up to it, hasn't he? If we agree it would land us in Stan's power. That's what he's after.'

Rob stood up abruptly, anger on his face. 'I'm well aware of my brother's dubious activities,' he said brusquely and then his expression relaxed. 'I know more about them than you realize. He's skating on the very edge of the law. Please believe me, Lucy. I have no connection with his businesses, not even the pub he owns in Port Tennant – none whatsoever.'

'Lucy, it's a place to live,' Sylvia said persuasively. 'We've only got one wage coming in now. Rob's offer could be our salvation.'

And her downfall, Lucy thought worriedly. Any connection with Stan Naylor, no matter how flimsy, filled her with dread and distaste.

'Why don't you come and meet Nora tomorrow?' Rob suggested. 'Make up your mind then.'

As it happened Lucy had asked Mario Benucci for the following morning off to look for new lodgings so nothing stood in her way except doubt and suspicion.

Sylvia was looking at her pleadingly. 'Please, Lucy,' she said. 'For my sake.'

Lucy's shoulders drooped. How could she ignore that plea? Sylvia had set her heart on this. Lucy thought about what could have happened earlier that morning and shuddered. Thank heavens her mother was safe.

'All right,' she said cautiously. 'We'll look into it. But I'm not making any promises.'

Eleven

Lucy was disconcerted when Rob turned up on their doorstep immediately after breakfast the next day. She had hoped not to see him again. Sylvia on the other hand was keen to go along with him to Fleet Street to the house where Nora Naylor lived.

It was one of a long row of terraced two-up, two-down cottages, the front door opening directly on to the pavement. Rob led the way down the narrow passage to the back living room with a small lean-to scullery beyond.

'My mother is upstairs,' Rob said. 'She never comes down unless I carry her.'

Lucy looked around. The place was clean enough, although shabby. The living room looked as though it hadn't been decorated for some time.

'I'll take you up to her,' Rob continued.

Lucy then noticed a narrow staircase in the corner of the room. Rob climbed the uncarpeted stairs, Sylvia and Lucy following.

Rob's mother occupied the front bedroom overlooking the street below.

'I've brought some visitors with me, Ma,' Rob called out before entering the room, while ushering Sylvia and Lucy in.

Nora Naylor was sitting up in bed. She was a pale fragile-looking woman probably in her sixties, a hand-knitted shawl around her thin shoulders. She looked up eagerly as they came in.

'Oh, there you are, Rob, *bach*,' she said.

'Ma, this is Sylvia and her daughter Lucy,' he began. 'I'm hoping Sylvia here will agree to come and look after you.'

'Oh, hello to you both,' Nora said smiling at them. She had small, neat features and her sweet guileless expression disarmed Lucy immediately.

'Hello, Nora,' Sylvia said, going forward to the bed. 'How are you?'

'Can't grumble,' Nora said. 'He's a good son, my boy here. He does his best for me.'

'I'm sure he does,' Sylvia said. 'If you think we'll get on together, I'd like to take the job of looking after you.'

'That would be nice,' Nora said pleasantly. 'But you know we can't afford to pay you much.'

'That's all right,' said Sylvia. 'Lucy has a wage coming in and Rob says we can live here rent-free in lieu of wages.'

An expression of apprehension crossed Nora's face.

'What about Stan?' she asked, a quiver in her voice. She looked at Sylvia. 'Stan, my stepson, likes to make trouble for us,' she said. 'Did Rob tell you how Stan diddled him out of a share of what their father left? He'd like to see me dead so that he can take this house, too.'

'Oh, no!' Sylvia exclaimed. 'That's dreadful.' She glanced doubtfully at Rob. 'I have to protect Lucy, Rob. I can't put her in any more danger from Stan Naylor.'

The muscles in Rob's jaw tightened. 'You leave Stan to me,' he said ominously. 'I'm just about fed up with him. If he starts anything I'll make some rough trouble for him.'

'Oh, be careful, *bach*,' Nora said nervously. 'Stan's no good. You don't know what he'll do next.'

'Don't worry about it, Ma,' Rob said persuasively. He looked at Sylvia. 'Will you take the job, Sylvia?'

Even though Nora's plight had touched her heart, Lucy was still not sure that they should get involved with Rob and his mother. It worried her that she might be exposing herself to Stan Naylor's advances. It seemed foolhardy to take the risk.

'Mam, I think we should talk about it privately before you decide,' she said quickly.

'Nonsense!' said Sylvia. 'I feel at home here already.' She looked at Rob. 'Would it be all right if we moved in at the weekend?'

He grinned. 'That'd be fine,' he said.

'Mam, are you sure?' Lucy was stumped.

'Very sure,' Sylvia said confidently. She turned to Rob. 'Now, I don't want to seem bossy,' she continued, 'but I think some changes should be made.'

Rob looked startled. 'Like what?'

Sylvia glanced around. 'The bed should be taken downstairs. Nora can use the front room for a bedroom. She'll be able to see what's going on in the street.'

'My parlour turned into a bedroom?' Nora looked uncertain.

'It's wasted at the moment,' Sylvia said persuasively. 'When you're downstairs neighbours can call and visit you during the day. You must be very lonely all alone up here.'

'That's true,' Nora agreed. 'But the parlour? We never use it except at Christmas.'

'All the more reason to make use of it now,' Sylvia said emphatically.

Lucy could see her mother was warming even more to the job and knew it would be no use to argue with her, so said nothing further against it.

'I've got a man working for me at the smallholding,' Rob said. 'He and I can move Ma's stuff this afternoon.' He smiled at Sylvia. 'I wish you were moving in before the weekend.'

'We've paid the rent on our flat until Friday,' Lucy told him quickly. 'I'm not letting our landlady get away with that.'

As they made their way back to Marlborough Road, Lucy's doubts returned. 'Are we doing the right thing, Mam?'

'I'm certain of it.'

'We may be playing right into Stan Naylor's hands.'

'Rob looks a young man who can take care of himself,' Sylvia said confidently. 'I'm sure he'll take care of us.'

'The debt is growing month by month.' Lucy hated having to remind her mother about that fact. 'We've no way of paying it off.' She knew in her heart Stan Naylor was past the point of accepting money as repayment. 'Rob's brother isn't a man who lets go. By moving in with Rob we're baiting him. Stan Naylor will take his revenge, Mam.'

'It's going to be all right, Lucy,' Sylvia insisted. 'Things are going our way for once. I trust Rob and he did save my life.'

After six weeks of living in Fleet Street, Sylvia was pleased and gratified when Lucy admitted to her that she'd been right after all. Moving in with Nora was the best thing they could have done, despite the underlying threat of Stan Naylor finding out.

Nora was patient and undemanding, and seemed grateful for everything Sylvia did for her. Sylvia found herself growing fond of the older woman, whose sweet nature could touch anyone's heart.

Rob called in daily after work to see his mother, and Sylvia noted that Lucy was obviously revising her opinion of him. She was less sharp with him. She listened when he talked about his work and began to show some interest in his cultivation of flowers.

'He seems a decent enough bloke,' Lucy admitted to her mother one evening after he had gone.

'Of course,' Sylvia agreed. 'He's doing the best he can. It isn't his fault that he has Stan Naylor for a brother. The two are as different as chalk and cheese.'

It was midmorning the following Wednesday when Stan Naylor made an unexpected appearance at Fleet Street. Sylvia had washed some sheets and was in the back yard hanging them on the line when she heard Nora's high-pitched tones from the house. She rushed in through the scullery but came to a stop when she heard Stan Naylor's voice.

'I've got a tenant for this place,' he was saying. 'You're in my way, Nora.'

'You can't throw me out!' Nora replied in a quavering voice. 'Your father wouldn't have wanted that.'

'You ought to be dead, you old bag of bones,' he said nastily. 'Someone ought to put you out of your misery.'

Nora gave a little cry of fear. 'Your father would turn in his grave if he knew how you treat me,' she retorted weakly. 'He'd curse you for speaking so cruelly.'

Sylvia was about to intervene but halted as Nora continued, 'I'm all alone in the house, Stan, a helpless old woman. But there, you always were a bully.'

'Dad left this house to me,' he said angrily. 'But it's a useless asset while you're still alive.'

'I don't know why you hate me so much, Stan.'

'You took my mother's place,' he rasped. 'You made Dad forget her.'

'Your mother had been gone eighteen months when I met your father. He was lonely,' Nora said. 'I was a good mother to you, Stan. I treated you no different to my own.'

'I never wanted you for a mother,' he said scathingly. 'You're nothing to me, Nora, except a bloody nuisance.'

'Get out or I'll knock the wall to call a neighbour,' Nora gasped breathlessly. 'You know I've got a bad heart.'

'I'm going, but I'll be back,' he said. 'And I'll keep coming back until you're out, feet first preferably.'

'I'll tell Rob about this,' Nora said.

'Huh! If he starts anything with me I'll beat him to a pulp,' Stan said. 'You tell him that.'

Sylvia heard him come from the room and dodged back behind the scullery door. He went out, slamming the front door behind him.

Sylvia rushed in to Nora. She was lying back on the pillows, her face ashen.

'The beast!' Sylvia said hotly. 'Are you all right, Nora dear?'

Nora couldn't seem to catch her breath to answer. Sylvia hurried to the cupboard, brought out a bottle of brandy, poured a tiny tot into a glass and held it to Nora's lips.

'Take a sip, dear,' Sylvia coaxed. 'It'll help soothe your nerves.'

Nora took a sip or two and then pushed the glass away. 'I'm all right now, Sylvia,' she said weakly. She caught at Sylvia's hand. 'Not a word to Rob about this, please,' she said. 'Stan will hurt him if he gets a chance.'

'We ought to tell the police about him.'

Nora shook her head. 'This is Stan's house. He has every right to call in when he likes.' She looked earnestly into Sylvia's face. 'He'll get his wish soon enough,' she said simply.

'No, no,' Sylvia said distressed. 'Don't say that, dear.'

Nora gave a quiet smile. 'You're a good soul, Sylvia,' she said. 'You've been though the mill yourself, I know that.'

Sylvia patted Nora's hand. Yes, she had suffered, but she had her health and strength. Now she was ashamed of what she had tried to do; to end her life. She wished she had half of Nora's courage.

'I'll make a bit of dinner for us,' Sylvia said. 'We'll feel better for it.'

The following Wednesday morning Lucy awoke with a sore throat and a head full of cold. She felt groggy as she got out of bed and went downstairs where Sylvia was putting a match to the fire in the kitchen range.

'Oh, Lucy, you look awful,' Sylvia said. 'You must go back to bed.'

Lucy sneezed loudly and clamped a handkerchief to her nose.

'What about the Benuccis?' she managed to ask thickly. 'I can't let them down.'

'And you can't risk giving them your cold either,' Sylvia cautioned. 'Maria is so delicate, and the old lady is susceptible, as well.'

'I suppose so,' Lucy agreed. 'I do feel mouldy, too.'

'Back to bed,' Sylvia ordered. 'I'll bring you a cup of tea and then I'll go to the phone box on the corner of Rodney Street and ring Mr Benucci. He'll understand.'

Lucy went thankfully back to bed, glad to get beneath the blankets again. Sylvia brought her a cup of tea as promised. It tasted dreadful but Lucy drank it dutifully.

'Mr Benucci says stay off work until you're better,' Sylvia said. 'He'll manage.'

'He's a very understanding employer,' Lucy said throatily and blew her nose.

'Nora's had her breakfast,' Sylvia told her. 'After I've washed her and made her comfortable I'll be popping into town to Swansea market for a few provisions. I won't be long.'

'I'll keep an eye on her,' Lucy volunteered.

'She'll probably sleep until I get back, so there's no need for you to worry about her.'

'All right, Mam,' Lucy said drowsily, snuggling back under the bedclothes. 'But leave my door open so that I can hear if she calls.'

Lucy was dreaming of their old home in the Mumbles, wandering through the rooms and garden like a ghost. But there was a disturbing echo in their old home, a threatening voice. She stirred uneasily and woke up in the bedroom in Fleet Street.

The threatening voice hadn't disappeared with the dream. It was real. It was a man's voice from downstairs.

Lucy got out of bed, slipped into her dressing gown and stood on the small landing, listening.

'I've had enough of this. I'm putting you in the workhouse!' the man shouted, and with a shock Lucy recognized Stan Naylor's voice.

'No! You can't do it!' Nora's pitiable cry of fear struck at Lucy's heart.

'I can do anything I like,' Stan bellowed. 'I could get a good rent from this place if it wasn't for your mouldering carcass still hanging about here.'

'Leave me alone!'

'I'll not leave you alone, you old bag,' Stan shouted. 'I'll pester you until you leave or die. Either way, I don't care.'

It was too much for Lucy. Nora needed her. Without stopping to think of the consequences of revealing herself she raced down the stairs, through the living room, along the passage and fetched up with a skid in the front parlour.

Bending over the small figure of Nora, cringing back in the bed, Stan Naylor's tall broad-shouldered form was overpowering and seemed to fill the room.

'Stop browbeating Nora, you beast!' she cried out. 'How could you torment your stepmother like this? It's abominable, inhuman.'

Straightening up, he turned and stared at her, his jaw dropping loosely in incredulity.

Lucy was shivering from head to foot, but it wasn't her fever, it was fear of him. Determined not to show it she moved swiftly to the other side of the bed away from him, trying to pull herself together. His astonished gaze never left her face.

'Get out before I call a constable to you,' she shrilled at him across the bed.

'You again!' he said at last. 'You're everywhere!'

Lucy straightened her shoulders and lifted her chin haughtily, but the aloof effect she wanted was spoiled when she had to wipe her dripping nose.

'What the hell are you doing in my house?' Stan demanded.

For the first time she was struck by his physical likeness to Rob. They had the same strong build, but the anger that contorted Stan's face now was quite unlike Rob's normally pleasant countenance.

Nora began to cry at his angry tone. Lucy went closer to the bed to comfort her but was afraid to get too near because of her cold.

'I said, what you are doing here?' he thundered, obviously over his surprise.

There was nothing else to do but tell the truth now, she realized.

'Rob employs my mother to care for Nora in exchange for lodgings,' she told him reluctantly.

'The hell he does!'

He scowled at her, his glance running over her dressing gown and bare feet. Lucy pulled the edges of her dressing gown more tightly at her throat, feeling suddenly embarrassed and vulnerable.

'I'm not a fool, Lucy. I can see what's going on here,' Stan shouted furiously.

Nora's whimpering increased, and Lucy was alarmed, realizing the seriousness of the strain of this confrontation on the older woman's heart.

'You're frightening Nora,' she said severely. 'You know she has a bad heart.'

She leaned over and grasped Nora's hand, squeezing it gently. 'It's all right, Nora. Don't be frightened,' she said. 'Mr Naylor is just leaving.' She released Nora's hand and straightening up gave him a challenging look. 'You'd better go.'

'Huh! Like hell I will. This is my property and I want an explanation.'

'I don't know what you're getting at.'

'Don't act innocent with me,' he said gutturally, his lips narrowing. 'It's you and Rob together, isn't it? You've just got up from his bed. You're Rob's woman. He's using this place as his whorehouse. That's it, isn't it?'

'No, it's not.' Lucy was appalled and angry. 'How dare you accuse me of that? I'm no one's woman.'

'You could've been mine,' he said throatily. 'I offered you anything you wanted. I'd have set you up in the best part of town. Nothing would have been too much for you, Lucy. Anything, anything could be yours if only you'll come to me.'

'Oh, my goodness! Such words,' Nora muttered, scandalized. 'Your father would be disgusted with you.'

Lucy felt embarrassed and deeply offended. 'You insult me by even mentioning it,' she said angrily. 'I have my principles. I wouldn't lower myself to become any man's mistress, no matter what he had to offer.'

His scowl deepened. 'Oh, no? Well, you moved into this hovel with my brother quick enough. So much for principles.'

'You're the landlord here,' Lucy burst out. 'If it is a hovel then you're to blame.'

'You chose Rob over me,' he accused, disbelief in his voice. 'What can he offer you that I can't?' His jaw worked in growing rage. 'You've both done this deliberately to get one over on me. You'll pay for it!'

'You're mad! Why would I do that?' Lucy tossed her head disparagingly. 'I despise you too much to give you a moment's thought. My mother and I have a business arrangement with your brother and that's all there is to it.'

'I don't believe it.'

'Believe what you like,' Lucy flared. 'I'll tell Rob you've been here today and what you've done to Nora.'

His mouth tightened. 'Don't worry,' he said in a low voice. 'Rob will be hearing from me, all right. He'll answer to me for this too.'

'Get out.'

He took a quick purposeful step to come around the bed towards her. She did not like the look in his eyes and hurriedly stepped back.

'If you lay a hand on me I'll scream the house down,' Lucy cried. 'The neighbours will come in.'

He halted at her words. 'You're going to be very sorry for double-crossing me, Lucy,' he said through gritted teeth. 'You owe me.'

She thought he must be referring to the debt Sylvia owed.

'You can do your worst about the debt,' she said bravely, sure her mother would agree with her sentiments.

'Oh, no,' he said. 'That's my hold over you.' He gave a thin cold smile. 'I could haul your mother through the courts if I had a mind to, remember that.'

'What, with the rate of interest you charge?' Lucy scoffed, putting a handkerchief to her nose hastily. 'You practise usury, and any court in the land would condemn that.'

He looked furious again.

'Besides,' Lucy continued quickly, 'I'm prepared to stand up in court and declare that you are using the debt to gain sexual favours. Can you risk that?'

He sneered. 'Your name would be mud after.'

I've already experienced that, she thought ruefully.

'And your business would be finished,' she reminded him.

He gave her a sour look, and Lucy had the feeling that he believed he was being cheated. She and Sylvia did not want to cheat anyone, not even the likes of Stan Naylor.

She swallowed hard before speaking again. 'My mother doesn't want to do you down over the debt, Mr Naylor,' she said cautiously. 'She wants a reasonable settlement. If you agree to let us pay off what we can each month, I swear we'll do everything we can to clear the debt.'

'I don't want your money. I want you!' he blurted savagely. 'I want you, body and soul.'

'Well, you can't have me!' Lucy cried out, disturbed at the passion in his voice and his expression. There was something frenzied in his look which frightened her. 'Never!' she cried out, all of a tremble.

He was silent for a moment staring at her. Then a gleam of cunning came into his eyes. 'I have Eva,' he said slyly after a moment. 'And an eager little bed companion she is too.'

'Oh, dearie me!' Nora whispered in shocked tones.

Lucy was mortified. 'How dare you!' she said in fury, taking a step forward, longing to slap his sneering face. She saw anticipation in his eyes and stopped, realizing she was playing into his hands.

'My mother will be back soon,' she warned shakily, retreating.

'You tell her I haven't finished with her,' Stan said. 'It's you or her, Lucy, remember that.'

He turned abruptly and strode out of the room and down the passage, slamming the front door as he went.

Lucy had been holding her fear in tight control but as he left she almost collapsed with relief.

'Lucy!' Nora said nervously. 'I'm so frightened.'

'I know,' Lucy said shakily. 'But he's gone now. He won't be back.'

At least not today, Lucy thought, but she realized that now he knew she was at Fleet Street he would be back again and again. She was nervous herself at the thought, but was even more frightened for Nora. Her heart could not stand such torment.

Sylvia was also worried when Lucy related what had happened, and then told Lucy about Stan's previous visit.

'Mam!' Lucy was astonished that she had kept it to herself.

'You should've told Rob. He must do something to stop Stan coming here.'

'Nora is afraid there'll be trouble and Rob will get the worse of it,' Sylvia said in a harassed tone. 'Stan Naylor is unscrupulous. He doesn't care what damage he does.'

'Well, I'm going to tell Rob about what happened today,' Lucy declared. 'Nora could have had a heart attack.'

Rob called in on his way home from Swansea market that evening. Sylvia had prepared a meal for him.

'Let him eat first before telling him about Stan,' she whispered to Lucy as they were together in the scullery.

Lucy's nose had stopped dripping but she was still feeling mouldy; however, her simmering anger against Stan Naylor was bolstering her up, and she could hardly wait for Rob to finish his meal.

Rob sat back from the table looking satisfied. 'That was a treat,' he said. 'You're a good cook, Sylvia.'

'I aim to please,' Sylvia said with a smile. 'Lucy's a good cook too, you know.'

Rob glanced in amusement at Lucy. 'I think your mother is trying to do a bit of matchmaking,' he said with a grin.

Lucy was still too angry to be embarrassed by her mother's machinations.

'Rob, there's something you should know. Stan has been here today, making trouble. Nora was frightened.'

'What!' He jerked forward in his chair, his expression stormy.

'He knows Mam and I are here now,' Lucy continued. 'I had to intervene when he was bullying Nora.'

Rob jumped to his feet, his face a mask of hatred. 'I'll kill him, the bastard!'

Lucy was startled by the vehemence in his voice and was reminded momentarily of Stan Naylor.

Rob reached for his jacket and began to shrug into it, his expression thunderous.

Lucy rose to her feet, too. 'Wait, Rob!' she exclaimed urgently. 'Violence isn't the answer. He must know you'll come after him. He'll be waiting. If anything happens to you, Nora will be at his mercy.'

He paused, looking at her, his jaw working in his fury. 'I know you're right, Lucy,' he said tensely, 'but I can't let him get away with it. Trouble has been simmering between us for years. This is the last straw. I've got to settle with him once and for all.'

'Can't we take Nora to a safer place,' Sylvia asked, 'and avoid further trouble?'

'I wanted to do that all along,' Rob said tensely. 'Ma won't have it. She came to live in this house when she was first married. Us kids, Stan and me, grew up here. Ma reckons she'll die if she has to leave.'

'She can't have any more stress,' Sylvia said. 'It would be the end of her.'

'What the hell can I do?' Abruptly, Rob smashed one of his big fists into the palm of his other hand. Lucy jumped at the violence of it and so did Sylvia. 'God damn him!' he raged. 'I feel like smashing his skull in, brother or no brother.'

Watching his simmering rage, Lucy realized Rob could be just as reckless as his brother if pushed too far.

'You must change the lock on the front door for a start,' Lucy suggested quickly in an attempt to bring calm to the situation. 'And put a big bolt on it. We'll keep it locked and bolted all the time.'

Rob nodded agreement. 'I'll do that first thing tomorrow,' he said. He hesitated, looking at Lucy uncertainly. 'I think I should spend the night here, just in case.'

Lucy felt relieved. 'I'll go in with Mam tonight,' she suggested. 'You can have my room.'

'Thank you,' Rob said simply.

'It's a good thing you don't have a horse with you,' Sylvia remarked. She laughed. 'I don't know where we'd stable it for the night.'

Lucy looked at him curiously. 'How do you bring your produce into town?' she asked.

'You've met Ted Locke who works for me. We bring the horse and cart into town each morning, unload the flowers for the market stall and then Ted takes the horse and cart back.' He shook his head. 'I couldn't afford the cost of stabling a horse daily in town.'

'How do you get back to Tycoch of an evening?'

He smiled. 'Shanks's pony,' he said.

'That's a long way on foot.'

'I'm used to it,' he said. 'Done it for years. Keeps me fit.'

He did look fit and his skin was nut-brown from being out in all weathers. She could not help compare him with his brother. Whenever she had seen Stan Naylor he always had a cigarette dangling arrogantly from his lip.

Her mother was right. Although similar in looks, the brothers were very different. Rob was a clean-living man, and she found herself warming to him. She knew he could be a good friend to her if she let him.

Lucy's cold was better the following morning and she decided she must go to work. Mr Benucci had been very patient with her absence.

She went downstairs early to fetch up a pitcher of water to wash in Sylvia's bedroom instead of washing in the stone sink in the scullery as she usually did.

Rob was already up, dressed and shaved when she appeared. Lucy felt self-conscious in her dressing gown.

'I've made a pot of tea,' he said, hardly glancing at her. 'Sylvia has taken a cup in to Ma. There's plenty left.'

'Thanks.'

She was about to pour out the tea when there was a loud knocking on the front door. Lucy saw Rob tense, and his expression was forbidding.

'If that's Stan, I'll not be responsible for my actions,' he said.

'I'll answer the door,' Lucy said bravely. The last thing she wanted was a fight in the house. Nora would be terrified.

Lucy answered the door to find a small wiry-looking man in his fifties on the step wearing labourer's clothes and a flat cap. She recognized Ted Locke.

'Is Mr Naylor here?' he asked urgently, snatching off his cap at the sight of her.

Rob was in the passage behind her. 'I'm here, Ted,' he said quickly. 'Come on in. What's up?'

Lucy stood aside to let Ted in.

'Mr Naylor, there's trouble at the holding,' Ted said in an agitated tone. 'I got here as quickly as I could.'

Rob frowned. 'What trouble?'

Ted swallowed hard before continuing. 'When I got to work early this morning – you remember, I was going to replace those two panes of glass that got smashed by those kids throwing stones . . .'

'Get on with it, Ted.'

'Someone's been and smashed up the place.'

'What?'

'Everything, Mr Naylor. The three greenhouses, every bloody pane . . . oh, excuse me, miss!' Ted glanced at Lucy in embarrassment and then back at Rob. 'They've trampled all the plants, every one of 'em, and ransacked the cottage as well.' He shook his head sorrowfully. 'It's a hell of a mess, Mr Naylor. They've done for the lot.'

Rob just stared without speaking, obviously numbed with shock.

'Who's done this?' Lucy asked.

Ted glanced at her. 'Dunno for sure, miss,' he said. 'But a pal o' mine was passing near the holding last night and saw a gang of men there.' He looked at Rob. 'Good job you wasn't there, Mr Naylor. They might have beat you, too.'

Rob's jaw muscles hardened. 'That swine Stan,' he said tensely. 'He's done this.'

'You can't be sure,' Lucy said cautiously.

'I'm sure,' Rob said tensely. He reached for his coat and cap hanging behind the kitchen door. 'He's gone too far this time,' he said between gritted teeth. 'He's asked for trouble, now he's going to get it.'

'What are you going to do?' Lucy was alarmed.

'I'm going to give him a beating he won't forget. I've wanted to do this for a long time for the way he treats Ma.'

'Don't do it,' Lucy begged. 'You're playing into his hands, Rob. Obviously Stan has supporters who'll stop at very little. They'll attack you.'

'Oh, aye! He's brave when he's got his cronies around him,' Rob agreed. 'But he'll be alone at his office this morning. Let him face me man to man.'

Sylvia came out of Nora's bedroom. 'What's all the fuss?' Lucy told her quickly.

'Oh, my goodness!' Sylvia said, clutching her hand to her throat in fright. 'Will that terrible man never leave us alone?'

'He will after today,' Rob promised with determination. 'I'll beat him until he begs for mercy.'

'Rob, it's not safe,' Lucy persisted. 'Think of Nora. If anything should happen to you . . .'

Rob shook his head. 'I can't stand by like a coward and let

Stan walk all over me, Lucy,' he said. 'He's destroyed my livelihood, Ma's and mine. It has to be settled between us today, once and for all.'

'I'll come with you,' Lucy declared.

'No, Lucy!' Sylvia exclaimed in fear. 'It's no place for a woman. You could get hurt yourself.'

'Your mother's right, Lucy,' Rob said seriously. 'What happens today is not something a woman should witness.'

'You're wrong, Rob,' Lucy exclaimed in determination. 'Stan has done this because of me. He believes we're . . . living together.' She felt embarrassed at saying such a thing. 'He believes I've slighted him. It's as much my quarrel as yours.'

'Lucy, I'd rather you stayed here,' Rob said.

'I'll come with you, Mr Naylor,' Ted Locke offered quickly.

Rob reached out and shook the man by the hand. 'I appreciate that, Ted,' he said, 'but I want you to get back to the holding and start the clear-up. We need to get the place going again as soon as possible.'

'I *will* come with you, Rob.' Lucy was adamant.

He stared at her determined expression for a moment, and then nodded reluctantly. 'Go and get dressed, then,' he said. 'But be quick.'

Twelve

Ted took the horse and cart back to the smallholding in Tycoch. Rob and Lucy caught a tramcar into town. Rob was mostly silent on the journey, obviously worried and wrapped up in his own thoughts; his expression was grim whenever Lucy ventured a glance at him.

She had a lot to think about too. This whole terrible situation was on account of her and her refusal to give in to Stan Naylor's disgusting demands. She was deeply sorry that Rob had to bear Stan's revenge because of it.

They got off the tram near the middle market gates in Oxford Street. Stan's office was just at the top of Union Street. When they got to the corner, Rob stopped outside the Exeter Hotel.

'This is as far as you go, Lucy,' he said. 'I won't put you in any more danger.'

She was not looking forward to the confrontation but knew that she must go through with it. Stan Naylor had humiliated Sylvia and herself, and what was worse he had ruined Eva and had been so blatantly smug about it.

She did not like to admit that there was thirst for revenge in her own heart, but it was there. Perhaps here was a chance to be rid of the yoke that Stan had placed on them all.

'This is as much my fight as yours,' she told Rob defiantly. 'I have to face him, too.'

Rob gave a heavy sigh. 'All right, but as soon as there's trouble I want you to get out, and quick. When I'm facing Stan's fists I don't want to be worrying about you too.'

Lucy nodded. 'I understand, Rob.'

Reaching the top of the street outside Stan's office, Rob hesitated only a split second before climbing the stairs two at a time, leaving Lucy panting as she ran up after him. He waited for her to reach him on the landing before throwing the office door open and striding in.

Stan Naylor was standing with his back to them beside the safe, which was open. 'Haven't you heard of knocking first, whoever you are?' he shouted and, slamming the safe's door shut, swung around to face them.

He was startled when he saw who was standing there, and he sprang forward tense and alert, feet apart.

'Oh, it's you,' he said to Rob in a sarcastic tone. 'I was expecting you but not so soon.'

'You rotten swine!' Rob burst out in fury. 'Why did you do it?'

'Do what?' Stan's glance alighted on Lucy, still near the open door. 'What's *she* doing here?'

'You know what I'm talking about,' Rob continued. 'Why did you smash up my place? You knew I'd come after you.'

Stan gave a mocking laugh. 'Yes, but I didn't think you'd bring reinforcements. Need a woman's skirts to hide behind, do you, little brother?'

With a howl of fury Rob leaped forward but before he could reach him, Stan swiftly bent down to retrieve something hidden under the desk and stood erect brandishing a cudgel. He was smiling as he let the thick head of the weapon tap the palm of his other hand.

'Did you think I wouldn't be prepared?' he asked with a sneer. 'You were never a match for me, Rob, and you never will be.'

'I don't need a weapon to deal with you, Stan,' Rob said through gritted teeth. 'We're not boys any more.'

Stan's glance slid to Lucy. 'Are you going to let your woman see me bloody your head?' He smiled. 'Perhaps she likes the idea of two grown men fighting over her.'

'Stop it, you beast!' Lucy cried out, coming further into the room. 'I'm here only because you involved me with your shaming accusations.'

'You chose him over me!' Stan thundered; losing his composure.

'I've chosen no one,' Lucy flared. 'I'm my own woman.'

'And where did my brother spend last night?' Stan's lips twisted. 'I know you both spent the night under the same roof, so don't deny it.'

'You think every man is as corrupt and lecherous as you,' Lucy said. 'But Rob's not like you. He's a decent man.'

It was true. Every day she saw Rob in a new light. He was honest and trustworthy, and her admiration of him was growing. Rob Naylor was a man worthy of her respect.

She felt a little jolt near her heart, suddenly realizing that her feelings went deeper than respect. She had never felt such strong emotion towards Lewis Saunders, the man she had agreed to marry. Rob was a man worthy of her affection.

Perhaps Stan was right in a sense. She had chosen Rob. Her new knowledge surprised her and she felt confused by her feelings.

'You could have had a good man in me,' Stan said furiously. 'A real man.'

'Rob's worth twenty of you,' she blurted out. 'You're not fit to clean his boots.'

Stan's lips drew back in a snarl. 'You little slut! Don't you talk to me like that.'

He took a step forward and in that unguarded moment Rob sprang at him and tried to take the cudgel from his hand. They wrestled savagely for possession of it, swaying around and bumping into the desk and chairs.

Lucy retreated to the door out of their way, her knuckles between her teeth, willing herself not to scream. She dared not think what would happen if Stan regained possession of the weapon.

With a shout of triumph, Rob took the cudgel from Stan's grasp and threw it into the corner of the room. The brothers sprang apart, panting and eyeing each other like wolves.

'You'd better get out of here, Rob,' Stan panted. 'Before I kill you.'

'I'm got going anywhere until I see you flat on your back with a bloody nose.'

With a yell of fury Stan leapt at him, throwing punches at Rob's head. But Rob was giving as good as he got. And then he threw a lucky punch, catching Stan full in the face. As though hit by a brewer's dray Stan went crashing down on to his back, and lay sprawled there, blood spurting from his nose.

Rob stood over him triumphantly, fists still clenched.

'The way you live has made you flabby and weak, Stan,' he said scathingly. 'Remember this beating and keep away from me and my property, or else. I mean it, Stan. You'll get much worse if you trouble me again.'

Stan made no attempt to get to his feet but lay stretched out and silent, his hand to his nose and blood smearing his face.

'Let's go, Rob,' Lucy said anxiously from the doorway. 'He's learned his lesson.'

'You don't know my brother like I do, Lucy,' he said, but he stepped away from the prone form. 'You better listen to me, Stan. Next time I'll put you in hospital.' He walked away and came to Lucy standing at the door.

'Come on,' he said abruptly. 'Let's leave him to it.'

They went downstairs to the street where they stood for a moment, unmoving. Rob still looked angry as though his vengeance had still not satisfied him. He kept glancing up the stairs as if he was in two minds whether to go back.

'Do you think he's badly hurt?' Lucy ventured to ask.

'He can be dead for all I care.'

There was such hatred in his voice that she was concerned. 'You don't mean that, Rob.'

'I do,' he said. 'When I think of the way he has treated Ma . . .' He hesitated. 'And now he's wrecked my livelihood. Any man would feel as I do.'

Lucy felt self-conscious as she looked up into his face. She was beginning to care for him, but there was nothing in his expression to reveal how he felt about her. And she should not expect it, she told herself sadly. Perhaps he knew about her illegitimacy, and for all he knew she might have encouraged Stan's attentions.

'I didn't lead him on, Rob, if that's what you think.'

'What?' He glanced at her in a vague way as though he had forgotten she was there. 'No, of course, not,' he said in that same distracted way. 'Stan needs no encouragement where women are concerned.'

He turned to walk away. Lucy hurried to catch up with him.

'What happens next?' she asked, trotting at his side as he strode forward at a pace.

'I rebuild the smallholding,' he said. 'Or try to. It'll take time, and money, which I don't have.'

'I want to help,' Lucy said. 'I feel partly responsible. Stan acted in revenge because of me.' She swallowed. 'He thinks we're together . . .'

She had given him an opening. If he felt anything for her

surely he would make it plain now. Instead he scowled, and Lucy's heart sank.

'He has a dirty mind,' Rob said angrily. 'He spends his time with scum, so what can you expect.'

They walked on in silence. When they reached the tram stop near the market, Rob turned to her. 'You'd better be getting back to your job,' he said, 'or you'll get the sack.'

'No, I'm not going back to that work,' Lucy said determinedly. Mr Benucci could find someone else to take care of his family. 'I want to help you rebuild the smallholding.'

'That's man's work,' Rob said. He paused to look at her then and smiled. Lucy was disappointed to see it was a smile of friendship only. 'I can't have you getting calluses on your hands.'

'I'm strong, Rob, even if perhaps I don't look it,' Lucy said eagerly. 'And I want to learn about growing flowers.'

He raised his brows. 'You want to learn about horticulture?'

Lucy nodded. She'd learn anything just to be with him.

'I'm not an expert,' he warned. 'All my knowledge about growing flowers and cultivating gardens has been self-taught, learned by trial and error.'

'But you could teach me,' Lucy said breathlessly. 'I could be your apprentice. Please.' She tried to make her plea as appealing as possible.

He frowned, looking doubtful. 'It's an unusual occupation for a woman, and it's hard work, you know, Lucy.' He smiled. 'It's not about arranging flowers in vases.'

She felt hurt that he was making light of her request.

'Couldn't you take me on a trial?' she asked. 'Don't dismiss the idea altogether, Rob.'

He studied her face for a moment more, and Lucy looked for signs of warmth in his eyes, but his gaze, while sincere, lacked that special light that she was hoping to see, and her spirits dipped.

She saw and tasted the irony. The brother she despised felt desire for her, but the other, who could mean all in all to her, did not care or perhaps even know how she felt. The truth was a bitter draught to swallow.

'All right, Lucy. I can see you're enthusiastic to learn,' Rob said at last. 'We'll give it a try, although you realize I can't pay you much of a wage.'

'I'll manage.'

He nodded. 'Before I can teach you about the cultivation of flowers, we have to deal with the disaster Stan created. That will take long hard toil.'

'I'm ready to work, Rob. You won't be disappointed in me.'

A tram arrived that would take Rob as far as the square in the Uplands. It was a long walk to Tycoch from there. Lucy made to board the tram with him.

'Hadn't you better go and see your employer first,' he said in a steadying tone. 'You can start at the holding tomorrow. Ted will come for you with the cart.'

'I can telephone Mr Benucci to explain this evening,' Lucy said eagerly. She could not bear to be parted from him.

'Tomorrow, Lucy,' he said firmly.

The tram moved off and Rob disappeared inside without a backwards glance.

It was midmorning and Eva, still in her nightdress, knelt on the stone-flagged floor of the lavatory next to the kitchen, her head hanging over the china bowl.

She felt so awfully ill, and was glad, not for the first time, that Stan's house in Ffynonne had the novelty of indoor plumbing.

Her innards in spasm again, she wretched and groaned weakly. For three mornings running she had had this nausea and vomiting, and could not account for it. It couldn't be food poisoning, she reasoned, because as the day wore on she usually felt better. It was only in the mornings that she felt she was dying. It was times like these that she missed her mother. Mam would know what to give her to ease it.

The door opened abruptly behind her.

'I thought as much!' a woman said sarcastically and Eva recognized the voice as that of Mrs Price, who Stan employed as housekeeper in Ffynonne.

'Are you spying on me?' Eva rallied to ask.

'Huh! You don't have to spy in this house to know what's going on,' Mrs Price said. 'He's put you up the spout. Well, that's what you get for loose ways, my girl.'

'What?' Eva was so jolted at the notion she fell sideways on to the cold flagstones. 'What are you taking about?' she squeaked peering up at the woman's tall gaunt figure dressed in black.

'You're in the family way, you foolish girl,' Mrs Price said scornfully. 'I knew it would come to this eventually.'

'You're talking rubbish!'

Mrs Price folded her arms across her narrow chest, nodding sagely. 'Morning sickness, it is,' she said. 'Didn't your mother ever tell you the facts of life?'

Eva was horrified. She'd fallen for a baby? It couldn't be true! 'I'll tell Stan – Mr Naylor – about the gossip you're spreading,' she whimpered. 'You'll get the sack. He'll sling you out.'

'Huh! I'm not the one who's in the pudding club, am I?' Mrs Price retorted. 'If anybody's going to be slung out it's you, my girl.'

'No,' Eva protested. 'Stan loves me. When I tell him about the baby, he'll leave his wife.'

Mrs Price gave a hooting laugh. 'You're dafter than I thought,' she said scathingly. 'Stan Naylor will never leave his wife. She's got too much money, and she knows how to hang on to it. Maisie Naylor is no man's fool.' She gave Eva a mocking look. 'Unlike some.'

Eva gave a little sob. 'You're wrong,' she murmured. Surely Stan would stand by her.

'Tsk!' Mrs Price was impatient with her. 'You don't really believe you're the first girl he's brought to this house, do you?' she asked with a sneer. 'I've been housekeeper here for five years. I've seen them come and go in that time. You're no different, my girl.' She shook her head. 'Stan Naylor is a no-good swine where women are concerned.'

Eva sat there helplessly, the cold of the flagstones striking through the thin cotton of her nightdress, and then she burst into tears at the awful truth of it.

'Oh, come on,' Mrs Price said more kindly, bending to help her to her feet. 'Like I said, you're not the first and you won't be the last.'

Eva could not find much comfort in that old adage. What was she to do? If what Mrs Price said was true, Stan would be angry with her; he would blame her.

Mrs Price helped her climb the staircase and took her back to her bedroom, assisting her back into bed. 'I'll fetch you a cup of tea,' she said and shook her head. 'You've had a shock, I can see that.'

Mrs Price left the room and Eva lay back on the pillows, clutching the counterpane up to her chin, hardly able to believe the mess she was in. She was expecting a baby. It was incredible and frightening.

What would happen to her now, if Stan did reject her? Her mother and sister would be horrified to find her in this condition and would blame her. She would get no sympathy from them. She felt as though the bottom had dropped out of her world, which had looked so rosy up until now.

'What am I to do, Mrs Price?' Eva asked tearfully when the housekeeper brought the tea.

'Do you really want this baby?'

Eva shook her head. She was too young, and a child would spoil the life she had envisaged for herself. No man would look at her with a brat in tow, especially an illegitimate brat.

'I don't blame you.' Mrs Price folded her arms. 'Only thing to do is to get rid,' she said. 'But it'll cost money if you want the best.' She sniffed. 'I wouldn't suggest one of these cheap backstreet johnnies. Too many poor girls have lost their lives because of them.'

'I haven't got any money,' Eva said, biting her lip with misery.

She had been sitting pretty, living here in luxury for these last few months. She had found Stan exciting, and generous on the whole. She had a wardrobe full of fashionable clothes, jewellery such as she'd never seen before. But he had never given her money.

'Mr Naylor has plenty,' Mrs Price said flatly. 'After all it's him that put you up the spout, it's only right he pays to get rid. Ask him, I would.'

'Suppose he won't pay.'

'I think he might,' Mrs Price said sagely. 'Men like him would rather pay to get rid than have a bastard kid running around, making demands on him later in life.'

Eva winced at the epithet. She was illegitimate through no fault of her own and she had already seen what that label could do to ruin a girl's life.

'And then there's his wife's standpoint,' Mrs Price continued, a thoughtful expression on her face. 'She won't like the idea of another woman having Stan's sprog.'

Eva felt even more despondent. Stan never talked about his wife or their life together. For all she knew he had children.

Mrs Price seemed to read her mind. 'There aren't any kids,' she said. 'And that's a real bone of contention between him and his missus.'

'How do you know all this about his private life?' Eva asked.

Mrs Price sat on the edge of the bed. 'My niece works as maid to Maisie Naylor.' She shook her head. 'Many the quarrels she's heard between them about it. *She* wants kids. He doesn't.'

Eva gave a whimper. That information did not bode well for her situation. Stan would be furious. He would probably tell her to leave his house immediately.

Again Mrs Price seemed able to read her expression. 'He'll pay up, my girl, if you approach him the right way,' she said. 'Mark my words.'

'But even if he does, I don't know anyone who does that sort of thing,' Eva said. 'How can I find out?'

Mrs Price studied her for a moment. 'I'm going to give you a name in confidence. But you mustn't tell anyone else. Right?'

Eva nodded.

Mrs Price looked smug. 'It's not only working girls who get knocked up, you know,' she said. 'I could tell you tales about the high and mighty families who live around here. Daughters of the well-off are just as likely to get themselves ruined as the likes of us.'

'Who do they go to?'

'Well, there's this doctor I know of. Struck off he was for doing abortions some years back, but he's still at it. Believes it's a woman's right, or some such nonsense. Anyway, he'll do it for five hundred pounds.'

'What?' Eva was appalled. He might as well ask for the crown jewels.

'He's a trained doctor, after all,' Mrs Price said. 'He knows what he's about. Dangerous complications are less likely with him.'

'Stan will never agree to that amount of money,' Eva murmured despondently.

'You can but ask.' She told Eva the name of the doctor and where in the town he could be found. 'Remember, you mustn't bandy that name about,' she warned gravely.

Forlornly Eva watched the housekeeper leave the room carrying the empty cup and saucer, her mind full of what was before her. She would have to face up to Stan as soon as he visited, which he did each evening, not leaving her usually until well after midnight.

She would be extra nice to him this evening and say nothing until after he had had his fun. He would be in a mellow mood then and full of whisky. She might be able to coax the money out of him.

It struck her then that if he did give her the money it would show how much he really cared for her. Mrs Price was wrong. Stan did value her, she was sure of it.

Stan arrived about seven o'clock that evening. Eva was feeling much better and was ready to make a great fuss of him.

He came into the sitting room where she was sitting on the chesterfield waiting for him, and without glancing at her or speaking a word, moved straight to the sideboard to pour a glass of whisky.

She was surprised and curious to see bruises on his face and the blood-caked split in his right nostril looked particularly painful.

'Who's been bashing you about?' she asked in an amused tone.

'Shut your face!' he snarled.

'Stan!' Eva was startled at the simmering rage in his voice. Getting him into a bad mood was the last thing she wanted at this time.

She got to her feet immediately and went to him, thrusting her body against his, and slipping her arm around his shoulder.

'Don't be nasty to little Eva, darling,' she said pouting prettily and then smiled up at him seductively. 'I only want to make you happy. Let's go upstairs. I'll be especially nice to you tonight; everything you like.'

'Get away from me!' To her consternation he pushed her away roughly.

Eva was aghast. 'Stan! What's wrong? What've I done?'

'It's that sister of yours,' he said between clenched teeth. 'And my bloody brother. Curse him to hell!'

'My sister? What has she got to do with anything?'

He looked down at her, his lips twisted in scorn.

'Everything,' he said. 'You're a poor substitute for Lucy.'

Eva took a step back glaring at him. 'I'm nobody's substitute,' she said angrily. 'I've been good enough for you these last few months.'

He walked away from her, whisky glass in hand, and went to stand before the white marble fireplace. 'You've been a handy distraction, that's all, Eva,' he said bluntly. 'I never wanted you. I want Lucy.'

Eva was stunned as though he had slapped her in the face. How could she have been such a blind fool? Anger welled up, making her incautious.

'Well, I'm here and she isn't,' she said loudly.

His glance at her was grim and she realized she must curb her rising fury. The last thing she needed was to quarrel with him. She had to get that money.

'I'm here willingly, Stan,' she said more quietly.

'Yes, well that ends now,' he said forcefully. 'I want you out of this house by midday tomorrow.'

'What?' Eva could not believe she was hearing those words. 'Why? What have *I* done?' Had he guessed her condition? 'You don't mean that, Stan.'

'You silly little bitch, of course I mean it,' he snarled. 'I never intended for you to stay this long anyway. I was bored with you after the first fortnight.'

'You're lying!' Eva shouted. 'You've come to my bed almost every night since I came to live here.'

'You're easy meat, that's why,' Stan said mockingly. 'What man wouldn't take what's offered so blatantly?'

'You bastard!'

'That's rich coming from you, Eva,' Stan said, with a sarcastic smile. 'With your background.'

Eva was incensed but felt helpless. How could he treat her like this, especially after the mess he had got her into? She had to face him with it now, she decided.

'You can't throw me out,' she said lifting her head high. 'Not when I'm carrying your child.'

He stared at her, his mouth slack. It was some moments before he spoke. 'What did you say?'

'You put me in the family way, Stan,' Eva said airily. 'I'm your responsibility now.'

'You're lying, you cheap little tart.'

'Ask Mrs Price if you don't believe me.'

'What's she got to do with it?'

'She caught me vomiting in the bathroom this morning. I'm up the spout all right.'

'What do you expect me to do about it?'

'You can pay for me to see someone to get rid,' Eva said, trying to keep desperation from her voice. 'All I need is five hundred pounds.'

Stan began to guffaw. 'I wouldn't give you five pennies,' he said mockingly. 'I have no responsibility for you or your brat. I don't even know it's mine. You could have brought umpteen men to this house behind my back.'

Eva was dismayed at this suggestion. 'You know I didn't, Stan,' she said. 'The child is yours. Getting rid of it is as beneficial to you as me.'

He guffawed loudly again.

Eva stamped her foot. 'Don't laugh at me, damn you!' she cried out. 'I'll have this child, and it will always be making demands on you,' she threatened. 'How will your wife feel about that?'

His expression darkened. 'Leave my wife out of this,' he said. 'And never threaten me again, if you know what's good for you.' He gave her a narrow speculative look. 'Has your mother put you up to this trick? If she thinks she can get one over on me she's mistaken.'

Eva was taken aback. 'My mother knows nothing of it,' she said. Sylvia would be devastated if she knew the trouble she was in. 'This is between you and me, Stan. I'm pregnant with your child. You can't deny it.'

'Huh!'

'Question Mrs Price,' Eva said quickly. 'She knows no other man has been here.'

'I don't give a bugger!' Stan exploded. 'You and your bastard kid can go to hell for all I care.' He pointed his finger at her threateningly. 'You're to get out of my house by midday tomorrow, and what's more you take nothing from this house except the clothes you arrived in. Understand me?'

'I won't go!'

'Then I'll come and throw you out,' Stan declared. 'On the street where the likes of you belong.'

With that final threat he put the whisky glass on the mantelpiece and strode from the room. Eva heard the front door slam as he let himself out.

In total shock, she stood where she was for a moment and then walked unsteadily to the sofa to collapse on it. She could hardly believe what had just happened.

Thrown out? Where could she go? She felt a sudden chill of fear. She had no money; she had nothing.

She had no time for women who cried: they were weak. She was strong, but despite that determination tears were stinging the backs of her eyes.

There was no help for it. As humiliating as it was, she must throw herself on her mother's mercy. There would be recriminations, of course, but she had to wheedle her way back into her good books somehow or other.

She was dabbing at her eyes when Mrs Price came into the room.

Eva glared at her. 'Are you snooping again?'

'You weren't very clever, were you?' Mrs Price said evenly.

'I did my best.'

'Not good enough,' the housekeeper said laconically. 'But you've still got an ace up your sleeve.'

Eva sat forward eagerly. 'Have I? What is it?'

'Maisie Naylor,' Mrs Price said. 'It might be worth visiting her. Mind you, she knows about his women only too well, but how would she feel about his child, eh?'

Eva was thoughtful.

'Maybe she'd pay to help you get rid. She has pots of money. She's childless herself. It would be interesting to know what she'll do when she learns about your little problem.'

'She'll throw me out.'

Mrs Price nodded. 'It's probable.' She shrugged. 'But then again, you won't know for sure until you try. Besides, he wouldn't want Maisie to know about your baby, so telling his wife of him would be a nice revenge, wouldn't it?'

Eva agreed. She was beginning to feel more optimistic. 'You're right, Mrs Price. It would serve him right.'

Stan had thrown her away like an old shoe, but he hadn't heard the last of her. Eva gritted her teeth in suppressed fury. No man treated her that way. Stan had made her his enemy, and she was out for revenge.

Thirteen

Deciding that the confrontation with Maisie Naylor was better done as soon as possible, Eva was up early the following morning, wasting no time, not with eviction staring her in the face. At midday she would have to seek out her mother and throw herself on her mercy. She would have a better chance of being taken back if she could show she had a solution to her problem.

Mrs Price had furnished her with the Naylors' address in Walter Road, ironically not so very far from Stan's love-nest in Ffynonne.

Putting on her most fashionable outfit, Eva set off. The Naylors' home proved to be a substantial white-painted detached house set against a background of dark green poplars. Eva hesitated for a moment. She dreaded this meeting. She had no reason to expect Maisie Naylor would even see her, but she had to try. It was the only way out of her desperate situation.

Taking a deep breath, she approached the front door. A maid answered her knock.

'Yes?'

'I'm here to see Mrs Naylor,' Eva said with a lift of her chin, feigning arrogance she did not feel. It was no good showing timidity, she decided.

'Is she expecting you, miss?'

Eva straightened her shoulders. 'No, but I'm here on a most important matter; a personal matter.'

The maid paused, frowning. 'Are you collecting for the church mission, because if so, Mrs Naylor has already given.'

'Do I look as though I'm from the church mission, you stupid girl?' Eva snapped, compressing her lips. 'Now tell Mrs Naylor I'm here.'

'I – I don't know whether she's at home.'

'I'll wait in the hall,' Eva said forcefully pushing her way past the girl.

'But . . .'

'Tell Mrs Naylor I'm here about Stan.'

The maid looked startled. 'Yes, miss.'

Eva did not have to wait long. A tall, slender, good-looking woman came into the hallway and stared stonily at Eva without speaking.

Eva hesitated for a moment, taken aback at the coldness in the woman's eyes.

'Are you Mrs Naylor?' she asked, remembering to sound confident. 'I've come about your husband.'

The woman's gaze was still chilled, and despite her resolve to be strong and appear haughty, Eva was beginning to shake, all of a sudden nervous at what she was about to do. Every second she expected to be ordered out.

However, the woman's glance turned to the waiting maid. 'That will be all, Doris,' she said loftily. 'You may go.'

The maid scuttled away through a door at the back of the hall.

She turned back to Eva. 'I am Mrs Naylor,' she said. 'Who are you and what do you want?'

Eva did not like the superior way the woman was looking at her; complacent and so sure of herself. She felt piqued at such composure and decided to be as blunt as she could.

Lifting her chin she said airily, 'I'm Eva Chandler, Stan's latest, and I've some news which may be of interest to you.'

Mrs Naylor raised her brows and looked annoyed. 'You've got a nerve, coming here.'

'Yes, it is taking a bit of courage,' Eva admitted flatly. 'But Stan left me no choice.'

'I see.' Mrs Naylor's gaze flickered. 'Well, what is it you want to tell me?'

Eva glanced around her. 'Do you really want to talk about it in the hallway, Mrs Naylor?'

'Come into the sitting room.'

Eva followed her in. Mrs Naylor pointed to a chair. 'Sit down. I'll hear what you have to say.'

'Very wise,' Eva said with satisfaction.

Maisie Naylor sniffed. 'Don't be too sure of yourself,' she

warned in a hard voice. 'I might get Doris to throw you out yet.'

'Yes, you might well throw me out,' Eva said. 'After you hear what I have to say.'

She sized up the other woman. Maisie Naylor was probably in her thirties. But for all her handsome looks there was a hardness around her eyes and mouth which perhaps spoke of unhappiness. Eva realized she might be a difficult woman to deal with, but she had no choice.

Maisie Naylor took a seat opposite her. 'I believe you're here to tell me that you're in the family way?' she said forthrightly.

Eva's eyes widened. 'How did you know? Did Mrs Price tell you?'

'I guessed,' Maisie said flatly. 'Who is Mrs Price?'

Eva tightened her lips. She had expected anger and recriminations, but this calmness was unnerving. The wind had been taken out of her sails somewhat at such insight and frankness, but she managed to keep her nerve.

'Never mind about Mrs Price,' she answered shortly, clutching her purse tightly in her lap. 'But you've guessed right, Mrs Naylor, and I need help. I'm desperate.'

'Oh, desperate, is it?' Maisie lifted a shoulder nonchalantly. 'Why come and tell me?'

Maisie Naylor was too calm perhaps, Eva thought. She noticed the woman was twisting her fingers in her lap. The little gesture was revealing and it fuelled her courage to press on.

'Because it is Stan's child, that's why,' she said firmly.

'How do I know that's true?'

'Because I say so!' she cried out tetchily. 'I wouldn't be here otherwise, would I?'

'You might be trying to trick me,' Maisie said sharply.

'I'm not trying to trick you,' Eva said emphatically. Her nerves were beginning to get the better of her despite her resolve, and she was half wishing that she had not come here. 'I've been living with Stan for a few months now,' she continued swiftly, 'at his house in Ffynonne.'

Maisie looked jolted at last and clenched her hands tightly. 'So close!'

Eva nodded, pleased at the reaction. 'Last night Stan called at the house. He was in a foul mood. Someone had given him a nasty beating.'

A narrow smile broke the grim line of Maisie's mouth. 'Really?'

Eva stared with interest at her amused expression. 'Haven't you seen him? Didn't he come home, then?'

'No,' Maisie said. 'Who beat him?'

There was malice in her tone and it dawned on Eva that Maisie hated her husband, and that give her spirits a lift. Perhaps she could use that to further her own ends.

'I think he mentioned his brother being involved,' Eva volunteered.

She decided not to mention Lucy or Stan's obsession with her. It still rankled in her mind that he had dismissed her in favour of her sister. It had been the worse insult of all.

'Rob was responsible?' Maisie looked thoughtful. 'I wonder what Stan's done to deserve that?'

'He wouldn't talk about it,' Eva said evasively. 'Instead he turned on me and told me to leave the house by midday today.' She hesitated for a moment, overcome with self pity. 'When I told him about . . . my condition he was furious.'

Maisie lifted an eyebrow in a knowing way. 'I don't doubt it,' she said, bitterness twisting her lips.

'I want to be rid of it,' Eva blurted out candidly. 'But I won't go to any backstreet butcher. I know a struck-off doctor who will do it safely for five hundred pounds.'

'Why are you telling *me* this?' Maisie asked and then nodded. 'Ah! I see. Stan refused to give you the money, eh?'

Eva hung her head. It was all so hopeless. She could tell from the older woman's tone that there was no help for her here. Perhaps she should go. Time was running out and she must collect her few belongings from the house in Ffynonne.

Eva got to her feet. 'I've made a mistake coming here,' she said. 'I'll go.'

'Sit down,' said Maisie curtly. 'I haven't finished with you yet.' She paused. 'I don't know that it was a mistake in coming here, but it was certainly a risk. Stan might've been at home.'

Eva glanced around the finely appointed sitting room, obviously the home of well-to-do people. Stan lived here in luxury and yet he begrudged her the money to save her reputation and perhaps her life.

'I thought he'd be at business at this hour,' Eva said. 'He told me he always gets off early each morning.'

Maisie's nostrils flared. 'Pillow talk, eh?' There was bitterness in her voice again.

'I'll go,' Eva said and began to walk to the door.

'I said, sit down!' Maisie commanded in a loud voice. 'We have to talk. I will help you, but not in the way *you* want.'

Confused, Eva sat down again, staring into Maisie's face, who was smiling as though making an effort to be friendly. It was unsettling, and Eva felt nervous again.

'There's only one way to help me,' she said. 'Give me the five hundred pounds to be rid. I'll leave you in peace then.'

'Wouldn't you rather have a thousand pounds?'

'What?' Eva almost bit her tongue in astonishment and looked at Maisie anxiously. Was she barking mad?

'That's the amount of money I'll give you, Miss Chandler, if you'll agree to carry the baby to term.'

'*What?*' Eva shook her head in bewilderment. 'What are you talking about?'

Maisie edged forward on her seat. 'Listen to me,' she said, eagerness in her voice. 'All the years I've been married to Stan he's cruelly denied me the one thing I long for – a child.'

'Oh!'

'Yes, now you see, don't you?' Maisie continued briskly. 'You possess what I want and I'm prepared to pay for what I want.'

'Stan's child?' Eva shook her head, perplexed. 'But I got the impression you hate your husband. Why would you want his child?'

Maisie sat back. 'I loved him wholeheartedly once. But it didn't take me long to realize why he'd married me. A young, wealthy widow – I was fair game to him.'

Eva watched the other woman's face begin to crumble. Bitterness and unhappiness showed plainly now.

'For years I've put up with his womanizing and his shady business dealings,' she continued. 'I could live with that if only he had agreed to a child, someone who would love me . . .'

She paused before swallowing deeply and then she straightened her shoulders, gaining control of herself again.

'You understand what I'm getting at, Miss Chandler? I can have Stan's child through you, and when I do . . .' Her features hardened again. 'I'll be finished with him. He won't leave me because of my money, but I can leave him when I have the child. His child!'

Eva began to tremble. This was totally unexpected. It had never crossed her mind to actually give birth to a child. The idea was frightening.

'You're asking a lot of me,' she said tentatively. 'I'm not sure that it isn't against the law.'

'Who's going to know but you and me?' Maisie said.

'I don't think I can . . .'

'All right, I'll give you two thousand pounds now, today,' Maisie pressed quickly. 'You can't refuse that. It's a small fortune. I'll even take you up to the bank in the Uplands immediately and help you open an account.'

Two thousand pounds! Eva had never dreamed of so much money. She could live the life she'd always dreamed of; leave Swansea, go to London, even travel abroad . . .

But wait! Eva gripped the arms of her chair convulsively. Everything was going forward too fast. Many months would pass before she was free to do that, unless . . . a notion came into her head . . . unless she absconded with the money. She could have the abortion and be gone before anyone knew different.

'You're not very clever or principled, are you, Miss Chandler,' Maisie exclaimed, cutting into her thoughts. 'You're thinking of cheating me. I can read it plainly in your expression.'

'No . . .'

'Oh, yes.' Maisie nodded emphatically. 'But you haven't heard the rest of my terms. When the baby is born and you hand it over to me I'm prepared to give you a further two . . . no . . . three thousand.' She smiled thinly. 'Your obvious greed will keep you honest, I think.'

Five thousand pounds! Eva could not believe it. 'You must be mad,' she commented unwisely. 'No one has that kind of money to give away.'

'No, I'm not mad, and I'm not giving it away,' Maisie said firmly. 'I'm as desperate for that child as you are to be rid, and I'm prepared to pay for motherhood. I'm also out for revenge against my husband for all those years of unhappiness.'

Eva stood up. 'I'll have to think about it,' she said. She thought of Sylvia's reaction to such an agreement. 'I must speak with my mother.'

Maisie jumped to her feet. 'No!' she exclaimed loudly. 'No one else is to know of our agreement. I forbid it.'

'But my mother . . .'

'She needn't even know you're expecting,' Maisie said. 'You'll have the money. You can afford to go away until it's all over.'

Eva sat down. If she took the money she would not spend one penny of it until she was fit to enjoy it to the full. It was an opportunity of a lifetime.

'I can't go through all this without my mother's help,' she said cautiously. 'I'll have to throw myself on her mercy for the duration.'

Maisie made a sound in her throat, and Eva lifted a hand.

'You have my word I'll say nothing,' she assured. 'Do you think I want this chance snatched away from me now?'

'So, you agree?'

Eva stood up, to find her legs shaky. 'Yes,' she said. 'I agree. But, remember, agreements work both ways. You won't even glimpse the child until I've been paid in full.'

Maisie sighed. 'We understand each other.'

Eva nodded.

Maisie moved to a small writing desk before the window and sat down. She took a chequebook out of a drawer and then took up a pen.

'You've made a wise decision, Miss Chandler,' she said, her back turned. 'I wish you joy of the money. My joy will come later.'

'How are things going at the smallholding?' Sylvia asked as she and Lucy sat before the fire in the back room at Fleet Street. 'Will Rob be back in business soon?'

'It'll be a few weeks yet,' Lucy said, sipping her tea. 'Rob and Ted Locke are working like Trojans. It is unbelievable how much damage was done. I do what I can to help.'

'Well, you seem to be spending every free minute of your day at the holding,' Sylvia commented. 'I hope you're not doing too much, Lucy.'

Lucy stared into the glow of the coals. She could not do

too much for Rob Naylor. Apart from the warmth of her feelings for him, she could not throw off the sense of guilt at what had happened to his livelihood.

Stan Naylor had a lot to answer for, but she was thankful that there had been no repercussions from the beating that Rob had given him. This surprised her and she wondered if Stan was merely biding his time before striking again.

Lucy glanced at the clock on the sideboard. It was almost seven o'clock. 'Is Nora settled for the night?'

'Yes, poor old dear,' Sylvia said. 'I'm worried about her, Lucy. She lives in fear of Stan Naylor. It's not doing her heart any good.'

If truth be told, Lucy thought, they all lived in fear of Stan Naylor. The spectre of the debt they owed him hovered over them continually. At least the locks were changed, so he could not gain entrance and catch them unawares.

At that moment there was a loud knocking on the front door and Lucy, her mind on Stan Naylor, almost dropped her cup and saucer.

'Who's that at this time of night?' Sylvia stared across at her wide-eyed and Lucy saw the same fear she felt.

'I don't know.' She wished Rob had not gone back to Tycoch so soon. She stood up. 'I'll look through the front room window before I answer.'

'Don't disturb Nora,' Sylvia warned.

Entering Nora's bedroom quietly, Lucy cautiously parted the curtains and craned her neck to peer out to see who was at the door. She was astonished to see a familiar figure. Eva!

Immediately she went to the front door and opened it.

'Eva!' Lucy stared at her sister as she stood on the doorstep. 'What're you doing here?'

'Well, you could let me come in,' Eva said petulantly. 'Anybody would think I was a stranger.' She pushed past and walked down the passage towards the back room. 'Where's Mam?'

'Hush!' Lucy said quietly. 'Keep your voice down. We don't want to disturb Nora.'

'Who the heck is Nora?'

'Hush, will you!'

Before Lucy could warn her mother, Eva burst into the room. Sylvia jumped to her feet, shock in her expression.

'Eva!'

'Hello, Mam,' Eva said pulling off her gloves. 'I've had the devil's own job in tracking you down. Mrs Grant had no idea where you'd gone.'

'Eva, I can't believe you've come back,' Sylvia said in a hushed voice. 'I thought I'd never see you again. What's happened?'

'Yes, I'd like to know that, too.' Lucy came into the room and stood close to Sylvia. 'What exactly are you doing here, Eva, and at this time of night too?'

'You might offer me a cup of tea,' Eva said nonchalantly, as she took off her hat and dark red wool coat and sat down.

Lucy saw that it was the same coat her sister had been wearing on the day she had decamped from the flat in Marlborough Road to live with Stan Naylor. Immediately she guessed why Eva was there.

'He's thrown you out, hasn't he? Out on the street with nothing but what you stand up in.' Lucy nodded sagely. 'I told you this day would come.'

Eva tossed her head. 'He didn't throw me out,' she denied vehemently. 'I've left him, as a matter of fact. He's too possessive of me. I got bored with it.'

'You're lying, as usual,' Lucy said flatly. 'And you're hiding something. I could always read you like a book, Eva.'

'Mam, have I got to put up with Lucy's nasty comments?' Eva asked pouting. 'I can see she hasn't lost any of her spiteful ways since I've been gone.'

'You broke my heart, Eva,' Sylvia said quietly. 'And you don't seem to care.'

'Oh, fiddlesticks, Mam!' Eva tossed her head. 'You make a song and dance of everything. I'm back now. It's all over.'

'Oh, no it's not!' Lucy said forcefully. 'Do you realize Mam tried to kill herself because of you?'

'Don't talk rubbish!'

'She walked into the sea to drown herself.'

Eva stared for a moment and then shrugged. 'Well, obviously she didn't drown,' she said rudely. 'So what's the fuss?'

'Oh, you cold-hearted girl,' Sylvia exclaimed and Lucy could see tears glistening in her eyes. 'I would have died if it hadn't been for Rob.'

'Rob? Who's Rob and who's this Nora?'

Lucy hesitated. She hated to admit it but suddenly she felt a stab of jealousy. It was plain Eva was back to stay and undoubtedly she would throw herself at Rob as soon as she met him, especially if she realized Lucy had feelings for him.

'Rob Naylor,' Sylvia said before Lucy could speak.

'Rob Naylor?' A look of alertness and enlightenment appeared on Eva's face as soon as the name was spoken, and Lucy realized her sister had heard that name before. 'Of course,' Eva exclaimed as though to herself. 'I should've guessed.'

'I'm looking after his mother, Nora,' Sylvia continued. 'In exchange, Lucy and I live here rent-free.'

Eva glanced up at Lucy, her features stiff. 'Are you sure that's the reason it's rent-free?' she said, her lip curling with derision. 'Because I've heard differently.'

'What do you mean?'

Eva's lips were tight with anger. 'Stan and Rob were in a fist fight over you.'

Lucy was aghast. 'It wasn't over me,' she denied strongly. 'Stan wrecked Rob's smallholding; ruined his business. He's lost hundred of pounds in income because of it. It had nothing to do with me.'

'Not according to Stan.' Eva looked at Lucy with fury in her eyes. 'It was because of that fight that Stan turned against me. He blames you, Lucy, and because I'm your sister, he took it out on me.'

'Then I've done you a favour,' Lucy said lifting her chin. 'I said I'd save you from him and I have.'

'You spiteful cat!' Eva exploded, her face turning red. 'You did that on purpose. You put Rob up to it, just to get back at me because I was living high off the hog. You couldn't stand it.'

'Huh! And you're too stupid to see when a man is using you for his own ends,' Lucy flung back with equal passion. 'Stan Naylor never had any interest in you. You had to throw yourself at him before he noticed you.'

'Why, you bitch!' Eva sprang to her feet and rushed at Lucy, but Sylvia got between them, raising her hands.

'Stop it!' she cried out. 'Stop it, both of you.' Sylvia held both at bay. 'I can't bear this squabbling between you,' she continued, a sob in her voice. 'We're in the most desperate trouble and you can do nothing better than to fight each other.'

Lucy was immediately ashamed of her thoughtless behaviour. 'Mam, I'm so sorry,' she said quickly putting an arm around her mother's shoulders. 'I wasn't thinking. We shouldn't quarrel.'

Glancing at her sister she saw that Eva's anger had not abated, and decided to leave before another row broke out. Perhaps it was a good idea that Eva and Sylvia should be alone for the moment to sort things out between them.

'I'll look in on Nora,' she offered walking from the room. 'We might've disturbed her.'

In the semi-darkness of the room Lucy saw that Nora was still sleeping peacefully. Lighting a candle, Lucy looked at the woman in the bed. She looked small and frail, and even in sleep her face was pale. Lucy could understand Sylvia's concern.

Lucy sat down on a cane chair near the window for a moment, giving her mother and sister some privacy. All at once she heard a sharp cry from Sylvia, a cry of deep distress, and immediately she rushed into the back room.

'Mam, what's the matter?'

Sylvia was holding a handkerchief to her lips, tears streaming down her face. 'It's too dreadful, Lucy.'

Lucy glared at Eva. 'What have you done now?' she burst out.

'She got herself with child,' Sylvia uttered wretchedly. 'By that beast of a man, Stan Naylor. Oh, my God, Lucy, what are we to do?'

Lucy was speechless. She stared at Eva, but her sister's expression was defiant and haughty. Lucy could not see one mite of regret in her eyes.

'Oh, you stupid little fool,' Lucy said disparagingly. 'Now we know why you've turned up here with nothing but the clothes you stand up in. You didn't leave him. He threw you out; threw you to the wolves.'

'What are we to do?' Sylvia repeated her despairing cry verging on hysteria. 'An illegitimate baby. This is the end!'

'I'm going to have the baby,' Eva declared calmly. 'I've made up my mind.'

'I should think so!' Sylvia said, staring at her in horror. 'Anything else is unthinkable.'

Shocked though she was, Lucy was also suspicious of Eva's

motives. She knew her sister too well. If Eva was prepared to put herself through childbirth she had a good reason and it wasn't anything to do with love or mothering instinct. But what Eva's reason was she could not even begin to guess.

'I'm surprised you're not looking for a way to be rid of it,' Lucy said. 'You were never one to sacrifice yourself.'

'There's nothing else for it but to have the baby,' Sylvia said quickly. 'Eva knows that.'

'Stan Naylor won't change his mind, Eva,' Lucy continued, 'if that's what you're thinking. You and your child are less than nothing to him.'

'Lucy is trying to start a quarrel again, Mam,' Eva whined. 'Tell her to stop it. I have to be careful in my condition.'

'Lucy, please,' Sylvia said reproachfully. 'What's done is done. No more recriminations.' She took a deep breath of resignation. 'We'll have to come to terms with the situation; make arrangements.'

Eva glanced around. 'Obviously, I'll have to stay here for the term,' she said. 'I've got no money to find a place of my own. I'll need my family to support me.'

'Money is short,' Lucy said stiffly. They could not turn Eva away, but it would mean an even heavier burden on their small income. 'But I expect we'll manage.'

'I should hope so,' Eva said tossing her head. 'After all, I am your own flesh and blood.'

Lucy could understand the look of concern on Rob's face when Sylvia asked if Eva could stay, and told him haltingly and shamefacedly the reason.

His expression was grim as he looked at Eva. 'So, my brother has thrown you out because of your . . . condition.'

'Yes, Mr Naylor,' Eva said in a small voice looking pathetic and helpless.

Lucy sighed with exasperation as her sister, giving a little sob, dabbed at her dry eyes with a handkerchief. Eva's hypocrisy was sickening.

Rob glanced from Eva to Sylvia and Lucy, his expression serious. 'Because she's kin to you both, I'll agree for her to stay,' he said. 'But I can't say I'm happy that anyone associated with Stan is under this roof.'

'He tricked me, Mr Naylor,' Eva exclaimed in a complaining

tone. 'I was an innocent girl before he used his wiles on me. I didn't know what I was doing.'

Rob gave her a fleeting glance and looked away. Lucy could see he was embarrassed.

'We'll say no more,' he said.

Lucy was glad to get away to the smallholding each day; glad to get away from Eva's sullen face; glad to be able to spend time with Rob.

The repairing of the damaged greenhouses was getting along well. Two houses were ready for replanting and although autumn was gaining on them fast they pressed on with the planting of those hardy varieties which would flourish in the colder weather. Lucy gladly helped Rob with that work, eager to learn and even more eager to please him.

The days darkened early and the working day was shorter, but Rob took time to sit with her in the house at Fleet Street of an evening to explain the properties of various plants and how best to nurture them.

His enthusiasm for his vocation was contagious and Lucy listened avidly. Often the work was backbreaking but she liked it very much; she saw that there might be a future for her in horticulture and she was determined to learn all she could.

During these evenings while Lucy and Rob pored over seed catalogues he outlined his plans for the future of the smallholding.

'You make it sound so exciting,' she told him, exhilarated by his enthusiasm and wishing fervently she could be part of that future too.

He turned his head to glance at her, his expression slightly startled. 'You're the first person to see that, Lucy,' he said.

He returned his gaze to the catalogues before him, but she sensed a new thoughtfulness in his demeanour, and was heartened by it. Would her equal enthusiasm help him to see her in a different light? She wished wholeheartedly that it would.

All the while when she and Rob were together she was conscious of Eva hovering. Her sister made a point of interrupting their discussions as often as possible. She smiled and preened herself before Rob in such a blatant way that Lucy was disgusted.

Eva had always been wilful and flighty, prone to recklessness, but now Lucy saw that her attitude had gone beyond girlish self-ishness, and was disturbed by her overt coquettishness. She was troubled, too, by the thought that Eva would not submit to the more demanding aspects of motherhood. She was fearful that it would all end badly. The burden of Eva's folly would fall on her shoulders and on Sylvia's.

Lucy continued to worry about her mother and her ability to withstand further stress. Sylvia had gradually regained some of her confidence, but Lucy was afraid that added troubles would drag her down into the depth of despair again and would result in another attempt to end her life.

She could not forgive Eva for the misery she had brought them and she sensed there was more to come.

Fourteen

The weather at the beginning of November had turned bitterly cold, but Lucy had got up early as usual to go off to the smallholding. Eva did not envy her working in the open air, even if it did mean she was with Rob Naylor.

Eva lay in the bed she shared with Lucy thinking of Rob. He was attractive and it amused her to flirt with him to put Lucy's nose out of joint, but so far he had resisted her, which was disappointing. But if she couldn't get him she was certain Lucy stood no chance at all. All Rob thought about was his damned smallholding.

Eva turned over in the bed, enjoying the warmth, knowing she could stay there until midday if she had a mind to. For the moment life was reasonably good. She did not have to spend any of the money Maisie Naylor had given her and there was more to come.

She would not think too much about the months ahead and what lay before her. It would be worth it, she told herself. Once the baby was born and she passed it on to Maisie she would live the life she had always wanted, the life that she deserved.

The bedroom door opened and Sylvia stood there. 'Aren't you getting up, Eva?' she asked, reproach in her voice.

Eva did not move. 'What's for breakfast?'

'You'll have to get it yourself. I've got to go into town to the market for provisions. Nora's not very well this morning. I want you to be up and dressed to keep an eye on her.'

Eva snuggled further into the bed. 'I don't see why I should,' she said grumpily. 'That's your job, Mam. I can't stand sick old people.'

'I don't ask you to do much, Eva. And after all . . . you're getting bed and board free . . .'

Eva jerked into a sitting position. 'Mam! You sound as though you begrudge me,' she said putting a whine into her voice. 'And me in my condition, too.'

'Yes, well, the less said about that the better,' Sylvia said with unaccustomed severity in her tone. 'It won't hurt you to look in on Nora from time to time. Now get up. Oh, and lock the front door after me and keep it locked.'

Eva heard the front door close. Shivering, she got out of bed and struggled into a woollen dressing gown. She would get up, she told herself, merely because she was hungry, but she wouldn't dress. She would come back to bed after she had eaten. The old woman could call out if she needed anything.

It was warm in the back room with the fire well banked up with coal. Eva sat before the glow with a cup of tea and some toast. She thought of what she would do when she got her hands on all that money. She wouldn't stay in Swansea. There was no future for her here. London was the place to be where she could enjoy the good life.

Her musings were interrupted by a knock on the front door. Eva decided to ignore it. She didn't have to do anything in this house if she didn't want to.

Someone knocked again, louder, and then to her surprise the front door opened and heavy footsteps sounded in the passage.

'Caught you napping, haven't I, you raddled old hag,' a man's voice said aggressively. 'You're hanging on, but nobody wants you. Why don't you do everybody a favour and die?'

Nora gave a sharp cry of fear.

That voice was all too familiar. Astonished, Eva rushed into the passage to see Stan just about to step into Nora's room.

'Stan! Why are you here?' she asked loudly, staring at him, frowning with suspicion. 'Are you hounding me?'

He turned and looked at her, startled.

'You!' he exclaimed above Nora's whimpering. 'What the hell do you mean by coming here?'

'Huh! You slung me out, Stan, if you remember,' Eva snapped angrily. 'I had nowhere to go, not that you cared. I've taken refuge with my mother. Rob has agreed I can stay in his house for the time being.'

'*I* own this house, not Rob,' Stan told her forcefully. 'You're trespassing on my property.'

Eva stared at him. 'Your house?' She felt flummoxed.

'Yes,' he said. 'And I'm only waiting for that old bat in there to kick the bucket so I can rent it out.'

Nora started to cry and moan.

'I didn't know the house belonged to you,' Eva said strongly. 'Huh! I'd have thought twice about staying here if I had.'

'Well, you can pack up and go,' he said. 'As quick as you like.'

Eva stared at him angrily. 'You haven't given my mother or Lucy notice to quit, I see,' she said petulantly. 'And I know why. Still think you can persuade Lucy to share your bed, do you?'

'Shut your face!'

Eva gave him a mocking smile. 'You don't stand a snowball's chance in a bakehouse with her. She's crazy about Rob. Anyone can see that.'

'I said, shut up!' Stan struck her across the face with his open palm.

Eva reeled back against the wall, her hand to her smarting cheek. She stared up at him for a moment, her blood boiling.

It was on the tip of her tongue to tell him about the arrangement she had with his wife, but caution stopped her. He might put a spanner in the works, and she was counting on getting that money.

'You'll be sorry you did that, Stan,' she panted with impotent wrath. 'One day I'll have the last laugh on you.'

'And pigs might fly,' he said scornfully. 'I'm warning you. I want you out of this house today or I'll send someone around to manhandle you out.'

'How can you be so callous?' Eva burst out, furious at his indifference to her. 'I'm in the family way because of you, remember.'

'Huh! You won't be for long,' Stan said scornfully. 'Being up the spout will cramp your style.'

'Well, you're wrong,' Eva flared. 'As a matter of fact, I'm keeping the baby.'

He stared at her frowning as though trying to discern her motive. 'It won't do you any good,' he said. 'You can't prove it's mine. You've got no claim on me.'

'Your wife might be interested to know about it,' Eva said unable to help herself. 'I've heard she's desperate for a kid of her own. I wonder what she'll do when she knows you've got me pregnant instead of her.'

Stan lifted his fist, his face darkening with rage, and Eva shrank back.

'You stay away from my wife, do you hear me,' he said through clenched teeth. 'You're asking for a nasty accident to happen, Eva. I can arrange it any time.'

'Oh, you're so brave against two defenceless women,' Eva mocked. 'But I've got you worried, haven't I, worried your missus will find out about my kid? I reckon she'd leave you, Stan.'

'You stupid little slut, I could shut you up for good here and now.'

Stan took a step towards her, but stopped abruptly at a sound from Nora's bedroom. The old woman had found the strength from somewhere to rap repeatedly with her walking stick on the partition wall of the house next door.

'She's calling in the neighbours,' Eva told him quickly. 'They'll come running. They're good like that around here. I'll tell them you attacked me . . . just look at my face! They'll call a bobby to you. You'd better go, Stan.'

The expression of frustrated fury that passed across his features pleased her. As Nora's stick continued to hammer the wall, Stan turned abruptly and strode out through the door. Eva rushed forward and quickly bolted it, breathing a deep sigh of relief that he was gone.

She went to Nora's door. 'You can stop now,' she said. 'He's gone.'

Nora dropped the stick and fell back on the pillows. Her face was ashen and she was breathing in loud harsh gasps. She lifted up her thin arm and extended her hand towards Eva, who flinched.

'There's nothing I can do for you,' she said hastily. 'You'll have to wait until Sylvia gets back.'

When Sylvia returned Eva was up and dressed. Her mother noticed the marks on her face immediately. Eva was on the point of passing it off by saying she'd bumped her face on the edge of the door, but Nora was sure to tell her what really happened. She decided it was wise to get her side of the story in first. But she would not tell Sylvia that Stan had ordered her out immediately. Her mother might insist that she did go.

When Sylvia learned about their unexpected visitor, the colour drained from her face and then she looked angry.

'I told you to lock the door behind me, girl,' she said sharply. 'You never pay attention to anything I say.'

'It's not my fault. You didn't explain how important it was,' Eva complained.

'More trouble for us again,' Sylvia said sadly. 'Stan Naylor won't rest until Nora is dead and gone.' She paused looking suddenly very concerned. 'Oh my goodness! Nora must've been terrified.'

She left the room quickly and Eva heard her go into Nora's room. She tiptoed along the passage to listen at the door. What was Nora telling her? How much had she heard of her exchange with Stan? The last thing Eva wanted was to have Maisie's name mentioned. Sylvia was sure to ask questions.

Eva was back in the living room when her mother came out. Sylvia shook her head as she entered the back room.

'Nora's had a nasty shock,' she said. 'She's so breathless she can hardly speak. Did Stan Naylor lay a hand on her?'

'No,' Eva said smartly. 'I protected her and sent him packing. He didn't even go in her room. Nora is making too much of the incident.'

'She's a sick fragile old lady,' Sylvia exclaimed impatiently. 'She can't endure many more upsets like this.'

Eva said nothing. She did not want to come up against Stan again either, although she doubted he would make good on his threat to send someone around to manhandle her out. Now she had been warned, she would make sure the door was always bolted against him.

That evening, when Lucy came home from the smallholding, Rob Naylor was with her. Eva was suddenly apprehensive when Sylvia told them that Stan had been there and that he had gained entry to the house.

Rob was furious, giving her baleful glances.

'I didn't know,' Eva complained. 'Nobody warned me.'

Rob said nothing but went in to see how his mother was. When he had left the room Lucy rounded on Eva in fury.

'You're a lazy selfish little beast, Eva,' she exploded. 'Nora must be protected first and foremost. If you can't play your part in the household then you'll have to go.'

Eva tossed her head. 'Well, we all know why that's so important, don't we, and it's not because you care a fig really,' she sneered. 'While Nora's alive you and Mam live rent-free.'

Lucy's mouth dropped open with shock at such an accusation.

'That's a dreadful thing to say,' Sylvia exclaimed, distress in her voice.

'It's true, though.'

'Mam and I have more feeling than that,' Lucy retorted at last. 'But I wouldn't expect someone like you to understand that, Eva, self-absorbed as you are.' She turned to Sylvia. 'Perhaps it would be better if Eva found lodgings elsewhere, Mam, especially since Stan Naylor now knows she's living here.'

'It's not for you to say whether I stay or not,' Eva blurted angrily. 'It's Stan's house and it's Rob's mother. Rob has already said I could stay.'

Rob came back into the room.

'Isn't that right, Rob?' Eva appealed to him quickly. 'You said I could stay but Lucy wants me out.' She shook her head. 'What happened today wasn't my fault, really it wasn't. And I've no money for lodgings elsewhere.'

Rob glanced at Lucy before replying.

'I gave my word,' he said steadily to Eva. 'You can stay if only because I owe Sylvia a lot, but you've got to be more careful.'

'I will, I promise.'

Rob sat down at the table. 'We're no worse off than we were before, I suppose,' he said. 'But still, we'll all have to be vigilant.'

Eva turned away. She could mention Stan's threat, but Rob might hold it against her, and she would not risk it. Stan would never go that far.

Later that evening Stan walked into the Red Cow in the High Street and glanced around the saloon bar. The man he was looking for was leaning against the counter nursing a half-empty glass.

Stan strode towards him. 'Ben Hopkins! I want a word with you.'

Ben Hopkins jerked erect and whirled, his face turning pale. 'Stan!' He looked as though he was ready to bolt and Stan was puzzled.

'What's up, Ben? Expecting trouble? Coppers after you?'

Ben shook his head. 'No, Stan. I'm just standing here minding my own business.'

Stan leaned against the bar. 'You're a bloody hard man to find,' he said to his companion. 'I think I've been in every bar in town looking. Are you hiding or something?'

'No, like I said . . .'

Stan signalled to the barman and then looked at Ben.

'What'll you have?'

'Eh? Oh, same again. Thanks.' Ben swallowed deeply. An expression of relief was plain on his face and Stan wondered again at it.

'Pint of best,' Stan told the barman. 'And same again for him.'

Ben turned to face the bar again as though unwilling to meet his gaze.

Stan watched him covertly while they waited for the drinks to be brought. He had been in two minds to ask for help from a small-time criminal, but Ben knew the kind of low life he was looking for; the dregs of humanity who would do anything for money. For what he had in mind he needed such men; men who were not associated with him and did not know him personally.

Stan's jaw tightened. He still smarted at the humiliation of being bested in a fight in front of Lucy. Rob would pay for that and dearly. His half-brother needed a lesson he wouldn't forget and that slut Eva, too, must be taught not to threaten him.

The barman put the drinks on the counter before them.

'Cheers!' Stan said and then took a long swig.

Ben pushed his old drink to one side and took up the new glass. 'You were looking for me,' he said quietly. 'What for?'

Stan jerked his head. 'Let's sit at that table in the corner,' he suggested. 'I don't want to be overheard.'

Stan walked to the table, Ben following. They sat down. There was still wariness in Ben's eyes.

'What's the matter, Ben? You're as jumpy as hell.'

'It's nothing.' Ben shook his head. 'We're not exactly pals, are we, Stan. So why search me out?'

'I need a favour,' Stan said. He hesitated before saying more. He had to trust him to a certain extent. 'I want you to find me a couple of blokes who will do a job, no questions asked. Get me?'

Ben looked interested. 'What kind of a job?'

Stan pursed his lips. 'Now I don't ask you awkward questions when you come to me to fence those various little trinkets you pick up, do I?'

'I have to know, Stan, to make sure I find the right men.'

'You don't need to know anything,' Stan told him sharply. 'Just find me men who'll do anything for money and keep their traps shut afterwards. All right?'

'All right, Stan. Don't get shirty.' Ben's tongue flicked nervously over his lips. 'Look, be here at this table same time tomorrow. I'll send a couple of blokes along.'

Ben got up from the table. Stan noticed his drink had hardly been touched. He frowned, still puzzled. 'You're in a hurry, Ben.'

'I've got to see a man . . .'

Stan gave him a sneering smile. 'Pick a lock more like.'

Ben looked nervous again. 'I don't know what job you want done, Stan, but if anything goes wrong I hope there'll be no comeback on me.'

Stan stared at him. 'I wish I knew what's making you so bloody nervous,' he said. 'I'm beginning to wonder if I'm the one with something to worry about.'

Stan was at the Red Cow the same time the following evening. He managed to get the same table. Before sitting he sloped the backs of two chairs against the table edge to show they were taken, and then he waited.

He was reading the evening paper when he was aware that he had company and looked up to see two men standing at the table.

'Are you the cove who wants a job done?' one of them asked gruffly in an accent that wasn't local. He had a narrow pasty face, sunken cheeks and very unfriendly expression.

'Quiet!' Stan hissed in consternation.

He stared at the thin man and then at his companion. The other man had the mutilated face of a pugilist; a broken nose and a scar etched in his right cheek.

Stan mixed with some pretty rough customers but he realized these two men were more dangerous, the kind that lined the gutters in the mean streets around the docks. They stood out from the Red Cow's regular clientele like sore thumbs.

Stan folded his paper and stood up. He could not afford to be seen with such low life.

'He can have the table, mate,' he said loudly for the benefit of drinkers nearby. In an undertone he continued: 'Meet me in the lane behind the pub in ten minutes.' And then he strode out.

Stan waited for them somewhat nervously, he had to admit to himself. Finally they strolled into the lane, their shambling outlines lit by the nearest gas street light.

'Well, mister?' Pasty-face asked. 'What's the job? Or more important, how much will you pay?' He gave a laugh that sounded like the neighing of a donkey.

'A pony each, if it's done right,' Stan said.

'A pony each, eh?' said Pug-face. He sounded more than interested.

'If it's done right,' Stan repeated.

Pasty-face spat on the ground. 'Never had any complaints in the past, have we, Sid?'

Pug-face shook his misshapen head. 'Never.'

'All right,' Stan said. 'Tomorrow, midmorning, I want you to break in to a house in Fleet Street.' He told them the number. 'Get in the back way. The front is bolted. There's an entrance to the back lane by the side of Lippard's coal merchant's yard. Breaking down the back door should be easy enough.'

Pasty-face nodded. 'What you want done?'

'Smash the place up good and proper,' Stan said savagely. 'And put the frighteners on anyone who's there. There's an old woman. You'll find her in the parlour, and a young loud-mouthed slut. Don't worry about broken bones. The worse the better.'

'Women? Thrash women?' Pug-face shook his head. 'I dunno about that, mister.'

'Shut up, Sid,' Pasty-face snapped. 'We'd thrash our own mothers for a pony.'

Pug-face chuckled. 'Right!'

'Get this straight,' Stan emphasized. 'It has to be midmorning.' He did not want Lucy anywhere near the place when these men called. 'Do as much damage as you can.'

'All right, mister,' said Pasty-face and held out his hand. 'Where's your money?'

'I don't have it on me,' Stan said hastily.

'Pay first,' Pasty-face said nastily. 'We don't take kindly to being gypped, mate.'

'I'm not a fool,' Stan snapped. 'I don't carry that kind of money around with me. All I've got on me tonight is a tenner.'

He took the banknote out of his top pocket and handed it over.

Pasty-face cursed; his expression was sullen and dangerous.

'You'll get the rest of your money when the job is done,' Stan told them quickly. 'You can collect it from Ben Hopkins. You trust him, don't you?'

'You'd better be straight with us, mister,' Pasty-face snarled. 'We've got long memories.'

'You know what to do,' Stan said dismissively. 'Midmorning, remember.'

He sidestepped them and strode quickly from the lane. His ears were pitched to hear if they were following him, but when he turned to look back they were gone.

'I tell you he's planning something, Maisie,' Ben said worriedly.

He stood near the window overlooking the street, peering through a gap in the curtains. They were in his room at his lodgings. He had smuggled her in through the back entrance.

'He's always up to no good,' Maisie replied lazily. 'Never mind him. Come back to bed.'

Ben took a cigarette from the packet on the side table and lit up. 'Do you think he's found out about us?' he asked, looking across the bed at her. 'What do you think he'd do?'

'He's not going to find out anything,' Maisie said reassuringly. 'I'm too clever for him.'

'He's up to something.'

She raised herself up and leaning on her elbow, held out her hand for a cigarette. 'Stop worrying, Ben,' she said as he passed her the one he had just lit. 'He's too busy with his bits of skirt at that house he's got in Ffynonne. Huh! He thinks I don't know about that.'

Ben sat on the bed and lit another cigarette. 'He knows too much about me, Maisie,' he said. 'He could shop me to the coppers.'

'No he won't,' Maisie said. 'Stan's in too deep himself.'
She put a hand on his bare arm. 'When are you going to do
his safe at his office? It's been months and months since I
gave you the combination.'

'I've been thinking, Maisie. It's too dangerous.'

'You said you'd do anything for me!'

'Now don't get stroppy, love,' he said cajolingly. 'I didn't
say I wouldn't do it.' He looked at her. He didn't want to lose
her. She was the best thing that had ever happened to him,
but if Stan Naylor suspected . . .

'Well, when?'

'I want to find out what Stan's up to first,' he said, drawing
deeply on the cigarette. 'I have to go careful, Maisie.'

'Oh! Careful!' Her tone was scornful. She turned over in
bed, her back to him.

Ben said nothing more but continued to smoke. Maisie was
Stan's wife but she had no idea how dangerous he really was.
He would do the safe but in his own time.

Eva glanced at the alarm clock by the side of the bed. Ten to
eleven. Her mother hadn't brought her tea this morning. Mean!

She was hungry and she had to admit she was getting bored
with lazing about. Perhaps she would get up, get a bit to eat,
have a swill and go into town to look at the shops. Maybe
she could cajole Sylvia into giving her a bob or two spending
money.

Slipping into her dressing gown she opened the bedroom
door and was startled to hear a sudden commotion from
below. Nora was crying out in fright and Sylvia was shouting
hysterically at someone.

'Mam!' Eva called out. 'What's the matter?'

She ran down the stairs, hurried through the living room
and into the passage. The uproar was coming from the parlour
where Nora slept.

Cautiously Eva peered around the door jamb and gave a
gasp of fright. Two strange men were in there. One of them
had Nora by the shoulders shaking her violently as she lay in
the bed, while she cried out pitifully.

'Stop it! Leave her alone,' Sylvia screamed at them.

Eva saw her mother was brandishing a fire iron. She swung
it at the head of the man nearest to her, a big brute of a man

with a fighter's face. He dodged but the iron struck him on the shoulder and he let out a coarse oath. He rounded on Sylvia and tried to take the iron from her.

As they struggled Eva did not hesitate another second but ran to the front door, pulled back the bolts and raced into the street, hardly noticing the biting cold piercing her thin dressing gown.

'Help!' she shrieked at the top of her voice. 'Help us! Murder!'

Two men in labourers' clothes were passing on the pavement. They stopped immediately. 'What's the matter, miss?' one of them asked.

Eva pointed a shaking finger toward the front door. 'My mother is being attacked! Help her!'

Immediately they charged through the doorway, Eva right behind them. 'In the parlour!' she called out urgently.

She was in time to see Nora's attackers running down the passage to the back of the house. One of the labourers gave chase while the other went into the parlour with Eva.

Sylvia was on the floor, the fire iron beside her.

'Mam!' Eva screamed in sudden terror, sinking to her knees. 'Mam, are you all right?'

Sylvia responded with a moan and struggled to get to her feet, Eva and the labourer helping her upright.

'Nora!' Sylvia murmured dazedly. 'Have they hurt Nora?'

The labourer went to the bed to look closely at the figure huddled there and then came back to where Sylvia was swaying dazedly.

'I believe the old lady is a goner, missus,' he said gravely. 'Her colour don't look good for a start, and I can't feel a pulse.'

'Oh, no!' Sylvia cried out in distress. 'Nora! Oh my God! Who's done this?'

The second labourer appeared in the parlour doorway. 'They got away down the back lane,' he said panting. 'Couldn't catch 'em.'

'I think they've done for the old lady, Bill,' the other man said in a low voice. 'She looks lifeless to me.'

Sylvia tried to go to the bed side. 'We must fetch a doctor to her straight away,' she cried out.

Eva held her mother back. She could sense Sylvia was on the edge of hysteria.

Bill gulped in air. 'I'll go and find a bobby,' he said breathlessly and hurriedly left.

'We must get the doctor,' Sylvia insisted straining in Eva's hold. 'You stay here, Eva, since you're not dressed. I'll go for him.'

'No, Mam, you're still shaken from what that beast did to you,' Eva said firmly. 'I don't think a doctor can help Nora now.'

She looked appealingly at the labourer. 'You're sure she's . . . dead?'

'Bet a week's pay her heart has stopped, miss,' he said. 'Best wait for the coppers to come. They know what to do.'

'Oh, Eva, how will I tell Rob his mother is dead?' Sylvia cried out. 'He'll be heartbroken. He loves her so.'

'Come into the back room, Mam,' Eva urged, leading Sylvia away. 'I'll make you some tea.'

Eva's mind was in a whirl as she sat her sobbing mother in the chair by the fire and went to the scullery to make a pot of tea.

Stan's threat was uppermost in her mind. Could he have been responsible for this? Perhaps if she had been downstairs she'd have been beaten too. She felt a shiver go through her. Maybe Stan wanted her to miscarry. She wouldn't put it past him.

Would Nora's death have been avoided if she had been straight with Rob? She decided she must keep quiet about what she knew now. With Nora dead everything would change in the house in Fleet Street. Stan was sure to take possession immediately. They were homeless once again.

Fifteen

Eva had dressed by the time two constables arrived at the house. With Sylvia still so distressed Eva found she had to deal with proceedings and was annoyed and nervous about it. She was tempted to leave the house before the police arrived but was afraid of the consequences. For once she wished Lucy was here. Despite their differences, Eva had to admit that her sister was much more capable in a crisis such as this one.

The constables spoke first to the two workmen, who had obligingly hung around outside. Apparently satisfied with their statements the men were told they could go, pending further questions.

Much to Eva's annoyance a small crowd had gathered outside the house, neighbours, women, children and a few men.

'Can't you do something about them,' she said to one officer.

'All right, you lot!' the police officer bellowed, lifting an arm to wave them away. 'No loitering or I'll run you in,' he ordered. 'There's nothing to see, so push off.'

Some of the curious onlookers drifted away but came back as the police officers came inside again.

Shivering, Eva looked on anxiously from the doorway of the parlour as the constables once again viewed the pathetic body in the bed.

'We'll have to send for the police doctor,' one of them told her. 'Nothing must be touched.'

'Her son, Rob Naylor, doesn't know what's happened yet,' Eva volunteered. 'Perhaps you could send a man up to Tycoch to his smallholding to inform him.'

'Yes, leave that to us.'

One of the constables went to the telephone box on the corner of Beach Street to ring the police station to report the situation and ask for further instructions. Eva could tell by their grim expressions that they were taking the matter very seriously.

Sylvia was in the back room sitting by the fire when the remaining constable came to speak to her. She looked up miserably, her eyes and nose red from crying.

'Now, missus, you were here when the attackers gained entrance to the premises,' the man began in a stiff official tone. 'What happened?'

Sylvia drew a staggered breath and wiped her nose on a handkerchief.

'I was in the scullery preparing the midday meal. The back door was open because of the steam from the cooking.' She looked up at him. 'I have to keep the door open, you see, because condensation runs down the walls . . .'

'Yes, yes, missus, get on with it! I haven't got all day.'

'Can't you see she's upset,' Eva snapped at him.

'The law can't make allowances,' the officer said smugly. 'The quicker we know what happened the quicker we can catch the buggers.' He turned back to Sylvia. 'Now then, missus, what happened next?'

Sylvia swallowed. 'Before I knew what was happening two men burst in through the back door and ran down the passage to the parlour.'

'Did you know them?'

Sylvia shook her head.

'Did they speak?'

'No, they just ran straight through to the parlour,' Sylvia repeated.

'Straight to the parlour, eh?'

Thoughtfully, the constable put the stub of the pencil he was using to his lips to moisten it and then wrote something in his notebook.

'And what did you do, missus?'

'I shouted and ran after them,' Sylvia said simply. 'Then Nora began screaming. I was frightened so I picked up the poker from the fireplace.'

The officer scribbled furiously in his notebook.

'One of the brutes was attacking Nora as she lay in the bed,' Sylvia continued haltingly. 'I hit the other one with the poker, the one that looked like a boxer, but he turned on me, punched me in the chest and I fell to the ground.

I didn't know anything more until Eva came to pick me up.'

'Was anything taken?'

'No,' Eva cut in. 'It all happened in seconds really. I heard the commotion and ran outside to get help. Those two labouring men tried to give chase but the beasts had disappeared.'

Frowning, the police officer rubbed his thumb along his jaw, mumbling as though to himself.

'Funny time to attempt a burglary; broad daylight, house full of people. Straight to the parlour and nothing taken.'

'Hadn't you better start looking for them?' Eva asked impatiently. 'They could be on their way to Cardiff by now.'

She could follow his line of thought. Knowing what she did it looked more and more like Stan had a hand in this.

The constable ignored her. 'Do you think the deceased knew her attackers?'

Sylvia shook her head emphatically. 'Oh, no! Not their sort; rough and uncouth.' She gave a quick description of both men. 'Nora wouldn't know anyone of that ilk.'

The constable left them alone at last to take up duty outside the door and await the arrival of a senior officer and the doctor.

Sylvia looked exhausted.

'Mam, why don't you go up and have a lie down,' Eva suggested. 'I'll stay here and wait for Rob and Lucy.' What she really wanted was to get out of the house.

Sylvia immediately burst into tears again. 'Oh, how can I face Rob after this? He trusted me to look after Nora and I let him down.'

Eva was impatient. 'Don't be silly, Mam,' she said shortly. 'There was nothing you could do. You were lucky they didn't beat you too.'

The police surgeon came at last. The law gathered with him in the parlour while Eva and Sylvia sat in the back room. Eva was becoming more and more apprehensive.

When Rob heard the full story he was sure to suspect Stan and she could not help but worry that she would be involved too. The more she thought about it the more she was convinced that the attack on Nora had been only a part of it. Stan had wanted her hurt as well to the point of miscarrying.

She trembled at the thought of such malevolence against

her. She would have to get word to Maisie Naylor about her suspicions, although how she could help Eva had no idea.

The constable appeared from the passage.

'The doctor has finished,' he announced. 'We're about to take the body to the mortuary. There'll be a post-mortem, of course, and an inquest later.'

'But why?' Eva burst out. 'Nora was old. We all know she died of a heart attack.'

'That's as may be,' the constable said. 'But the authorities have to find out if it was the attack that caused her death. You'll be informed of the date, probably tomorrow.'

Sylvia jumped to her feet. 'Don't take her yet! Can't you wait until her son gets here?' she asked in distress. 'I'm sure he's on his way by now.'

'Regulations are regulations, missus,' the officer said loftily. 'The law waits for no man.' Then he was gone.

Sylvia collapsed into her chair, crying again. Eva watched her with a mixture of irritation and trepidation. She did not want to be in the house when Rob arrived.

'Mam, I'm going out.'

Sylvia looked up startled. 'What?'

'I've had a shock, too, Mam,' she complained. 'I've just about had enough. It's not good for the baby. I must get out into the fresh air, go for a walk.'

Sylvia looked concerned. 'Eva, of course, I'm sorry. It's been a strain on you too. Yes, you go. I'll wait for Rob and Lucy.'

Feeling relieved Eva donned her hat and coat and hurriedly left the house. What had happened to Nora was a dire warning. Eva decided she must disappear and if Maisie Naylor wanted this baby as desperately as she appeared to, she must help her.

The horse and cart stopped outside the house in Fleet Street and Rob jumped down immediately and hurried into the house. Lucy climbed down too.

'You'd better take the cart back to the holding,' she said quietly to Ted Locke. 'Come back in the morning to see if Rob needs you.'

'Right you are, miss.' He shook his head. 'What a terrible thing to happen. Rob's in shock by the look of him.'

Lucy nodded as she gazed up at him sitting in the driver's seat, the reins in his hands. 'He's devastated, Ted,' she agreed. 'He thought the world of his mother.'

Lucy turned away then to go into the house although she dreaded it. She was worried for Rob and sorry for his loss, but she was also worried about Sylvia.

The constable who had turned up at the smallholding to give Rob the bad news had assured her no one else was hurt, but Lucy knew her mother. Sylvia would take this to heart and blame herself. Lucy's one fear was that in her unsteady frame of mind she might do something drastic again.

Lucy went into the back room where Rob was standing with Sylvia, her hands in his. She was crying uncontrollably.

'Oh, Rob, can you ever forgive me?' Sylvia was saying tearfully. 'I've let you down.'

Rob shook his head. 'No, Sylvia—'

'Mam, Rob doesn't think that for a minute,' Lucy interrupted quickly. She hurried forward to put her arm around Sylvia's shoulders. 'What could you do against two men? Come and sit down and I'll make some tea.'

Rob sat down too, his face ashen and strained. She realized he had no idea that she was in love with him. Her heart ached for that and also to see such desolation in his eyes. She longed to hold him tightly in her arms to comfort him.

Lucy brought in the tea things and sat down with them. She handed Sylvia her cup and then passed one to Rob.

'Drink it while it's hot, Rob,' she said gently. 'It'll steady you.'

'I can't believe it, Lucy,' he said quietly, the cup and saucer shaking in his trembling hands. 'My mother is gone.' He looked appealingly at her. 'Why, Lucy? Why did it happen?'

Lucy compressed her lips, trying not to burst into tears. With so much grief in the home she needed to stay in control, although it was hard.

'I'm sure the police will get to the bottom of it, Rob,' she said gently. 'They'll find the ones responsible and they'll be punished.'

He shook his head as though she had not spoken. 'Why?' he repeated. 'There's nothing here worth stealing. Everyone who knew my mother knew she had little to her name. Even the house doesn't belong to her.'

A light suddenly flashed on in his eyes, and his expression turned hard, and Lucy was startled to see the abrupt change in him.

'What is it, Rob?'

'Stan!' he said, his nostrils flaring in anger. 'Stan is behind this.'

'Surely not!' Lucy was appalled. 'Not even Stan would attack his own stepmother in such a brutal way.'

'He wasn't one of the men,' Sylvia assured him. 'They were unkempt dissolute brutes of the lowest ilk.'

Rob's expression was savage. 'He's behind it, I know it. He wants this house and now he's got it.'

He stood up abruptly and Lucy rose to her feet too, holding out a hand to him.

'Please, Rob. Don't do anything rash,' she begged him. 'You have no proof; none. Nora wouldn't want you to get into trouble over this. Let the police deal with it.'

Rob sat down again, hanging his head, his shoulders drooping with misery and Lucy thought her heart would burst with feeling for him.

'I'll do nothing before the funeral,' he said, and she could hear the grief in his voice. 'But afterwards I'll get the truth . . .'

Eva hung around the Naylors' house for a while until she was certain Stan Naylor was not at home and then she went to the front door. The same maid let her in when she lied and said she had an appointment to see Mrs Naylor.

Maisie Naylor rose hurriedly to her feet, looking startled as the maid showed her into the sitting room.

'You shouldn't have come here,' Maisie said with her hand against her throat. 'Stan might've been at home.'

'I made sure he wasn't,' Eva replied.

She noticed she wasn't invited to sit, but she sat down anyway and took off her gloves. Maisie frowned at the gesture.

'What do you want, Eva? We have an agreement.'

'I'm in trouble,' Eva said.

Maisie's eyes opened wide with apprehension and she sat down opposite. 'It's not the baby, is it? Has something happened?'

'No, it's not that,' Eva said. 'It's your husband. He's trying to hurt me.'

'What?'

Eva described the attack on Nora and the tragic consequences. 'I'd have been beaten too,' she continued, 'if my mother hadn't fought back while I managed to call for help.'

'So Nora Naylor is dead,' Maisie said nodding. 'She's been a thorn in Stan's side for years.'

'Is that all you can say?' Eva asked angrily. 'What about me? I could've been badly beaten and lost my baby – your baby, Maisie, remember?'

'Stan couldn't care less about you or your baby,' Maisie said confidently. 'I think the attack was a coincidence.'

'Stan threatened me the other day,' Eva persisted. 'And he meant it, too. And now Nora is dead because of that.' She gave Maisie a keen glance. 'Are you willing to take the chance? How much do you want this baby of mine, anyway?'

'We have our agreement,' Maisie said stiffly. 'But I'm not open to blackmail, Eva.'

'Blackmail!' Eva jumped to her feet. 'Buying my baby was your idea,' she exclaimed angrily. 'But if you're not willing to protect your investment . . .'

'I never said that. Sit down,' Maisie said. 'This needs some thought. And we'd better be quick. Stan could return at any time. If he finds you here, it's all up. That would ruin my plans.'

'I need a place to stay,' Eva said. 'Somewhere where Stan can't find me. If you really want my baby, Maisie, then you'll arrange it.'

Maisie's lips thinned and Eva could see she did not like being spoken to in such straightforward terms, but she didn't care. She had to admit she was now afraid of what Stan might do.

Maisie was her only hope, except for the money she had tucked away in her bank account, but she was determined not to touch that just yet. That money was her ticket to a better life.

'A friend of mine has a boarding house on Oystermouth Road,' Maisie said thoughtfully. 'You'd be safe and comfortable there,' she went on. 'I'll pay the rent for you but you'll have to keep yourself to yourself. No gadding about town.'

'I want to go there now,' Eva said strongly. 'I'm not showing my face in Fleet Street again. Stan may have someone watching the house.'

Maisie looked around. 'I didn't see a bag with you?'

'I didn't stop for that,' Eva said. She gave Maisie a confident glance. 'Surely you can provide anything I need. After all I'll be going through labour just so you can have a child of your own.'

Maisie's lips thinned again. 'You're a greedy hard-faced little schemer, Eva,' she said. 'All right. I'll bear the cost, but within reason, remember that!'

'It's nine o'clock. She's been gone all day. Where can she be?' Sylvia stood before the fire twisting her hands anxiously. 'Oh, heavens! Something has happened to her, Lucy, I know it. What shall we do?'

Lucy was concerned that her sister had not returned from her walk, but at the same time was doubtful that anything untoward had befallen her.

'Mam, we would have heard if anything had happened to her,' she said. 'You know what Eva's like. She acts without bothering about the consequences or how you'll worry.'

Sylvia put her hands to her face. 'I'm still upset about what happened this morning.'

'Get up to bed,' Lucy suggested. 'You need to rest. It's no good driving yourself to the edge. I'll let you know when Eva comes home.'

Sylvia went upstairs reluctantly while Lucy quietly sat before the fire waiting for Rob to return. He had gone out earlier without saying where he was going and she was more worried for him than for Eva. He had said he would remain in Fleet Street until after the funeral or at least until Stan ousted them and she was glad of that.

With Nora gone Stan would now claim the house. Despite the tragic circumstances she expected him to turn up at any time to evict them.

But with the inquest and post-mortem to take place the funeral would be postponed for a week or maybe more. Would Stan be prepared to wait a decent interval? She doubted it, and she was worried how Rob would react. He was in such a state she was concerned he might take matters into his own hands and confront his brother. No good could come of that.

Eventually, to her relief, Rob returned to the house. Lucy quickly made him a meal and a hot drink and then sat with him while he ate. She had the sense to be quiet and not ask questions.

'I've been up to the smallholding to make everything secure,' he said at last. 'I won't be doing business until after . . .'

Lucy nodded but remained quiet.

He pushed his plate away. 'Sorry, Lucy,' he said. 'I'm not hungry.'

'I understand, Rob.'

'I can't make arrangements for the funeral until after the inquest.' He put his hands to cover his face. 'I knew my mother must die at some time, but not like this . . . in terror.' The muscles in his jaw bulged. 'I could kill Stan,' he said savagely.

Lucy reached out and put her hand on his shoulder. 'Please don't talk like that, Rob,' she said. 'If Stan is behind this he'll be punished.'

Rob put his hands on the table and looked at her. 'Not him, Lucy,' he said bitterly. 'He's too cunning. He'll have covered his tracks well.'

'Rob, please.' Lucy looked into his face earnestly. 'Let the law deal with it.'

He gave her a weak smile. 'I'm thankful I have you and Sylvia beside me to help me through this time.'

Lucy's heart quickened. She put her hand over his browned work-roughened one and felt the strength vibrate in it.

'I'll always be at your side, Rob . . .' She hesitated, embarrassed at her own words, her face flooding with colour.

That had sounded so forward and presumptuous. But loving him so, she had difficulty in hiding her feelings, especially at a time like this when he was so low in spirits.

'You're a good friend, Lucy,' Rob said evenly. 'I'm so glad fate brought us together.'

Disappointed, Lucy withdrew her hand from his. If he felt anything for her, this would be the ideal moment for him to speak, but he had called her friend and there had been nothing in his tone to indicate more.

Lucy rose from the table. 'I'd better go up now,' she said quietly. 'I'll go in with Mam. Eva hasn't come home and I doubt she will now, so you can have the room we share.'

He looked up questioningly. 'Your sister has left us?'

Lucy shrugged. 'Eva is a law unto herself,' she said. 'Mam

is worried but I'm inclined to think Eva is doing exactly as she wishes.'

Rob's features hardened. 'Do you think she has gone back to Stan?'

Lucy shook her head emphatically. 'Your brother is the last one she would turn to.' She hesitated. 'In fact, Rob, I think Eva is afraid of Stan now.'

She was beginning to wonder if Eva also suspected that the attack on Nora was of Stan's doing and was the reason why she had run off.

'My brother has a lot to answer for,' Rob said thickly.

There was a letter in the post the following morning and Lucy was not surprised to recognize Eva's handwriting on the envelope. She took it upstairs with Sylvia's morning tea.

Obviously relieved, Sylvia opened it quickly, the tension easing in her face.

'She's all right,' Sylvia told Lucy after reading the letter. 'She's staying with friends until after the birth of her baby.'

'I didn't know she had such obliging friends,' Lucy said sceptically, pulling back the curtains to let in the November morning gloom. Turning back she noticed Sylvia's eyes were filling up with tears. 'Mam, what is it?'

'She'd rather be with strangers at a time like this than with me,' Sylvia said in a hurt tone, the letter fluttering from her hand. 'I wanted to look after her. After all, I am her mother.'

Lucy felt anger towards her sister. Once again Eva was acting thoughtlessly, causing Sylvia pain and disappointment.

'It's months yet before the baby is due,' Lucy said. 'I wonder how long Eva's friends will put up with her. She'll come running back to you, Mam. Don't fret.'

It was midmorning when a police officer arrived at the house to speak with Rob, introducing himself as the coroner's officer. Lucy brought him into the back room where Rob and Sylvia were sitting, talking about Nora.

'I thought you'd want to know, sir, that the post-mortem was done last night,' the officer began. 'It is confirmed that the deceased died of a massive heart attack.'

'That's no news,' Sylvia said sharply.

'Yes, well, now it's official,' the officer said. 'The inquest will be on Wednesday next. The body will be released for burial the following day. Now you can make the necessary arrangements.'

'Why an inquest?' Lucy asked. 'This is a difficult time for Mr Naylor, for all of us, without the added strain of an inquiry.'

The officer looked at her. 'It has to be established whether the assault on the deceased was a contributing factor to the cause of death,' he explained patiently. 'Whether, in fact, a crime has been committed.'

Rob jumped to his feet. 'I don't need an inquest to tell me that,' he blurted out. 'And I know who is responsible.'

'Rob!' Lucy exclaimed. 'You're talking wild. You don't know anything for sure.'

The officer rose to his feet. 'If you have information which you have been holding back, Mr Naylor, that is a serious matter,' he said in an officious tone. 'You'd better speak up now.'

'I'm convinced my half-brother, Stan Naylor, is behind the attack.' Rob put his hand to his forehead and shook his head. 'But Lucy is right. I have no proof.'

'That's a serious allegation, Mr Naylor,' the officer said. 'However, now you have made it I must inform my superiors. It will be looked into.'

Rob shook his head sceptically. 'You'll find nothing,' he said. 'My brother is far too canny. But I know it's true. He thinks he'll get away with it but he won't.'

The police officer stood quietly for a moment, his gaze steady on Rob. 'You're under a strain, sir, but I must warn you not to take matters into your own hands.'

'Oh, he won't do that,' Lucy assured him quickly.

After the coroner's officer took his leave Rob put on his coat and flat cap. 'I'm going into town to make arrangements for the funeral,' he said in a subdued voice.

'I'll come with you,' Lucy offered.

Rob was in no mood to think straight and she dreaded the prospect that he might be tempted to go and see Stan at his office and there would be another fight.

He smiled sadly at her. 'I'm not going to do anything foolish, Lucy,' he said. 'Trust me.'

Rob, Lucy and Sylvia attended the inquest at the town hall, where Sylvia was a witness to what had happened. Lucy could see her mother was shaking with nervousness but she managed to answer all questions with some degree of calm.

The eventual verdict was manslaughter by persons unknown.

Rob's expression was grim as they came away from the proceedings.

'The verdict should've been murder,' he said harshly to them as they walked up Wind Street. 'Stan meant to kill my mother, and he succeeded.'

'But at least now the police will make every effort to find the men responsible,' Lucy said. 'If Stan is involved it will come out.'

They walked through the town making their way to Fleet Street. Already shopkeepers were making ready for the coming Christmas trade; butchers were displaying notices that they were taking orders for geese and ducks.

Christmas! Lucy did not want to think about it. There was Nora's funeral to endure first. And after that, where would they end up?

There would be no real Christmas for her and Sylvia. But that did not matter so much. What broke her heart was that once evicted from Fleet Street, she could not be with Rob. He was all she thought of these days, but obviously he did not feel the same way.

Lucy looked into a future without him and saw it looked very bleak indeed.

Sixteen

Nora's funeral was arranged for the last Friday in November, a miserably wet day which echoed the feelings of the chief mourners, Lucy felt. Although women were not normally expected to attend she and Sylvia were determined to go to support Rob.

Despite the torrential rain, the turnout for the internment at Dan-y-Graig Cemetery to bid Nora farewell was well attended. Two people conspicuous by their absence were Eva and Stan Naylor, but because of the bad feeling between the two brothers Lucy thought it just as well that Stan had stayed away.

Rob invited several of the wet throng, many of whom were neighbours and friends of the deceased, to come back to the house in Fleet Street for the traditional tea and ham sandwiches, which Lucy had prepared beforehand.

Quite a number accepted the invitation and the back room and parlour at Fleet Street were quite jammed with mourners in damp overcoats, standing shoulder to shoulder, talking, holding cups of tea and balancing plates of sandwiches.

Lucy watched Rob avidly as he edged his way among the throng, talking briefly with this one and that one. But even with the funeral over he still looked strained, the skin around his nose and mouth stretched as though with tension, and she was worried for him. She wished those present would leave so that he could rest and relax, but they continued to linger, chatting with an occasional laugh, perhaps forgetting why they were there.

The crowd had thinned an hour later, but some remained, perhaps neighbours who, having found chairs, were comfortable enough, and hoping for another cup of tea and what was left of the sandwiches.

Rob was sitting down at last in the parlour, talking in a low voice with Ted Locke and another man. Mrs Brown from next door was helping Sylvia with the washing up.

Lucy stayed in the passage hovering by the parlour door, her gaze on Rob. He had taken the manner of Nora's passing very badly and she was worried that he still intended to exact some kind of retribution against his half-brother.

She was standing there when someone knocked on the front door. She opened it and was startled to see Stan Naylor standing on the step. She started to close the door but he put his shoe on the threshold to stop her.

'What do you want?' she asked him in a low voice. 'You've no business to be here on this day.'

'I've every right,' he said loudly, putting his hand against the door and pushing. 'I own this house.' He was in the passage before Lucy could stop him and striding forward. 'Where's Rob?'

Rob could not fail to hear his brother's voice and he rushed from the parlour. Lucy stood by, her knuckles to her mouth in fear as the two men faced each other.

Rob's face was white with fury and hatred. 'Get out!' he bellowed. 'Get out now before I put you out.'

Stan gave a sneering smile. 'That's a coincidence,' he said smugly. 'I was about to tell you the same thing.' His smile disappeared abruptly. 'Get off my property, Rob, and take your women with you.'

'This is the day of Nora's funeral, your own stepmother,' Lucy cut in quickly, staring at Stan accusingly. 'How could you be so insensitive?'

He glanced at her. 'Nora meant nothing to me,' he said harshly. 'Now she's gone I want what belongs to me.' His expression changed suddenly. 'You don't have to leave, Lucy,' he said in a softer voice. 'You can stay here in my house as long as you want.'

Lucy grimaced in disgust at his words and tone. She felt cheapened and embarrassed by his base proposition in front of everyone present. 'How dare you suggest such a thing to me,' she cried loudly so that everyone would hear. 'I'll not stay one moment longer under this roof than I need to.'

'Your property!' Rob shouted. 'The property that you killed my mother for.'

Stan's nostrils flared and he looked at Rob in fury. 'You'd

better be careful what you say, little brother.' He glanced into the parlour at the seated figures, all staring at them in curiosity. 'Especially in front of witnesses.'

'I want witnesses,' Rob continued in a guttural voice. 'You sent those men here to cause Nora's death just so you could get your filthy hands on this house. I could kill you where you stand.'

Sylvia and Mrs Brown came hurrying into the passage at the sound of the raised voices; Sylvia's face was tight with fear.

'I had nothing to do with that attack,' Stan countered quickly. 'You're making a serious accusation which you can't prove.'

'I don't need proof,' Rob said almost spluttering in rage. 'I know you, Stan. I know what you're capable of. You're a dirty rotten murderer!'

There were exclamations of alarm from some of the men in the parlour and most of them got to their feet. Stan threw them a glance.

'He's lying,' he said loudly for their benefit. 'He's defaming my name. You're all witnesses. I could have him up for this.'

'You're scum!' Rob bellowed. 'The police will find proof, but I'm not waiting for that. I'll deal with you now. I'll kill you myself!'

His face white and distorted with grief and rage, Rob drew back his fist and struck out at Stan's face, catching him full on the mouth. Stan reeled back against the passage wall, his lip bleeding.

Ted Locke and another man, a neighbour, dashed out of the parlour; Ted clutched at Rob's arm, raised to strike again.

'Leave him! He's not worth it, boy,' Ted urged. 'It won't do no good.'

The neighbour stood squarely before Stan in case he intended to retaliate. 'You'd better go, Mr Naylor,' he said in a hard voice. 'This is no place for you.'

Stan stood erect, his hands clasping the lapels of his overcoat, pulling at them to straighten it on his shoulders.

'You'd better watch him,' he said, indicating Rob. 'He's dangerous. And I'm taking his threats seriously.' He looked around at everyone now clustered in the passage. 'You're all my witnesses. He threatened to kill me and I'm going to have the law on him.'

'No one will side with you, Stan Naylor,' Lucy cried out in ringing tones. 'Rob has something you don't have. Respect.'

Stan glowered at her for a moment and then he turned towards the door. 'I want you all out of this house by midday Monday,' he said harshly. 'Or else the bailiffs will throw you out.'

With that last threat he swung on his heel and strode from the house.

'I'll kill you!' Rob yelled at his retreating back and struggled in Ted's grasp. 'As God's my witness you are a dead man.'

'Rob, please!' Sylvia begged. 'Let's have no more of this, today of all days. Nora wouldn't want it.'

Rob's shoulders drooped and he ceased to struggle. Ted led him back into the parlour and he sat down, his head sunk forward.

Lucy followed them in and sat near watching him, her heart aching with love and pity. Why must Rob suffer like this? It wasn't fair.

Obviously embarrassed, the men present began to take their leave. Sylvia stood near the door thanking them as they left. Soon they were alone except for Ted Locke.

'What can we do?' Sylvia asked wringing her hands. 'There's no time for finding new lodgings before Monday.'

Rob raised his head, obviously trying to pull himself together.

'No need to look,' he said quietly. 'You can both stay with me at the cottage on the smallholding for the time being.'

'That's very good of you, Rob,' Lucy said eagerly. She did not care where she stayed as long as she was near him. 'But we don't want to put you to any inconvenience.'

'It may be you who are inconvenienced,' he said with a wry smile. 'The old place is roomy but I must warn you it's quite primitive otherwise, no sewerage or gas laid on. You may find it bleak.'

'Not at all,' Lucy said. 'The cottage is old but it has stout walls and Rob has made it very liveable.'

Sylvia's expression was dubious. 'I'm not sure we should,' she said hesitantly. 'Not because of the lack of amenities but . . .' She threw Lucy a meaningful glance. 'Well, I don't think it's proper for Lucy to sleep under the same roof as a single man. People might talk.'

'Huh!' Lucy countered. 'As if they're not talking already! And anyway, you'll be there, Mam.'

Sylvia sat down. 'I'm without work now,' she reminded Lucy. 'Tomorrow morning I'm going into town to see Mr Benucci. I'll ask for my job back caring for his family.' She absently fiddled with the hem of her pinafore, folding the edge over and over. 'I'm going to ask him if I can live in.'

'Mam!'

Sylvia looked stubborn. 'Perhaps you've forgotten the money I owe Stan Naylor,' she said in a strained voice, 'but I haven't. If I can live in at the Benuccis' house it will save paying rent on lodgings. I must make an effort to clear the debt.'

Lucy shook her head. 'Stan Naylor will never allow it to be repaid. He already refused to take Mr Benucci's offer to settle,' she reminded her mother. 'He'll hold the debt over us until I agree to be . . .' She was unable to continue.

Rob's expression was grim. 'It would be better for everyone if my brother were dead.'

'Rob, please don't say such things,' Lucy begged.

'If I do get my job back,' Sylvia interposed, 'I'll ask Mr Benucci if you can spend a few nights there too until you find suitable lodgings elsewhere, Lucy. I mean no disrespect to you, Rob, but Lucy cannot risk her reputation by living alone with you at the cottage. But thank you for your kind offer.'

'Mam!'

'Your mother's right, Lucy,' Rob said. 'It might be a mistake.'

'I think I should be the judge of that.' Lucy dipped her head and said nothing more.

Her mother was forgetting the label of illegitimacy was already on her, which meant her reputation was already tarnished in many people's eyes. She wanted to stay close to Rob, do all she could to look after him. He might not have feelings for her, but she loved him and all she asked was to be near him.

Sylvia went to see Mario Benucci the following morning, and came back to Fleet Street looking relieved and a little more cheerful than Lucy had seen her in a long time.

'I start work for Mr Benucci on Monday,' she announced after she had taken off her coat and hat and sat down before the range fire. 'And he's prepared to put you up, too, Lucy, for a day or two until you get fixed up with lodgings.'

Lucy lifted her chin stubbornly. 'I'm going to the cottage with Rob,' she said firmly. 'He has been good to us, Mam. I'm not going to desert him now.'

'But it's not proper,' Sylvia cried. 'It's not that I don't trust Rob. He's a good man, but people will talk. You'll get a name.'

'I already have one,' Lucy said bitterly. 'Bastard.'

'Lucy!' Sylvia clapped a hand to her mouth, obviously shocked to the core to hear that base word on her daughter's lips. Her eyes were round as she stared at Lucy and then they began to fill with tears.

Lucy immediately regretted that she had spoken in such a brutal way. 'Mam, I'm sorry!' She went to Sylvia and put a comforting arm around her shoulder. 'I didn't mean to imply you are to blame,' she said gently. 'You are as much a victim of Father's treachery as Eva and me.'

Despite Lucy's comforting Sylvia's tears began to flow.

'To what fate have I brought you both?' she wailed. 'You're about to bring more disgrace upon yourself and Eva . . .' She gulped. 'Eva is shamelessly with child and estranged from her family. Sometimes I wish Rob had not saved me from the sea,' she murmured piteously. 'I wish I were dead and gone.'

'Eva will come back to us,' Lucy said. She was close to tears herself to hear such words of abject despondency from her mother. 'She must. She has no one else to turn to.'

'Her friends . . .'

'Her friends, whoever they are, will not want to support her and her child for long,' Lucy conjectured. 'We will rise above her shame. We'll be a family again.'

'Not if you go and live with Rob,' her mother said provokingly.

'I'll not be living with him,' Lucy protested. 'I'll be his lodger and his employee. Mam . . .' She hesitated to reveal her secret but decided she must. 'Mam, I'm in love with Rob. I must be near him.'

'Lucy!'

'There's nothing for you to fear,' she went on hastily. 'I'll do nothing improper. Rob is a man of integrity. I'd trust him with my life – as you did.'

Sylvia put a handkerchief to her brimming eyes. 'Did your

father ever guess, I wonder, to what ignominy his actions would damn us?' She looked up into Lucy's face. 'Did he ever really love us, Lucy? Or were our lives a complete lie?'

Midday Saturday Maisie let herself in at the front door of a tall rundown lodging house in Lower Oxford Street. She hesitated, listening, before climbing the dusty stairs to Ben Hopkins' room on the second floor back. Reaching the door she tapped gently.

'Ben, it's me.'

The door opened immediately. 'Maisie! What the hell . . .'

He grabbed at her arm and pulled her inside quickly before giving cursory glances down the stairs and up the next flight.

He closed the door and stared at her. 'Maisie, you're taking a chance coming here. You could've been seen.'

'No one saw me,' she said impatiently.

She was exasperated with his caution. His landlady was as deaf as a post and half blind. Maisie suspected the old woman didn't give a fig what her lodgers got up to as long as they paid their rents on Friday.

'Well?' she continued eagerly. 'How much did you get?'

'Nothing,' Ben said and turned away.

'What!' Maisie caught at his arm and swung him around. She glared into his face suspiciously. 'You're not trying to diddle me, are you, Ben? Because if you are . . .'

'I'm telling you the truth, Maisie,' he said. 'The safe was empty. Not even a loose fiver.'

Maisie stared. 'But it couldn't be. Stan banks the week's takings on Saturday morning. The money is always left in the office safe on Friday night.'

'Maybe you don't know as much about Stan's routine as you think,' Ben said. 'I took a risk for nothing. I don't like doing that, Maisie.'

'But that day I managed to get the combination,' she said. 'You remember. I watched him in my powder-compact mirror. He opened the safe. It was full of bundles of banknotes. I saw them, Ben. I didn't imagine it.'

'That was months ago,' Ben reminded her. 'Maybe he saw you watching and decided to change tactics. Perhaps you're not so clever after all, Maisie.'

Maisie sat down. She had made such plans. She had prepared

herself to leave Swansea immediately after the burglary. She and Ben would get away – London, perhaps. Eva would stay with them, at least until after her baby was born. She had promised the girl three thousand more. Stan's money would have paid for that. It was only just.

Maisie jumped up. 'Stan, the cunning swine!' she exclaimed hotly.

Ben looked agitated. 'He knows by now that someone's been at the safe,' he said. 'Maisie, are you sure he doesn't know about us?'

Maisie did not answer. She wasn't so sure about anything any more, except that it wasn't over. 'I'm not done yet,' she said. 'I'm certain he doesn't have a safe at the house, but he must be hiding the money there somewhere. I'll have to find out.'

Ben shook his head. 'I'm not taking another risk, Maisie,' he said. 'Especially not breaking into his house.' He gave her a pleading glance. 'Let's skedaddle now with what we've got, love.'

'No, I want that money,' Maisie said determinedly. 'I want it for the girl. Stan is going to pay one way or another.'

Ben's expression changed. 'It seems to me that doing the dirty on Stan and getting hold of his money is more important to you than I am,' he said bitterly.

She gave him a cold stare. 'You don't know the half of what that man has put me through. His women, his dirty business dealings; my so-called friends laughing behind my back.' She shook her head. 'He was only ever interested in my money, but I made sure he never got control of it.'

He shook his head. 'I only hope you know what you're doing.'

Maisie smiled thinly. 'Stan has mostly ignored me throughout our marriage, but I swear he'll never forget me after I'm finished.'

Seventeen

Rob was up at five o'clock on the Monday morning they were to leave the house in Fleet Street. Lucy rose too to start breakfast. There would be a lot to do that day.

Ted Locke arrived with the horse and cart at half past. Lucy thought what a faithful friend he was to Rob. He sat down with Rob at the table and Lucy put mugs of hot tea in front of them and a cooked breakfast each.

Sylvia sat with them. She wanted nothing more than tea, she said. Lucy thought she looked strained and was worried for her. Sylvia had already packed what clothes she owned and other bits and pieces in a carpet bag and had placed it near the living-room door. She was to move into Mario Benucci's house in the Uplands that morning.

Straight after breakfast Rob and Ted began shifting what few possessions Nora had left. The iron bedsteads were dismantled and put in the cart with the mattresses. The kitchen chairs and the table went on next and an old sideboard that had seen better days and also a couple of worn-out armchairs.

While the men were busy with that Sylvia helped Lucy in the scullery packing up what was left. There was little in the way of china or other crockery, but Rob wanted to take as much as they could carry, being unwilling to leave anything of his mother's for Stan to dispose of.

Lucy could sense her mother wanted to say something, something she would not want to hear.

'Lucy, I wish you'd think again about moving into the cottage with Rob,' Sylvia burst out at last. 'It just isn't right. It's . . . degrading.'

Lucy was angry. 'It's nothing of the sort,' she said quickly. 'I've told you, Mam, I'm Rob's lodger and employee, nothing more. If people have evil minds it's not my fault.'

'But think—'

'No, Mam,' Lucy said firmly. She lowered her voice. 'You know how I feel about Rob. I love him and I sense he needs me.'

She did sense that, even though she knew Rob himself was unaware of it. It did not matter that he did not feel the same about her.

'I don't want to see you hurt and ruined, Lucy, my dear girl,' Sylvia said. She sounded as though she might burst into tears at any moment.

'Mam, you're talking as though we won't see each other again,' Lucy said. 'I'll not let a week go by without seeing you. And I'll always consult you before I do anything.'

Sylvia folded up a tea towel and put it in a cardboard box Lucy was packing.

'I'm worried about Eva, too,' she said. 'I'm afraid that when she needs me she won't be able to find me.'

'Eva can well look after herself,' Lucy said with confidence. 'She has done so far.'

Sylvia went to get her hat and coat. Lucy saw there were tears in her eyes as she buttoned up her coat against the cold morning air.

'Mam, don't worry about either of us,' Lucy said. 'Eva and I have come a long way since we learned the truth about Father. We've grown up, each in our own way.'

'It'll be Christmas soon,' Sylvia said sadly. 'What kind of a Christmas can we expect, separated as we are as a family?'

Lucy went to her mother and embraced her warmly. 'There'll be other Christmases,' she said kindly. 'And next Christmas there'll be Eva's child to fuss over. Think of that, Mam.'

They kissed and then Sylvia picked up her carpet bag and said goodbye. Lucy heard her speak to Rob and Ted as she went. It was beginning to get lighter. The workaday world outside was beginning to bustle about its business.

Rob and Ted came into the house. Rob looked around at the bareness of the room.

'Well, that's the lot,' he announced, his voice echoing in the emptiness. 'We're done here.'

'We've got until midday,' Lucy said. 'I thought I might scrub around a bit.'

'Leave it,' Rob commanded in a hard tone. 'Stan wanted the house, well, he's got it.' He stood thoughtful and silent for a moment. 'Come on,' he said at last. 'Let's go. We've got to get you settled into the cottage.' He raised his cap and scratched his head. 'I don't know where we can put all Nora's furniture, though.'

They went through the house to the street for the last time. Ted Locke was ready on the cart. Rob placed the door key in the lock on the inside and then ushered Lucy out on to the pavement.

She stood watching as Rob paused as he was about to close the door. He stared down the passage with its worn linoleum, which Nora had once polished with pride until it shone like glass.

'I grew up in this house,' he said quietly. 'And so did Stan. I never dreamed as we scuffled around as boys that one day it would come to this.'

'Families,' Lucy said. 'They change.' She was thinking of Sylvia, Eva and herself and how their paths appeared to be diverging. And there seemed to be no way to prevent it.

Rob closed the door with a snap. 'You're right, Lucy,' he said. 'There's no point in reliving old memories. Stan and I are enemies now. That will never change. He's gone too far.'

He helped her on to the seat of the cart and pulled himself up beside her. Ted Locke shook the reins and clicked his tongue and the obedient horse began to amble forward.

Lucy felt exhilaration and a degree of independence. The horse was taking her into a new life. Rob was at her side. She could feel the warmth of his body seep into hers as he sat next to her.

Without making it obvious she stole a sideways glance at him. The outline of his face was strong; a well-developed nose, a determined chin and a wide sculptured mouth. It was the face of a man who could be trusted and loved.

She probably loved him in vain, she thought, and felt a little pain around her heart for a moment. Would he ever look at her with loving eyes and speak the words she longed to hear him say?

Inwardly she scolded herself. She should ask no more than to be with him and be thankful for it.

Ted Locke helped them unload at the cottage. Having worked at the smallholding for the past few months, Lucy was familiar with the dry privy behind the cottage, which Rob kept scrupu-lously clean, the big galvanized bucket always smelling of creosote. She had often made tea for them in the big kitchen at the back but had seen little of the rest of the cottage.

The front door opened into a very large living room which had a wide fireplace at one end, tall enough for a man to stand up in. The makings of a fire had been laid earlier by Ted. Rob put a match to it and placed a log on the coals. It was soon ablaze.

A narrow staircase was at the other end of the room leading to the bedrooms, three in all. Lucy chose the one she wanted, which overlooked the side of the cottage where there was a small orchard.

By midday everything had been sorted out; Nora's bits of furniture fitted in without bother. The atmosphere of the place was good, Lucy decided, with no hint of dampness.

Lucy made some food for the three of them and then Rob told Ted he could leave. 'We'll be open for business tomorrow at seven sharp.'

Ted touched his cap in an old-fashioned salute. 'And I'll be here at six as usual, Mr Naylor,' he said cheerfully.

Lucy was uncertain of what was expected of her after Ted was gone. 'Shall I do some potting in one of the greenhouses this afternoon, Rob?'

'Leave work for today, Lucy,' he said. He sounded tired. 'Tomorrow will be soon enough to get back to normal.'

When dusk fell Rob lit the oil lamps. They sat in Nora's old armchairs either side of the fireplace. To Lucy it felt so right being there with him.

She listened avidly to his every word as he told her again of his plans for the smallholding.

Lucy let her thoughts run free, imagining the rest of her life here with him. It was just a dream, she knew, but it cost nothing to wish for such happiness.

'I'll build a house one day too,' he said. 'When I can afford it.'

'This is a good well-built cottage in a pretty location,' Lucy ventured to say. 'Perhaps you could extend here. Spend the money instead in bringing in the sewerage and gas.'

Rob looked across at her. 'You know, Lucy, that's not a bad

idea,' he said. 'This old place was built about a hundred years ago. I reckon it'll stand another hundred.'

He yawned then and looked apologetic. Lucy realized what a great strain he was under. He should be resting instead of sitting here talking.

'I think I'll go up now, Rob, if you don't mind,' she said feeling suddenly awkward. 'We've both got an early start tomorrow.'

'You're right, Lucy.' He rose to his feet. 'You go. I'll just lock up.'

'Goodnight, then.'

'Goodnight.'

Lucy turned towards the staircase.

'Oh, Lucy,' Rob said. 'There's something I want to say to you.'

Lucy whirled around to stare at him, her heart suddenly thudding in her breast. Was he about to speak of his feelings?

'I want you to know that I'm not like my brother Stan. I respect you, Lucy. I would never take advantage of our situation. You have nothing to fear from me.'

Lucy smiled at him although it was difficult to keep her deep disappointment from showing on her face.

'I know that, Rob,' she said quietly. 'I have no doubts. I wouldn't be here otherwise.'

'Thank you,' he said simply. 'Goodnight, Lucy. Sleep well.'

Eighteen

One Week Later

Lifting the oil lamp high, Maisie descended the stone steps down to the cellar, raising her skirts gingerly to avoid the dust underfoot. She had not been down here for years and did not want to now, but she had searched the rest of the house without finding Stan's hidden cache. If she failed to find it, he was probably hiding the money in the house in Ffynonne and she would have to rethink her plans.

Reaching the bottom of the steps, she looked around. The cellar was bigger than she remembered and filled mostly with old junk from years ago, now draped in white cobwebs.

In the flickering light of the lamp she caught glimpses of wine bottles stacked on shelves against the wall at the far end. There was a clear path towards them through the rubbish and bric-a-brac. Stan was the only one who ever came down here. The thought was hopeful. His devious mind would think this was just the place to hide his secrets.

She made her way towards the bottles. She stopped, her heart taking a jolt when she saw the perambulator. She hadn't thought about it for a long time; it was an impulsive buy in the early years of her marriage when she had believed, at least for a week or two, that she had fallen with child.

She stared at it, her mouth tightening. Stan deserved all he was going to get. She would leave him high and dry, make a laughing stock of him. It would soon get around town that his wealthy wife had bolted; had deserted him for her lover. That would pinch his pride.

She peered down. Something stood in the space between the wall and the side of the tall wine rack. It was square and bulky and covered by a piece of sacking.

She gingerly pulled the sacking away and then gave a little

laugh of triumph. A safe! A fair-sized one, too. She pulled at the handle. It was locked as she expected.

She was thoughtful. Now when did Stan have this put here? She looked closer. Old dusty cobwebs were thick in the narrow spaces between the back and sides of the safe and the wall. This had been here some time, perhaps years.

Maisie was furious. The crafty swine! The office safe was a decoy. This is where he hid most of his money, away from the prying eyes of the tax man.

But why hadn't he told her about this safe in the cellar? The answer was plain. He didn't trust her. But did he suspect her? That day at the office when she had spied on him in the mirror of her powder compact, had he seen through her actions? There had been money in the office safe that day. Had it been a trick?

She decided it hadn't been. Stan did not believe she had the gumption or the brains to outwit him. She was just the shallow inconsequential rich widow he had married for her money. Well, he was going to learn.

She looked at the safe again before replacing the sacking. Ben could open this, she was certain. Now all she had to do was decide which night would be safest for him to try.

When Stan came home much later, Maisie was in the sitting room. She had been waiting impatiently and was still piqued that he had kept the safe a secret from her, his own wife. But she could not resist revealing her knowledge to show him that she wasn't such a fool as he thought.

'I've been down in the cellar this afternoon,' she said, her tone sharp.

'That was the highlight of your day, was it?' he said mockingly. He walked towards the decanter on the sideboard and poured out a measure of whisky. 'You should take up voluntary work, Maisie. You need something to fill your days.'

It was on the tip of her tongue to blurt out that soon she would have a child to love and fuss over, but she bit back the words. Stan must know nothing of that.

'I saw the safe, Stan. What's it for? You've got a safe in the office.'

He paused, the whisky glass halfway to his lips, and looked keenly at her. 'Funny you should mention that, Maisie,' he said. 'Last week some bugger broke into the office and opened the safe.'

Maisie had the wits to look surprised, even shocked. 'You never said anything to me, Stan,' she said. 'How much was taken?'

He smiled widely at her. 'The bugger, whoever he was, got bugger-all.'

His look was keen and she wondered how much he really knew about her activities of late.

'Well,' she said feeling rather breathless, 'that was fortunate. You'd already banked the money, then?'

He shrugged. 'Some of it.'

'And the safe in the cellar?' Maisie asked and then lifted her chin. 'I'm surprised you didn't tell me about it. After all, this house is mine. I have a right to know what happens on my property.'

'You own the house, Maisie. You don't own me.'

'Is there much money in it?' Ill at ease at asking the leading question, Maisie touched her hair. 'I ask only because the thought of there being a lot of money in the house makes me nervous. It attracts intruders.'

'No one knows that safe is there.' His glance was keen again. 'Only I know. And you, of course, now.'

She glanced away. 'All the same, I wonder why you need two safes.'

'Use your head, Maisie,' he said scathingly. 'My legitimate businesses are doing well, but I make a hell of a sight more with my sidelines.'

Maisie was scornful in turn. 'You mean, fencing stolen goods?'

His lips tightened at her forthright words but he answered.

'Exactly. I can't bank the surplus in the usual way,' he said. 'The Inland Revenue and the law might start taking an interest.'

'So there's quite a lot of money in the safe, then?'

His look was guarded for a moment.

'There's no need for you to worry your head about it, Maisie,' he said. 'I can't bank the money but I can buy property with cash. It's just as secure. That's what I intend to do with the contents of the safe very soon.'

Contrarily, his frankness made her angry. 'Houses to keep your tarts in, you mean,' she burst out passionately. 'You're making me a laughing stock amongst my friends.'

'Friends? Oh, I'm sure you have other – consolations.'

Maisie was suddenly wary. 'What do you mean?'

Did he know about her and Ben? Did he suspect Ben of being the safebreaker?

He turned away. 'I won't be here for dinner,' he said casually. 'And I'll be home late, very late.' He walked to the door and then turned and smiled mockingly at her. 'Don't wait up.'

Maisie sat fuming at his mockery and her determination to revenge herself was fuelled by it. One day soon Stan would be laughing on the other side of his face.

Rob and Ted Locke left the smallholding midmorning, taking the cart to fetch some building supplies. Lucy had come in from working in the greenhouses, washed her hands and begun thinking about getting something cooked by the time the men returned.

Rob had got her an oil-fuelled stove from somewhere and she was becoming a dab hand at using it. It cooked fruit cakes brilliantly and meat dishes too.

Lucy felt she was very lucky. Her life seemed idyllic at the moment. Working all day with Rob and then sharing his confidences and dreams as they sat before the fire in the evenings was all the life she ever wanted. She wondered how long it would last, and prayed that one day he would love her as she loved him.

She was peeling potatoes when she heard the sound of a motor car come into the yard in front of the cottage. Thinking it might be a customer, she wiped her hands and walked through the big living room to open the cottage door. With a welcoming smile she stepped outside to greet whoever it was.

The driver had already got out and was walking towards her. She was disconcerted to realize it was Stan Naylor.

Lucy turned on her heels and rushed back to the cottage, but she wasn't quick enough. Stan was right behind her and barged his way in.

'What do you want?' she cried out angrily. 'This is private property. Get out!'

'I want to talk to you, Lucy,' Stan said, taking a step towards her. 'You must listen to what I have to say.'

'You're wrong,' Lucy exclaimed hotly stepping back. 'Nothing you say can be of interest to me. Leave now before Rob gets back.'

'He won't be back for a while,' Stan said with confidence. 'We're quite alone, Lucy.'

He pushed the door closed with his foot and stood with his back to it. Lucy watched him with a growing fear. His mouth was set in a determined line. What did he intend to do?

Trembling, she moved so that the big kitchen table was between them. 'You've no right to be here,' she said lamely, her heart thudding painfully against her ribs. 'Have you no sense of decency?'

'To hell with decency,' Stan said loudly. 'I'm here to give you one last chance to come to your senses.'

'My senses? Oh, I'm in my right senses, all right,' Lucy said. 'I know the kind of man you are, and I despise you.'

'You don't even know me,' Stan said. 'You haven't given me a chance.'

Lucy nodded. 'I know enough.'

'Well, you're going to listen to what I have to say now,' he said passionately. 'Don't be a strait-laced little fool, Lucy. Leave Rob and come to me. We'd be good together.'

'Rob's worth twenty of you,' Lucy flared. 'You're not fit to lace his boots.'

Stan grabbed the back of a chair and hauled it roughly out of his way, moving forward again.

'Listen!' he said angrily. 'My brother has nothing to offer you. I can give you everything.'

'A man like you?' Lucy shook her head. 'I want nothing to do with you,' she said shakily. 'You've already disgraced my sister. How many more times must I refuse your disgusting proposition?'

'Eva was willing enough, too willing,' Stan said with a sneer. 'But she isn't what I want. I want you, Lucy.' He took another step forward. 'You don't realize how much I want you. I can't get you out of my mind, day or night.'

'Stop it!' Lucy cried out. 'I don't want to hear such words. Don't you understand? Nothing on earth would make me give in to you.'

The muscles in his jaw tightened. 'There's the debt,' he said. 'It's mounting every day. I could drag your mother through the courts. Her name would be mud.'

'You're too late,' Lucy cried out. 'My father dishonoured her name a long time ago. He put a label on Eva and me.' She gave a sob at the truth of it. 'I doubt a little thing like money can besmirch our name more.'

He stood silently for a moment looking at her. A muscle in his jaw was working furiously and his colour rose.

'I could take you here and now,' he said tensely. 'Nothing to stop me.'

Lucy gave a frightened cry and recoiled.

'But that's not what I want,' he continued hastily. 'I'm in deadly earnest about what I feel for you. This isn't lust anymore. I love you, Lucy, I swear I do. I'll . . . marry you, Lucy, if that's the only way I can have you.'

Lucy's mouth dropped open with astonishment and she stared at him in silence for a moment. 'Marry me?' she said at last. 'Do you take me for a fool? You already have a wife.'

'I'll divorce her,' he said eagerly. 'I'm pretty certain she has another man, anyway. I'll get proof of her adultery.'

Appalled Lucy took a step back, placing both her hands to the base of her throat in a protective gesture. 'You're despicable! I'd rather perish than marry you.'

'Lucy, you're pushing me too far,' he snarled. 'I'm not a man who takes no for an answer. You and I were meant to be together. I must have you.' He banged his fist down on the table top. 'You will come to me!'

He moved purposefully towards her but at that moment Lucy heard the sound of a heavy motor vehicle drawing up outside the cottage. Stan heard it too and hesitated in his advance.

'That's a delivery of fertilizer we've been expecting,' she said breathlessly. 'I only have to scream, Stan. The driver would be in here in a minute. I'll tell him you attacked me and the police will be called.'

His face hardened with fury but he backed off.

'This is not the end of it, Lucy,' he said in a heavy tone. 'I'll have what's due to me any way I can.' He gave her a narrow mirthless smile. 'Maybe your precious Rob will have a nasty accident.'

'Don't you dare harm him,' Lucy said quickly.

Stan's brows lifted as though with enlightenment. 'Well now,' he said with satisfaction. 'I've found your weak spot, have I?' He nodded, a bitter smile on his face. 'What happens to Rob depends on you, Lucy. If you want to keep him safe you know what you have to do. I'll give you one week.'

'You're insane!'

'You'll come to me of your own free will or else Rob ... I'll leave the rest to your imagination, Lucy, my dear.'

The driver of the vehicle outside honked the horn impatiently.

'You'd better see to that,' Stan said. 'See you soon, Lucy.' He turned towards the door, opened it and stepped outside.

Stunned at his words, Lucy could only stand there like a statue. Stan had actually threatened Rob's life, all for the sake of his vile obsession with her. She sank on to a nearby chair, putting her head in her hands. What was she to do?

The motor horn sounded again. She lifted her head, suddenly sure of one thing. She must not tell Rob that his brother had been there or what had been said.

Fear gripped her heart. She dreaded to think what might happen if the brothers came face to face. That could only end in one of them being badly hurt – even killed, if Stan's threat was to be taken seriously. And she did take him seriously.

Maisie was watchful over the next week, noting Stan's comings and goings, particularly in the evenings. It was obvious he had replaced Eva with another floozy in the house in Ffynonne.

Stan had a set pattern. He would leave home about seven o'clock most evenings and not return until the early hours. On a Friday he did not return until midday Saturday.

This suited Maisie's plans well. Ben would do his work with the cellar safe on Friday evening. There would be ample time to catch the last train for Paddington. They would probably be well hidden in London even before Stan realized he had been robbed.

Ben was argumentative and seemed reluctant when Maisie told him that their scheme was set for the following night, Friday. She had already given Doris, their maid, the weekend off.

'Be at the house about half eight,' she told him. 'Walk. Don't use a hansom.'

'I don't know about this, Maisie,' he said edgily. 'It seems too easy. Maybe Stan has set a trap. He's a devious bugger.'

'I thought you wanted to be with me,' Maisie said belligerently. 'You've told me you love me often enough. Was that a lie?'

'Of course not!' Ben was agitated. 'I do love you, Maisie. It's just that I don't trust Stan.'

'Well, trust me!' Maisie said with energy. 'I know exactly what I'm doing. Eva Chandler will be coming with us, of course.'

'What?' He stared at her looking perturbed. 'My God, Maisie, this is turning into a circus. Does the girl have to be included?'

Maisie's lips thinned. 'The baby she's carrying belongs to me now. I've already given her money for it and promised her more.'

'But taking her with us . . .'

'I'm not letting Eva out of my sight,' Maisie declared. 'Don't you understand? It's Stan's child!'

Ben's face fell. 'You still love him!' he accused. 'Otherwise you wouldn't want anything to do with his sprog.'

'You fool! You don't understand women,' Maisie said. 'Stan wishes the child never existed. I'll bring it up making sure it knows who its father is. It'll be something to hold over Stan's head any time I want.'

Ben was silent staring at her with a puzzled expression.

'Don't look at me like that,' Maisie flared at him. 'The child will have a good life with me. I'll treat it as though it were my own.'

Maisie called on Eva at her lodgings the following day. She did not beat about the bush, realizing the girl was far too bright to be fooled by flimflam.

'Eva, I'm leaving Stan tomorrow night for good,' she said. 'I'm travelling to London on the last train.'

'What about me?' Eva looked angry. 'You promised me more money. Don't you want my baby?'

'Our deal still stands. That's why I'm here. You're coming with me to London.'

'Oh!'

'Pack a small bag tomorrow and meet me at the corner of Phillips Street at about eight o'clock in the evening. There'll be a hansom waiting. I'll be in it.'

'I'll be there, don't worry,' Eva said eagerly. She gave a little laugh. 'London, I can't believe it.' Abruptly her expression became puzzled and she frowned. 'If we're catching the last train then eight o'clock is a bit early to leave for the station, isn't it?'

Maisie paused. 'We'll go back to the house and wait there,' she said. 'I have something important I want to do before we go.'

Eva's eyes widened. 'But Stan . . .'

'I can guarantee Stan won't be there. He'll be far too busy at Ffynonne.'

'Ah! I see.'

'Listen, Eva,' Maisie said gravely. 'You're to tell no one about this. Do you understand me?'

Eva hesitated, licking her lips in uncertainty. 'But I can't just disappear,' she said. 'I should tell my mother where I'm going.'

'No one is to know!' Maisie exclaimed loudly. 'In a couple of weeks' time you can tell your mother where you are. Trust me, Eva. I know what I'm doing.'

The following evening, Eva sat on the soft leather chesterfield in Maisie's lavishly furnished sitting room, her small carpet bag at her feet. She watched her benefactress with keen interest as she walked ceaselessly about the room, stopping now and again to part the curtains of the tall windows to peer out.

'Stan won't come back, will he?' Eva asked, uneasy at Maisie's restlessness.

'What?' Maisie sounded vague as she peered out of the window.

'Are you watching for Stan?'

'No, no,' Maisie said. 'I told you. He's busy elsewhere.'

'What time is the last train?'

'What? Oh, eleven.'

Eva looked at the ormolu clock on the mantelpiece. It said the time was just gone half-past eight. 'Why are we meeting so early? Maisie, is there something wrong? You seem on pins.'

'Everything is all right,' Maisie snapped. 'Pour yourself a drink.'

Eva was about to get up when the door bell sounded, making her almost jump out of her skin.

'At last!' Maisie said with obvious relief and hurried from the room.

'Is that Stan?' Eva called after her quickly her heart in her mouth. She could not face him again. She got up quickly and went to stand just behind the open sitting-room door listening.

Maisie let the caller in, talking excitedly in the hall. A man's voice answered but it wasn't Stan and Eva was weak with relief.

They came towards the sitting room. Eva hurried back to her seat on the chesterfield, waiting expectantly to see who the newcomer was.

Maisie came into the room, her face wreathed in smiles now. She was followed by a man Eva had never seen before. He was small and slight with a pale narrow face. The gaze from his dark eyes darted here, there and everywhere about the room. He looked as nervous as Maisie had been earlier.

His gaze finally rested on her and to her surprise he showed plainly by his scowling expression that he was not pleased to see her there.

Eva was piqued. 'Maisie, who is this?'

'This is Ben Hopkins,' Maisie said. 'The man I'm running away with.'

Eva stared. 'You never said anything about him.'

'Why should I tell you anything,' Maisie said curtly. 'Now be quiet. Ben has work to do. We'll be back soon.'

'What's going on?' Eva asked angrily.

'I don't like this, Maisie,' Ben said. 'I think—'

'You concentrate on cracking that safe,' Maisie interrupted him shortly. 'Leave the thinking to me.'

Ben sent Eva a shifty glance. 'Can we trust her?'

Maisie nodded, her smile grim. 'I've promised her a fair sum. Eva knows when she's on to a good thing. Come on. Let's get on.'

They left the room. Whatever they were up to it was no business of hers, Eva told herself firmly. Besides, Maisie was dead keen to have her baby. Eva felt certain she need not mistrust her.

She went to the chiffonier to pour out a glass of sherry and returned with it to the chesterfield.

So Ben Hopkins was Maisie's lover. He appeared a weak little squirt compared to Stan. Eva was musing over Maisie's choice when she heard an all-too-familiar voice in the hall and Maisie's loud exclamation of dismay.

'Stan!'

Aghast herself, Eva hurried to take a position behind the door again, almost spilling the sherry, feeling very frightened.

'What are you doing home?' Maisie's excited tones verged on the hysterical. 'I thought you'd gone for the night.'

'So did I,' Stan answered. 'You'll probably laugh your head off when I tell you, Maisie.'

'Stan, I—'

He interrupted her with a coarse expletive, his tone thick with anger. 'That dirty little slut I put in at Ffynonne has been double-crossing me,' he said wrathfully. 'I caught a man sneaking out of the house just as I arrived. She's been using the place as a whorehouse, that's all.'

'Stan, listen . . .'

'I smacked her silly, of course,' he continued. 'And then slung her out. The dirty bitch!'

He marched into the room and went straight to the chiffonier. Eva pressed herself against the wall behind the door, staring transfixed at his back. He was bound to catch sight of her when he turned around but her feet seemed rooted to the spot.

He poured out two fingers of whisky, threw it into the back of his throat and immediately poured out another measure. Eva could see he was really riled up.

He turned, glass in hand. 'I suppose you're pleased about this, Maisie, eh? A woman getting one over on . . . me . . .'

He stopped, catching sight of Eva behind the door.

'What the hell . . . !' He turned an astonished glance on Maisie. 'What's *she* doing here?' he exploded. 'What's going on?'

Maisie visibly pulled herself together. She straightened her shoulders and lifted her chin defiantly. 'I invited her here. This is *my* house, after all.'

His eyes narrowed. 'But why? What possible interest could you have in this little tramp?' He flashed a sudden glance of understanding at Maisie. 'No! You wouldn't be so stupid.'

Maisie nodded, a gleam of glee in her eyes. 'Yes, the baby,

your baby; the baby you have always denied me. I'm finally getting my way, Stan.'

A look of utter fury creased Stan's face, his skin turning a dull red. 'You can't do that. It's illegal.'

'Don't make me laugh, Stan,' Maisie said mockingly. 'When did you ever care about what was legal?'

There was silence between them for a moment.

Eva came out from behind the door and stood behind Maisie for protection. It was in her mind to make a dash for the door but the thought of the money Maisie had promised kept her still. She deserved that money.

'I forbid it!' Stan bellowed at last. 'You're not bringing her bastard into this house.'

'You're right, I'm not,' Maisie hurried to agree. 'Eva and I are catching the last train to Paddington. I've had enough of your womanizing and your shady deals. We're finished. I'm leaving you, Stan, tonight.'

'The hell you are!' Stan shouted. He looked at Eva, jerking his thumb towards the door. 'Get out, you scheming little tart,' he ordered. 'Before I throw you out, you and your bastard kid.'

'Stay where you are, Eva,' Maisie commanded. A sound came from the hall. 'Ben!' Maisie shouted loudly. 'Come in here. We've got a surprise visitor.'

Ben Hopkins shuffled reluctantly through the door, his face paler than ever. He was carrying a large carpet bag that bulged alarmingly. It looked heavy too.

Stan stared at him in astonishment. 'Ben Hopkins?' He gave Maisie a puzzled look. 'Don't tell me you invited him here too?'

'As a matter of fact I did,' Maisie said, her voice strong and confident now. 'Ben is my lover.'

Stan raised his eyebrows in surprise. 'I suspected there was some bloke,' he said with incredulity in his tone. 'But Ben Hopkins?'

'Yes, Ben.' Maisie nodded. 'He's the man I love. We're leaving Swansea tonight; the three of us.'

Frowning, Stan stared at the carpet bag in Ben's grasp and then looked at the man. 'You're the swine who broke into my office safe,' he said stonily. He turned to stare accusingly at Maisie. 'You've been planning this flit, you cunning conniving bitch!'

Before Eva realized what was happening Stan lunged at Maisie, his arm raised, his fist clenched. Dropping the carpet bag, Ben darted forward and grasped at Stan's uplifted arm to restrain him.

Stan turned on him then, throwing punches. The smaller man clung to him desperately, trying to avoid the blows, but Stan hurled him against a bookcase then went after him viciously, raining blows on his face.

'Stop it!' Maisie screamed. 'Stop it, Stan. You'll kill him.'

'I'll kill the bastard all right,' Stan panted the threat, continuing to beat at his smaller opponent.

Eva watched in horror, too afraid for her own safety to do anything. But she saw Maisie dart towards the fireplace to pick up one of the fire irons and then she rushed at the struggling men, the heavy iron raised high above her shoulder. Without hesitation she swung it at Stan's head.

Eva experienced a moment of déjà vu. This was the second time in the last few weeks she had witnessed such a thing. First Sylvia battling the intruders at Fleet Street and now Maisie attacking her own husband.

The iron struck Stan forcefully on the side of his head. He went down like a felled tree. As he measured his length on the carpet his head struck the decorative mouldings of the brass fender around the fireplace, and he lay there as still as death.

Maisie threw the fire iron on to the carpet. 'That's for all the years of neglect and unhappiness,' she said harshly.

Eva had forced her knuckles into her mouth to stifle a scream, now she bit down on them in sheer terror, staring at the prone man.

There was silence in the room. Ben had been crouching under Stan's blows; now he got gingerly to his feet and after a moment went over to the fallen man. He knelt down beside him and put his fingers against the side of Stan's throat. He stayed like that for a few moments more and then looked up at Maisie.

'He's a goner, Maisie,' he said in an awed whisper. 'We're done for. They'll swing us all for this.'

Terrified at the thought, Eva could not prevent a scream erupting in her throat.

'I don't want to be hanged,' she cried out loudly. 'I've got to get out of here. I've got to get out!'

Maisie stepped forward and smacked her across the face. Eva recoiled, even more frightened.

'Be quiet!' Maisie hissed, her eyes flashing dangerously.

Eva clutched at her stinging cheek, staring at Maisie as though seeing her for the first time. The woman had just killed her own husband but Eva could see no remorse in her. What kind of a woman was she?

Eva began to edge towards the door, her gaze fixed on Maisie's expressionless face. 'I'm going home,' she said. 'I can't stay here.'

Maisie darted forward and seized her arm. 'Stay where you are, Eva. We have an agreement, remember.'

Eva gave a sob and was afraid to move again. She had never been so frightened in her life. How could she trust Maisie after this?

Ben stood upright. 'None of us can stay here,' he said in a low voice. 'I don't want to swing either, not for something I didn't do.'

'No one is going to swing,' Maisie said still holding on to Eva's arm. 'We've got what we wanted and we're going to do as we planned.'

Ben looked at her and Eva saw fear in his eyes too.

'I've done all that you asked me to do, Maisie,' he said shakily. 'But I never thought it would come to murder. You've gone too far.'

'What are you worrying about, Ben?' Maisie snapped. 'No one but the three of us knows about this. We're all in it together and we're not going to talk about it to anyone else, are we?'

'I'm sorry, Maisie. I won't have anything to do with it.' He moved quickly to where the carpet bag lay on the floor and picked it up. 'I'm getting out. I'm getting away now while I can.'

'What are you doing, Ben?' Maisie cried out. 'Leave the bag.'

'No,' he said. 'I've earned this, Maisie.'

'Ben! Don't leave me. What about us? You can't just walk away and leave me.'

'Sorry, Maisie. This is too much for me. I'm off.' With those words he rushed out of the door.

'Ben!' Maisie cried out in anguish, but Eva heard the front door slam behind him.

She turned frightened eyes on Maisie still standing next to her, a stunned look on her face. She stole a glance at the man stretched out on the floor, a pool of dark red blood seeping into the carpet around his head, then quickly averted her gaze, feeling sick to her stomach.

'Maisie, I want to go home,' she said tearfully. 'This is a nightmare.'

'Sit down and be quiet. I have to think of a way out for us.'

'But I'm not involved,' Eva said miserably. 'I've done nothing wrong.'

Maisie stared at her. 'You're involved all right, Eva,' she said sternly. 'And the law will think you guilty just for being here when Stan died.'

Eva sank into a nearby chair, covering her face with her hands. 'Oh, no! I had nothing to do with it. You know that, Maisie. You can tell them.'

'You little fool!' Maisie exploded. 'I'm not taking the blame.' She stood with her fingers to her mouth for a few moments, thinking. 'I'm going to tell the police the name of the real murderer.'

'What?' Eva stared at her, wondering if she had gone out of her mind.

'I'll tell them Rob Naylor killed Stan.' She gazed about her at the wreckage of the earlier struggle. 'They had a fight right here. I'll say I witnessed the whole thing. The police will believe me. Why wouldn't they? I'm a grieving widow.'

Appalled, Eva jumped to her feet. 'You can't do that! They'll hang him.'

'Most likely,' Maisie said. 'After all, people have heard Rob threaten to kill Stan more than once.'

'But he's innocent. Maisie, you can't do it.'

Maisie's glance at her was cold. 'It's his neck or ours,' she said heavily. 'Is there any real choice?'

Eva sat down again, numbed by shock and fear.

'Now listen. You go back to your lodgings straight away. Make sure no one sees your bag. You stay there and you keep your mouth shut. Do you understand me?'

Eva nodded.

'I'll continue to support you, and our agreement can continue. With Stan gone, I have no need to leave Swansea.

Everything that was his is now mine. I'm free to do as I please.'

'Maisie, I'm afraid . . .'

'Walk up as far as the Uplands Hotel,' Maisie continued as though Eva had not spoken. 'You'll find a hansom round about there. Here's money for the fare. Go now.'

Eva jumped up with alacrity, longing to get out of the house and away from Maisie.

Maisie went with her to the door. There she gripped Eva's arm strongly, making her wince.

'Keep your mouth tight shut about what happened, Eva,' she warned in a hard voice, 'or you'll find yourself in deep trouble too.'

Eva hurried from the house and walked on trembling legs up Walter Road towards Uplands Square, her mind in a whirl. She had seen a side of Maisie she never dreamed existed. Cold, calculating and dangerous.

Eva paused by the wall surrounding St James's Church and leaned against it weakly. She could never trust the woman again. She was safe while she was carrying, but once the child was born Maisie would have no further use for her, and now she knew too much. She would never be safe. She whimpered at the thought.

Should she tell what she knew? She shied away from that step. She could be implicated in Stan's death too. The thought of hanging terrified her. No, she must keep quiet for her own safety, but at the same time she must go where Maisie could not find her again.

Eva looked about her. She had heard that her mother was now living at Mario Benucci's house in the Grove. It wasn't far away. She pushed herself away from the wall and continued towards Uplands. She would throw herself on Sylvia's mercy and beg to be taken in. But she would keep all her secrets and never tell the truth.

Nineteen

L ucy had just cleared away the tea things when Ted Locke appeared at the cottage. She hardly recognized him, all dressed up.

'Hello, Ted,' she said with a smile. 'Are you going to a dance or what?'

He laughed good-naturedly. 'Well, it is Christmas next week. I'm meeting my brother for a seasonal drink. It's the only time of year his wife will let him out on his own.'

Christmas! Lucy had hardly thought about it lately. It could never be the same as it once was while she, Sylvia and Eva were separated. Her only family now was Rob. She made up her mind then to get a goose for next week and try to make a Christmas just for Rob and herself.

Rob came in from the back of the cottage where he had been splitting logs for the fire. He smiled at seeing Ted. 'My goodness! Who's this gentleman, then?'

Ted grinned. 'It's good of you to offer me a lift to the Uplands, Mr Naylor. It's a fair old trek on foot.'

'It's my pleasure, Ted,' Rob said. 'You work hard for me all year. I'll pick you up at closing time.'

'Much appreciated,' Ted said.

'You're going to the Uplands?' Lucy asked quickly. 'Could I come too? I'd like to visit my mother as it's almost Christmas.'

'It's no trouble, Lucy,' Rob said. 'Go and get ready.'

Lucy took off her apron, hastily swilled her face and combed her hair and then put on her hat and coat. This was an unexpected treat. She and Sylvia kept in touch by letter, but it would be wonderful to see her in person. She missed her mother so much and perhaps she had news of Eva.

The early evening air was crisp and cold as Lucy rode on

the cart, but she did not mind it. At last the horse was making its way down Windsor Hill into Uplands Square.

Rob pulled on the reins at the kerb outside the Uplands Hotel. Ted jumped down and then helped Lucy safely to the pavement.

'I'll pick up both of you here just after ten,' Rob said.

'Why don't you come in for a quick drink, Mr Naylor,' Ted suggested. 'The horse will be all right for a short while.'

'Thanks, but I'll get back to the smallholding,' Rob said cheerfully. 'I've got a couple of jobs to do.' He saluted them. 'See you later.'

He clicked his tongue and shook the reins and the horse and cart moved off. Ted and Lucy stood on the pavement watching it go.

'Well, Ted, have a good evening with your brother,' Lucy said. 'I'm going to Mr Benucci's house up in the Grove. See you later.'

With a wave, she walked away. The Grove was just around the corner, a square with trees and tall gabled houses. Lucy approached the door of the Benucci house and knocked. A young maid answered.

'I'd like to see Mrs Chandler, please,' she said. 'I'm her daughter.'

The girl opened the door wider and Lucy stepped inside. The girl led the way to the back of the house and into the large kitchen and then retreated. Sylvia was sitting at the table drinking a cup of tea. She jumped up at the sight of Lucy.

'Oh, Lucy, love,' she exclaimed with joy. 'I was just thinking of you, and Eva, too; thinking that this is the first Christmas that we've not been together as a family.'

Lucy went forward quickly to kiss her mother's cheek, feeling a lump of emotion rise in her chest.

'Happy Christmas, Mam,' Lucy said, trying not to let her feelings crack her voice. If she started weeping then Sylvia would too but she wanted to keep this occasion as happy as possible.

'Happy Christmas, love,' Sylvia responded, hugging her. 'Although it will be a very strange one with the three of us spending it apart.'

'Have you heard from Eva?' Lucy asked as she sat at the table.

Sylvia put a cup of tea in front of her and Lucy accepted it eagerly.

'Not a word,' her mother said sadly. 'Oh, I'm so worried, Lucy. A girl in her condition should be with her mother, not with strangers.'

'Well, she said she was with friends,' Lucy said. 'So I suppose she's all right.'

Sylvia sat down again shaking her head. 'It's a sad thing we've come to, Lucy,' she said. Her eyes were glistening and Lucy knew her mother was near to tears and she could not blame her.

Lucy covered her mother's hand with her own. 'I know, Mam,' she said softly. 'But we have to believe things will get better next year.'

'Do you think Eva will come back to us when her baby is born?' Sylvia asked forlornly.

'I think she'll have to,' Lucy said practically. 'She'll need to earn a living and she can't do that with a baby in tow.' She looked at her mother speculatively. 'You know she'll probably expect you to step in and look after her child.'

'I won't mind that,' Sylvia confessed. She glanced away. 'I've already sounded out Mr Benucci,' she said. 'If Eva comes here he said she can stay. There's plenty of room, after all.'

'That's very good of him,' Lucy said. Mario Benucci had proved himself to be a good friend to them all. 'I don't know how we'll repay him for all his kindness.'

Sylvia filled their teacups again and they chatted about times past, a time when they had a real family, or at least they believed they had.

'I'll have to watch the clock,' Lucy said. 'Rob is picking me up outside the Uplands Hotel at ten o'clock.'

'Oh, there's plenty of time yet,' Sylvia said. 'It's only quarter past nine. Have another cup of tea.'

The front door bell rang. Lucy heard the maid's footsteps along the passage as she went to answer. Within minutes the maid was walking into the kitchen and behind her walked Eva carrying a carpet bag.

'Eva! Oh, love!' Sylvia jumped up, clearly overcome. She rushed towards her youngest daughter and enveloped her in a hug.

Lucy stood up too glad to see Eva again, but noticed immediately that her sister's face was very pale and drawn; her eyes were wide and her expression almost fearful. Lucy put this down to her condition, which was now quite apparent. Obviously Eva was frightened at what was before her.

'Hello, Eva,' Lucy greeted warmly. 'Happy Christmas. How are you?'

Her sister mumbled something in response as Sylvia took Eva's bag, helped her out of her hat and coat and sat her down at the table offering tea.

Eva's hand shook so much it made the cup rattle on the saucer. She put them down on the table quickly as though conscious of Lucy's speculative gaze.

'Happy Christmas, Eva, love,' Sylvia said.

'Happy Christmas, my foot!' Eva said with a little more spirit. 'I've been turfed out of my lodgings and at Christmas time, too.'

'Oh, Eva, what a terrible thing to happen,' Sylvia said sympathetically.

Lucy frowned. 'I thought you were with friends,' she said.

Apart from her paleness Eva had a shifty expression in her eyes and Lucy had a strong feeling her sister was not telling them the complete truth. Perhaps she had outstayed her welcome, Lucy thought, and her friends had made it plain that they wanted her gone.

'Yes, I was with friends,' Eva said quickly. 'You don't know them,' she added hastily. 'But my friends' father found work in Durham. It was all of a sudden, like. The whole family has to move up there before Christmas. So, I had to go.'

'You must stay here,' Sylvia said. 'I've already asked Mr Benucci, just in case you needed me.'

Eva looked extremely relieved and a little colour came back into her cheeks. 'I won't be any trouble, Mam,' she said. 'I just want to stay quietly out of the way. No one need know I'm here.'

Lucy found that a very odd thing for her sister to say. Was she still afraid of Stan Naylor?

'Where do your friends live?' Lucy persisted. She was curious about the whole thing.

Eva shrugged. 'The other side of the river,' she said in an

off-hand way as though she wanted no further discussion about it.

'I'm so glad to see you, Eva,' Sylvia interposed. 'I've been worrying.'

'Well, I'll be all right now I'm here with you, Mam,' Eva said. She took Sylvia's hand and clung tightly to it, looking up into her face.

Lucy watched with interest. There was something Eva wasn't telling them. It was as though she was in some kind of trouble.

'Is your baby all right?' Lucy asked in concern. 'You're not ill, are you?'

Eva turned an irritable gaze on her. 'I'm tired, that's all.' She looked at Sylvia again. 'Mam, can you show me which room I'll be sleeping in. I want to get to bed.'

'Of course, love,' Sylvia said and picked up Eva's bag. 'Come on, I'll take you up.' She turned to glance at Lucy. 'Don't go yet, Lucy,' she said. 'Wait until I come down.'

'You're not going to talk about me behind my back, are you,' Eva exclaimed in a high nervous voice.

'Of course not,' Sylvia said soothingly. 'Come along, love. Get some rest. You look worn out.'

When she came back downstairs it was almost ten o'clock.

'I've got to go, Mam,' Lucy said. 'I don't want to keep Rob waiting.'

Sylvia hugged and kissed her. 'I'll miss our Christmas together,' she said sadly.

'Well, at least you've got Eva back,' Lucy reminded her. 'You don't have to worry about her any more.'

Lucy wondered how true that was as she hurried down to Uplands Square to meet Rob. She felt in her bones that there was something behind Eva's sudden return; that there was trouble in store for them all.

'I hope you don't mind, Lucy,' Rob said at the breakfast table the next morning, 'I've ordered a goose for Christmas dinner.' He grinned. 'I know it's a bit of a cheek on my part expecting you to cook it.'

Lucy grinned back. 'I'll give it a go,' she said. 'But I must warn you I've never cooked a goose before.'

'I've always spent Christmas at Fleet Street,' he said sadly.

'Relying on neighbours to help out, but now with there being two of us here . . . oh, and of course, Ted; I've invited him to dinner, I thought I should make an effort.'

'Quite right,' Lucy agreed cheerfully, smiling at him.

She was looking forward to the festivities, limited as they might be. She would be with Rob and that was all she wanted.

He got up from the table and reached for his coat and cap behind the door. 'I'll spend today working on the new greenhouse,' he said. 'Perhaps you and Ted could start clearing out the big greenhouse. Spring will be on us before we can look around. I want to be ready for planting.'

As Rob opened the door, a cart horse pulling a large black enclosed carriage trotted into the front yard. There was something ominous about the vehicle and for some reason Lucy felt a shiver go through her.

The driver reined the horse in and climbed down. Lucy stared to see he was in a policeman's uniform. At the same time the back of the vehicle opened and several uniformed men got out together with a man in plain clothes. He wore a long black overcoat and a bowler hat. The group advanced towards the house.

'Are you Robert Naylor?' the man in the overcoat asked.

'Yes,' Rob said in a puzzled voice. 'What can I do for you?'

'We have some questions for you,' the man said heavily. 'We'd better go inside.'

'What's this all about?' Rob asked again, turning to go into the house. 'Why are all these policemen here?'

'I'll ask the questions, sir,' the man said.

When they were inside the man spoke again. 'My name is Detective Inspector Edwards,' he said. He indicated the nearest man in uniform. 'This is Sergeant Thomas.'

Inspector Edwards glanced at Lucy. 'Is this your wife?'

'No, Miss Chandler is my employee and lodger,' Rob said.

'I see.' Inspector Edwards raised his brows. 'Perhaps you'd leave us, Miss Chandler.'

Lucy took off her apron and was about to go outside when Rob spoke. 'Lucy, stay where you are,' he said angrily turning to the police inspector. 'This is my house. I give the orders around here. Now what the hell is this all about.'

Edwards nodded. 'Pleading ignorance, are you?' he said. 'Well, that's as good a defence as any, I suppose. I've never met a criminal yet who would admit to anything.'

'Criminal?' Rob glared looking mystified. 'I'm no criminal. I'm an honest hard-working businessman.'

Edwards stared at him silently for a moment. 'Where were you between eight o'clock and ten o'clock last night?'

'He was with me,' Lucy burst out without thinking twice. 'All night long, and I'll swear to that on a Bible.'

She was aware that Rob was staring at her in amazement and she was amazed at herself too but some deep feeling of dread and premonition had prompted her to lie.

'Lucy?' Rob said. 'Why on earth did you say that? There's no need.' He turned to the inspector. 'As a matter of fact, after I dropped my two employees in the Uplands about seven to seven thirty—'

'Uplands?' Inspector Edwards interposed sharply and darted a glance at his sergeant, who was writing furiously in his notebook. 'You admit you were in Uplands last night, sir?'

'Yes, I gave Lucy – Miss Chandler – and Ted Locke a lift,' Rob said. 'From there I went up to Prosser's farm in Fforestfach. It's that farm down behind the Marquis's Arms pub.'

'I know where it is,' Edwards said shortly. 'What were you doing there?'

Rob glanced at Lucy. 'I heard Prosser was selling Christmas trees. I went to buy one to brighten the place up a bit for Christmas.'

Lucy felt a wave of tenderness for him at his thoughtfulness.

'At that time of night?' the inspector snapped.

Rob shrugged. 'He was doing good business even though it was late,' he said. 'The tree is out the back. You can see it for yourself.'

'Huh! That's no proof where you were,' Edwards said. 'You could have purchased it at any time.'

Rob looked flummoxed.

'Can you prove you were there last evening?' Sergeant Thomas asked. 'Do you know the farmer Prosser personally?'

Rob shook his head. 'No, and there was a crowd of men buying trees. I doubt Prosser would remember any of us.'

'So, you can't prove your whereabouts last evening,' Edwards said heavily. 'It so happens that I can. I have a witness that puts you at your brother's house in the Uplands during the hours in question.'

'That's nonsense,' Rob said energetically. 'I was nowhere near there.'

'Come now, Mr Naylor,' Inspector Edwards said harshly. 'You've already admitted you were in the Uplands last evening.'

'Yes, but I didn't go near my brother's house.' He hesitated. 'I wouldn't.'

'Why not?'

Rob hesitated a second time. 'We don't get on,' he said quietly.

'No, in fact you threatened to kill him, didn't you, on more than one occasion,' Edwards said. 'And I have witnesses to those threats too.'

'Now look here,' Rob said angrily. 'Those words were spoken in anger. I didn't mean it and if Stan is saying I was making trouble at his house last night he's lying in his teeth.'

Edwards pursed his lips as he studied Rob. He spoke at last in a low voice.

'Your brother is not in a position to say anything, Mr Naylor. He's dead, murdered.'

'Oh, no,' Lucy could not help but cry out and then covered her mouth with her hand. The dread she was feeling grew, cold and dense around her heart.

'Stan is dead?' Rob looked stricken.

'You know he is, Mr Naylor,' Inspector Edwards said evenly. 'It was you that did him in.'

'No!' Rob exclaimed.

'Oh, yes.' The inspector insisted nodding his head confidently. 'I have a very reliable witness who saw you perpetrate the crime.'

'It's not possible!' Lucy cried out in horror. 'Rob couldn't do anything like that. Who is this witness, anyway?'

'The victim's widow, Mrs Maisie Naylor, your sister-in-law, Mr Naylor. She saw you strike the killing blow with her own eyes.'

'Maisie!' Rob looked around at them all. 'Why would she lie? I don't understand.' He stared at the police officer. 'Look, take my fingerprints,' he suggested. 'You won't find my prints at the house because I was never there.'

'Mrs Naylor told us you were wearing gloves.' Inspector Edwards squared his shoulders. 'Robert Naylor,' he began in an officious voice. 'I'm arresting you for the murder of Stanley Naylor. You don't have to say anything but I must warn you that anything you do say will be taken down and may be used in evidence.'

Rob shook his head in bewilderment as two policemen advanced on him and, placing his arms behind his back, hand-cuffed him.

'You're making an awful mistake, Inspector,' Lucy cried out. 'Rob didn't do this terrible thing. You must believe him. He's innocent.'

'I've got my duty to do, miss, so don't interfere.' He gave her a cold stare. 'You may be called as a witness.'

The group of men moved outside, Rob in their midst. Lucy wrung her hands in fear and helplessness.

'Rob!'

'I didn't do it, Lucy. I swear.'

'Oh, Rob!'

Twenty

E va lifted the tray and put it on the table at the side of the bed. Her mother was spoiling her with breakfast in bed and she loved it.

She had made a shrewd move in appealing for Sylvia's help. It was more than she had hoped for; free bed and board thanks to Mario Benucci's kindness.

She lay back on the pillows, smiling. She suspected it was more than kindness on his part. Mario had a soft spot for Sylvia, she was sure of it. He might even be in love with her. Well, why not? Her mother was comparatively young and still a handsome woman. Sylvia could make a very comfortable nest for herself here if she played her cards right.

Not that she would, Eva judged. Sylvia was too stiff and starchy for anything risqué. Not like herself, she thought. In taking a risk with Stan Naylor she had grabbed at a better life.

At the thought of him a picture flashed into her mind's eye; Maisie wielding the fire iron, bringing it crashing down on his head, him falling to his death.

Eva sat up in bed with a jerk. Would she never get that image out of her head? It terrified her. Maisie terrified her.

She could forget the further money that Maisie had promised her. The woman couldn't be trusted.

Eva climbed out of bed and went to stand before the dressing-table mirror, staring at her reflection, her abdomen bulging beneath her nightdress. She was safe while she still carried the child but afterwards . . .?

She grabbed her dressing gown and put it on. Maisie mustn't find her again. She knew too much about her. The woman had killed once. She might kill again to save her own neck.

Suddenly cold with fear, she sat down on the stool before the mirror and began to brush her hair like an automaton. She must stay closeted here in the house until the whole thing blew over. That could be months, of course.

Eva paused in her brushing. What was happening? Had anyone found out that Stan was dead? This evening she must try to get a copy of the *Cambrian Leader* to see if the story was in the paper.

A new frightening thought struck her. Suppose someone found out she had been in the house at the time, that she had witnessed the killing? Her stomach contracted at the thought and she clutched frantically at her abdomen. No one must ever know.

Later Eva was just coming out of the bathroom and returning to her room when she heard a commotion downstairs: her sister's voice, high-pitched and fearful. She looked down over the banister and saw Lucy cross the hall accompanied by Sylvia. They went towards the back of the house where the kitchen was.

Eva was filled with curiosity. Collecting the breakfast tray from her bedroom she went downstairs and into the kitchen. She paused in the doorway, startled to see Lucy sitting at the table, her face streaming with tears.

'What's going on?' Eva asked.

Lucy looked up her eyes brimming. 'Rob has been arrested for murder,' she said with a choking sob. 'They say he killed his brother Stan.'

In shock Eva's fingers lost their grip on the tray and it slipped, crashing to the flagstone floor.

'Oh, Eva, look what you've done!' Sylvia exclaimed angrily, rushing forward to clear up the mess.

'They've already arrested Rob?' Eva exclaimed. Feeling her legs were about to give way under her she clutched at a nearby chair for support. 'No! I never thought she really . . .' Eva stopped. She had almost given herself away then.

'What?' Lucy said vaguely. She appeared too overwrought to follow up her question.

'I'm stunned at the news,' Eva said evasively. She must be more careful what she said in future. 'Do you think Rob really did it?'

'He's innocent,' Lucy cried out miserably. 'I know he is.'

'Well, you can't actually know that for sure,' Eva said

quickly to cover her earlier faux pas. 'You were here with Mam at the time, weren't you?'

Lucy looked at her with a puzzled expression. 'The police have told me nothing,' she said. 'They haven't even said exactly what time Stan was killed.'

'Well, I don't know that either!' Eva exclaimed hotly. 'I know nothing about it whatsoever.'

'Lucy, love,' Sylvia interposed. 'Are you sure Rob is innocent? I mean there was a great deal of bad blood between them. Stan was responsible for Nora's heart attack. One couldn't blame Rob if he took revenge.'

Lucy looked at her mother with a horrified expression. 'Mam, how can you talk about Rob that way – the man who saved your life, remember.'

'Even good men do bad things sometimes,' Sylvia said. 'Look at what your father did to us.'

Lucy jumped to her feet. 'Don't you dare compare Rob to my father. Father's behaviour was despicable and I hate him for it.'

'Lucy! Don't say that.' Sylvia looked even more upset.

Her guilty knowledge weighing heavy on her, Eva rushed to support her mother's reasoning.

'Lucy, be sensible,' she said. 'The police wouldn't have arrested Rob unless they had good reason. After all, the evidence of a witness is very damning.'

Lucy jerked her head around to stare at her.

'A witness?' she repeated loudly. 'How did *you* know there was a witness?'

Eva started guiltily, appalled at her slip. 'You said so just now. I heard you.' Confusion was making her head spin and she felt fear clutch at her heart.

'No, I didn't!' Lucy was staring hard at her. 'Eva, I know you of old,' her sister said forcefully. 'The corners of your mouth always turn down when you're lying.' Her eyes narrowed speculatively. 'You've got that look now.'

Eva bristled to cover her fright. 'I don't know what you're talking about. Stop badgering me.'

'You know more than you're saying,' Lucy insisted. 'You and Stan practically lived together for months, so you must know all about him. Did ever meet his wife?'

'No!' Eva turned away, all of a sudden terrified. Every time she opened her mouth her guilty knowledge caused her to say the wrong thing.

'Where have you been these last weeks, then?' Lucy continued. 'Did you go back to Stan?'

'I told you, I was with friends.'

'I don't believe you!'

'Lucy,' Sylvia exclaimed angrily, 'don't shift the blame to your sister. I know you're upset over Rob, but that's no reason to accuse Eva of underhandedness.'

'Mam, our Eva is a devious little witch!' Lucy burst out in fury. 'She can't be trusted about anything. She has no scruples or morals either. Look at the way she latched on to Stan in that shameful way.'

'That's in the past,' Sylvia said plaintively. 'I've forgiven her. She's learned her lesson.'

'Has she?' Lucy glared at her sister. 'She knows something about Stan's murder, I'm sure that she does.'

'I know nothing about it!' Eva cried out desperately. 'How could I?'

'I don't know,' Lucy said darkly. 'But I can feel it in my bones.'

'That's rubbish, Lucy,' Sylvia exclaimed in a shocked tone. 'You're clutching at straws.'

'Mam, I'm telling you I don't know anything about it,' Eva repeated. 'How dare Lucy accuse me?'

Eva saw Lucy's lips clamp together in a straight line, and recognizing that look was filled with alarm. Her sister had the idea of her implication in the murder fixed in her head and nothing would shift it.

'I will not be bullied!' Eva shouted in defiance. 'I'm in a delicate condition. Tell her to stop, Mam. She's making me ill.'

'Delicate, my foot!' Lucy said hotly. 'You made a strange remark earlier when I gave you the news of Rob's arrest. I was too upset to take it in properly. But now I'm calmer.' She pointed a finger at Eva. 'You said – you didn't think *she* really . . .' She glared at her sister. 'What did you mean, Eva? Who is *she*?'

Eva turned to her mother, her hand outstretched for protection.

'Mam, Lucy is browbeating me. Tell her to stop.' She put

the back of her other hand against her forehead in a dramatic gesture. 'She's making me feel faint.'

'Oh, stop acting the innocent!' Lucy said angrily. 'You've proved you're as hard as nails by throwing yourself at Stan Naylor in that shameful way.'

'I'm ill!'

'There's nothing wrong with you. You're perfectly healthy,' Lucy insisted. 'If you're telling the truth give me the names of these friends of yours.'

'Why should I?'

'Why wouldn't you, Eva,' Sylvia asked. Her mother was looking at her sternly now. '*Do* you have something to hide?'

Her mother's gaze on her was uncertain and Eva realized she could lose Sylvia's support if she wasn't careful. She let her face crease as though to cry and feigned a sob. It did the trick. Sylvia went immediately to her and put her arm around her shoulders.

'There, there! Don't get upset, love.'

Eva took a quick peek at Lucy's face. Her sister looked furious.

'I think I'd better go back to bed, Mam,' Eva said in a small voice. 'I'll get no peace down here.'

'Oh no you don't,' Lucy shouted. 'I'm going to get at the truth if it takes all day.'

'Mam!' Eva squealed an appeal but Lucy pointed an accusing finger at her.

'Maisie Naylor, Stan's wife, has told the police she witnessed the killing.' Lucy glared at her. 'Somehow you knew she said that, didn't you? You mentioned a witness earlier. You knew that witness is Maisie Naylor.'

'I feel faint! I must lie down in a quiet room.'

'There's only one thing for it,' Lucy said in a firm tone. 'I'm going to tell the police that you are withholding information. They'll get the truth out of you.'

'No!' Eva screamed in horror. 'I could go to prison. They might even hang me.'

'What?' Sylvia looked stunned. 'Eva, what are you saying?'

Eva couldn't help bursting into genuine tears, and collapsed helplessly on to a nearby chair. What was the use? She could no longer hide what she knew. Maybe if she told the truth and gave Maisie up, the police would go easy on her. After all, she had done nothing wrong herself.

'Well?' Lucy demanded to know in a stony voice.

Her mother knelt down beside the chair to hold her hand. It was very comforting and she clung on tightly.

'I was there,' Eva admitted, emitting a deep heartfelt sob. 'I saw it all. It was horrible.'

'What did you see?'

'I saw Maisie Naylor strike Stan over the head with a fire iron. She killed him and now I'm hiding from her.' Eva sobbed again. 'I'm afraid she'll kill me too because I know too much.'

Lucy gave a huge sigh and sank into a chair opposite.

'At last, the truth,' she said. 'I knew in my heart that Rob was innocent.'

'What happens now?' Eva looked pleadingly at Lucy. She had a feeling her ordeal was far from over.

'We're going immediately to the central police station in Alexander Road,' Lucy said positively. 'You can repeat what you've told us to the police.'

'I'm afraid!'

'Are you going to hide from Maisie Naylor for the rest of your life?'

Eva saw the sense of that. She was thankful too that Lucy had not asked the vital question as to why she had been at Stan's house in the first place.

The last thing she wanted was to reveal to her mother and sister that she had had an arrangement with Maisie; that she had sold her unborn baby. If that came out Sylvia would turn against her completely.

At the police station Eva was terrified, especially when Inspector Edwards would not allow either Sylvia or Lucy to remain with her in the interview room while she was being questioned.

She told them in detail everything she could remember of that awful night; in fact it all poured out like a tap being turned on. They were particularly interested to learn about Ben Hopkins's involvement and the robbery.

Later on, when the inspector began to probe her connection with Maisie Naylor, Eva was glad not to have her family present. Even so, she had no intention of telling the complete truth about that.

Inspector Edward's expression was cold and austere when he asked: 'Did money change hands over the child?'

Eva shook her head vehemently and lied in her teeth. 'No. I wouldn't sell my baby. What kind of a person do you think I am?' She sniffed theatrically. 'Maisie felt sorry for me and wanted to help,' she continued stiffly. 'After all, it was her husband who got me into trouble.'

When they said she was free to go Eva was overwhelmingly relieved. But the inspector had a warning for her.

'I'm letting you go – for now,' he said sternly. 'You may be called as a witness. You may be liable for a charge, too.'

Eva trembled anew. 'What for?'

'You withheld vital evidence,' he said. 'And there's the question as to whether or not you sold your unborn child. Trafficking in children is a serious crime. The courts would be very harsh on that.'

'I tell you I didn't sell my baby!' Eva burst out.

'Yes, well, we'll be looking into it,' the inspector said.

Eva could not help bursting into tears.

'All right! Never mind the waterworks,' Edwards remarked unsympathetically. 'You can go home.'

Eva was thankful to escape. When she had agreed to tell all to the police she had not bargained on them poking their noses into her private life. Now she was glad she had taken Maisie's advice to bank the money in an account with a false name. Her secret was still safe.

Lucy and Sylvia were waiting in the station's front office. Eva rushed into her mother's arms, weeping.

'What about Rob?' Lucy eagerly asked the inspector as he followed Eva out. 'You'll let him go now, won't you?'

'Your sister's statement has to be verified. It could be a pack of lies, for all we know.'

'It's not!'

'Nevertheless,' Edwards said firmly. 'Robert Naylor is not in the clear yet by a long way. We have to find Ben Hopkins, who is known to us, and question Mrs Naylor. You'll be hearing from us again.'

A question burned in Lucy's mind as the three of them walked from the police station in Alexander Road to the Uplands, but she waited until they were in the kitchen of Mario Benucci's house before broaching the subject.

Sylvia put the kettle on immediately. They all needed a refreshing cup of tea. Lucy sat at the kitchen table opposite her sister. She was determined that Eva would explain her connection with Stan's wife.

'Now I want the truth, Eva,' Lucy began. 'How did you come to be connected to Maisie Naylor?'

Eva shifted uncomfortably in her chair and Lucy watched her avidly for signs that she was lying.

'It's nothing mysterious or underhand,' Eva said with a straight face. 'When Stan kicked me out I was very angry. I wanted to spite him, so I told his wife about the baby.' She spread her hands as though still surprised herself. 'I thought she'd be furious but instead she was sympathetic. She said Stan had treated me very shabbily, and she'd help me because she was sorry for me.'

Lucy stared at her disbelievingly. 'That's a very strange attitude for a deceived wife to take.'

Eva shrugged. 'Maisie Naylor is a strange woman,' she said. 'She did murder her husband, remember. You can't get stranger than that.'

'Well, that's certainly true,' Sylvia interposed. 'How did she help you, Eva?' she continued. 'Did she give you money?'

'No!' Eva denied vehemently, rising quickly from her chair before Lucy could read her expression and went to the larder to fetch the jug of milk.

'So it was Maisie you were staying with, then?' Lucy persisted when Eva returned to the table.

'After the attack on Nora I was afraid Stan would want to harm me too,' Eva said. 'Maisie helped me find safe lodgings and paid the rent.' She lowered her head. 'But I never took a penny piece from her, I swear.'

'I don't know why you'd want to stay elsewhere,' Sylvia said plaintively. 'I'd have taken care of you. A girl's place is with her mother.'

'Mam, please!' Lucy said. 'This is important.' She turned back to Eva. 'Why were you at Stan's house that night?'

Eva grimaced. 'It's a good thing I was,' she said archly. 'Or Rob would be done for.'

'Eva, you won't wriggle out of this by trying to be clever,' Lucy snapped.

Eva sniffed. 'Maisie wanted me to meet her gentleman friend, Ben Hopkins.'

'Why?'

'I don't know!' Eva said angrily. 'Just as I didn't know they planned to steal from Stan's safe. Stan caught them and that's why the fight started. Maisie finished it.'

'But . . .'

'I'm not answering any more questions,' Eva exclaimed hotly, rising to her feet again. 'I've had enough of that with the police. I've said all I'm going to say. I've done nothing wrong.'

With that she rushed from the room, her cup of tea untouched.

Alone Lucy sat dejected and despondent in Rob's cottage, elbows on the table, chin in hands. It was two days since Eva had visited the police station with evidence that would clear Rob of a murder charge, but he had still not been released. Now it was Christmas Eve.

She stared morosely at the fat goose on the table before her. She should be busy preparing it for tomorrow's dinner, but she did not have the heart or even the willpower to tackle it. Rob wasn't here to share and enjoy so what was the point in doing anything? Nothing mattered without him.

She had been looking forward so much to spending Christmas in his company, pretending in her secret heart that they were a married couple. Her heart ached to think of him languishing in Swansea prison; an innocent man.

Lucy looked at the clock on the mantelpiece. It was almost midday. She regretted sending Ted home early. He could've taken her on the cart to the police station in town, but if she started now she could walk it in an hour. She would demand to know why they still had Rob locked up.

She was walking down the lane towards the main road when she saw a hansom cab coming towards her. It slowed as it passed and the door swung open.

'Lucy!' Rob stepped down quickly and came to her. 'Lucy, they've let me go.'

Lucy could not help herself. She rushed at him and threw her arms around his neck burying her face against his shoulder.

'Oh, Rob, thank God!' She clung to him, conscious of his strong arms around her. 'Are you all right? Why did they take so long to release you? I was worried out of my mind.'

Lucy was then aware of another figure standing close to them and then she recognized Sergeant Thomas. She drew away from Rob and stared self-consciously at the policeman.

'Why are the police here?' she asked uncertainly. 'Surely the nightmare is over for us.'

'It's all right, Lucy,' Rob said soothingly. 'Sergeant Thomas brought me home.'

'It was the least we could do,' Sergeant Thomas said.

'What has happened?'

'I think we'd better speak at the cottage, Mr Naylor,' Sergeant Thomas said. 'I don't want to talk official business here.'

Lucy thought he was being officious and overly cautious. There was no one else about but them.

The policeman told the cab driver to wait and then they walked back to the cottage.

Sergeant Thomas removed his helmet once they were inside.

'Sit down,' Rob said to him. 'Lucy will make some tea.'

'Thank you, no, sir,' Sergeant Thomas said regretfully. 'I have the cab waiting.' He paused and then spoke to Lucy. 'Inspector Edwards thought you deserved a report of what has been happening, miss, since your family was involved to a degree.'

'Thank you. I was worried,' she admitted.

'You'll be glad to learn that Ben Hopkins has been apprehended. He confessed to two robberies, and he confirmed your sister's statement that Mrs Maisie Naylor struck the blow that killed her husband.'

'Oh, thank heavens,' Lucy said with feeling.

'Mrs Naylor has been arrested and charged. She broke down and confessed everything.' He paused a moment. 'As regards Miss Eva Chandler, our superiors have decided no charges will be brought against her because of her youth and – er – interesting condition.'

'I should hope not!' Lucy said energetically.

Sergeant Thomas inclined his head. 'Yes, well, Inspector Edwards was convinced she had sold her unborn child to Mrs Naylor. Now that is a serious crime . . .'

'What did you say?' Lucy burst out indignantly. 'Sold her

baby? I've never heard anything so outrageous! My sister wouldn't stoop to such monstrous behaviour.'

Sergeant Thomas's expression changed to one of haughty officialdom. 'Nevertheless, miss, it looked very much that way,' he said somewhat stiffly. 'However, Mrs Naylor denied it and we could find no evidence to the contrary, so the matter was closed.'

'And that's an end of it, Lucy,' Rob forestalled her quickly as Lucy opened her mouth to say more. 'Thank you, Sergeant, for bringing me home.'

The police officer left and Lucy felt her whole body relax with relief. She stood near the table, Rob close by. She turned to him, her heart so full of love for him that she could not contain herself.

'Welcome home, Rob,' she said. 'I thought I'd never see you again.'

'Glad to be home, Lucy,' he said smiling, his eyes bright. She thought there might be tears lurking there. Her emotions overwhelmed her at the notion.

'I don't know what I'd have done if you hadn't returned,' Lucy said.

'I am back,' he said gently. 'For good.'

She wanted to hold him again and kiss him. She could not contain her feelings a moment longer.

'Rob, I think my life would be over if anything happened to you,' she said in a rush. 'You mean the world to me.'

'Lucy!'

He looked so surprised, Lucy felt suddenly mortified and she turned away from him, her cheeks flaming. What must he think of her forwardness?

'I'm sorry, Rob,' she said quickly. 'I shouldn't have said that. I've embarrassed you with my presumption. Please forgive me.'

'Forgive you? What for?' He came and stood close behind her. 'Lucy, I had no idea you felt like that.' He put his hands on her shoulders and turned her to face him. She looked up into his eyes, and then at his face that she loved so dearly.

'I wish I'd known,' he said. 'We've wasted so much time.' He put his hand up to caress her face. 'Oh, Lucy, my dearest Lucy, I fell in love with you from the very first day we met.'

Lucy thought her heart would overflow at those words she had longed to hear. 'But you said nothing, Rob.'

'I was afraid,' he said. 'I didn't want you to think I was like Stan; I didn't want to drive you away. I love you so much.'

'Oh, Rob.'

She went into his waiting arms then and felt them about her, holding her tightly to him. She clung to him as though he was life itself. And then he kissed her, tenderly at first and then with growing passion. Lucy responded with a fire matching his.

They were lost in each other, the kiss lingering on so that Lucy had no idea of the passing of time.

At last Rob eased her away from him, breathless.

'Marry me, Lucy, please,' he said in a hoarse whisper. 'I can't live without you any longer.'

Lucy gave a cry of joy. 'Oh, Rob, I will marry you and let it be soon, my love.'

Twenty-One

Christmas Eve, 1911

R ob came into the cottage rubbing his hands. 'Hooh! It's cold today.' He took off his cap and coat and hung them behind the door. 'Any chance of a hot cup of tea, Lucy, my love?'

Lucy was preparing the goose for dinner the next day, but turned eagerly to him.

'Right away, dearest husband mine,' she said with a happy laugh. She went to swill her hands at the sink and then wiped them on a towel.

He came quickly to put his arms around her waist and kissed her on the back of her neck. 'Do you realize it's a year today since I told you I love you,' he said gently.

She loved him all the more for remembering that and wriggled around in his arms to face him. 'As if I could forget,' she said softly.

Memories of that day had been in her mind from waking that morning; her despair when she thought she would never see him again and then the overwhelming joy she had felt when he had taken her in his arms and told her of his love. It had seemed like a miracle.

'It was the happiest day of my life,' she continued. 'Except our wedding day in March last.'

'Any regrets?'

'I couldn't be happier.'

She hesitated, bursting to tell him of her suspicions that she might be in the family way, but it was too soon yet to be sure and she did not want to disappoint him.

He held her away from him smiling into her face. 'Well, a lot has happened since, hasn't it?' he said.

Lucy stood on tiptoe to kiss his cheek and then went to fill the kettle to make tea.

'I can't believe Eva's little Peter is four months old already,' she said. 'He's such a beautiful baby. I've got a lovely cuddly teddy bear for him as a Christmas present. Could we slip down in the cart to see them all later today, do you think?'

'Of course we can, love,' Rob said and sat at the table waiting for the tea. Lucy placed the cup in front of him and sat down to drink hers.

Yes, so much has happened, she thought. Eva had been lucky not to have been charged with something after Stan's death. She thought of the others involved – the guilty ones. Ben Hopkins had got five years for burglary while Maisie Naylor had managed to get her charge reduced to manslaughter. She had avoided the gallows but would spend the next fifteen years in prison. Lucy shivered at the prospect of such a fate.

A knock on the cottage door startled her out of her reverie and she jumped up to answer. She could not have been more astonished to see her mother standing on the doorstep, clutching a bundle in her arms.

'Mam!' Lucy gasped and then opened the door wide. 'Quick, come in out of the cold.'

Sylvia seemed to stumble as she stepped inside and, alarmed, Lucy clutched at her arm to steady her. 'Mam, what's the matter?'

Sylvia gave a little moan and swayed and Lucy quickly took the bundle from her. Her mouth dropped open in amazement as looking closely she realized the bundle contained a baby, Eva's baby, Peter.

'Mam, what's going on?' Lucy asked in agitation. 'Why on earth have you brought Peter out on such a cold day? Where's Eva? Has something happened?'

Rob came forward quickly and helped Sylvia into a chair.

'Sylvia, you look exhausted,' he said. 'I'll get you some tea.'

Staring at her mother, Lucy could see she had been crying; her eyes and nose were red, her features strained. She looked up at them both, tears filling her eyes again.

'It's Eva,' she said in a strangled voice. 'She's run off to London. She has abandoned her own baby.'

'What?'

'I found her note in the kitchen early this morning,' she

said with a sob. 'She's gone to London for good. She's never coming back.'

'How could she leave her baby? What kind of a mother is she?'

Sylvia took a handkerchief from the pocket of her coat and dabbed at her streaming eyes. 'I don't know how Eva could be so heartless, Lucy. Her own child! It beggars belief.'

'And where did she get the money for such a trip?' Rob asked.

Lucy looked at him. That was a fair question. Eva had no means of her own, so where did the money come from and what did she expect to live on in London?

Lucy lips tightened in anger. 'She lied to us all along,' she said. 'Maisie Naylor must have given her money, a lot of money. The unprincipled little witch!'

Peter began to whimper at her harsh tones and Lucy held him to her to comfort him. Then she sat down and placed him on her lap to release him from the bundle.

Freed from the confined of the blanket he kicked his podgy little legs and waved his arms, his blue eyes on her face. Lucy's heart contracted with a sudden rush of tenderness for him.

How could Eva bear to be parted from such a darling child as Peter? Her sister's nature was even harder than she realized.

'What am I going to do now, Lucy?' Sylvia said plaintively. 'Mr Benucci has been so good to us, letting Eva stay even after the birth. I can hardly expect him to keep me on now that I've got the responsibility of a baby. I don't know how I'll manage.'

Rob sat down next to her.

'Sylvia,' he said gently. 'No one expects you to bear this burden. Peter is my nephew. I'll be responsible for him. Despite the antagonism between me and Stan I owe it to my brother to raise his son as my own.' He looked at Lucy. 'It's our family duty, Lucy, love,' he said simply. 'Peter is your nephew, too.'

Lucy smiled at her husband, holding back tears. He was such a good man, admirable and full of integrity. She hoped she would always be worthy of his love.

'I would be proud to call Peter our son,' she said. 'I love him already as though he were my own.'

'Lucy, I don't deserve you as a daughter,' Sylvia said tearfully. 'I've brought nothing but trouble to you.'

'Mam, don't be silly,' Lucy said cuddling Peter in her arms. 'You're the best mother a girl could have and I love you very much. I only hope I'll be as good a mother to my child.'

Rob stared at her, his gaze suddenly alert.

She winked at him and smiled. 'Don't get excited yet, husband dear,' she told him mischievously. 'We'll see what blessings next year brings.'